Here's lookin' at you, kid...

"One of the gang of robbers—well, sir, I thought he was a youth—twelve or thirteen years old—but then he turned back, and I realized he was only a child. He'd dropped this."

Maxwell handed something across the railing, and Mr. Colquhoun took and examined it. It was no weapon, this, but a toy soldier made of metal.

Mr. Colquhoun had seen too much of the world to cherish many illusions, but he found something rather poignant about a child young enough to play with toys being put to work robbing banks instead.

"It's unfortunate, Mr. Maxwell, but not uncommon," he acknowledged with a sigh. "A child can get into places a grown man can't—through windows, gaps in the walls, even down chimneys, if he's small enough."

"Yes, sir, but this child—" He broke off frowning.

"Well?" prompted the magistrate, when his principal officer seemed disinclined to continue. "What of him?"

"This child—the light from the gas lamp was shining on him, you understand, and I got a good look at his face."

"Yes, Mr. Maxwell?" Mr. Colquhoun's voice held an edge of impatience. "What of it?"

Maxwell took a deep breath. "He looked just like Mr. Pickett."

Brother, Can You Spare a Crime?

Another John Pickett Mystery

Sheri Cobb South

To my dad, Bill Cobb, who taught me how to draw blueprints when I was a teenager—a skill that proved invaluable during the robbing of this bank, er, the writing of this book.

And to the helpful folks at the Bank of England, who, when I emailed them and asked for advice on how best to rob it, gave me an answer.

1

In Which a Crime Is Committed

Robert Maxwell sat in a public house in the Strand, nursing a pint (his third that evening, if memory served) and trying without success to hold the ghosts at bay. He had fared better than many of the men at Corunna, he knew; the fact that he was sitting here, and not buried under six feet of rocky Spanish soil, was proof of that. He had a good position, for his military service (along with a letter of recommendation from his commanding officer) had secured for him immediate entry to a place amongst the elite half-dozen Bow Street men known colloquially as Runners without his being obliged to languish for years on the Foot Patrol.

Granted, to call himself a "Runner" might be overly optimistic, as the French ball that had shattered his leg had left him with a tendency to limp unless he made a concentrated effort to even his gait. Still, the magistrate had been willing to take a chance on him, and Maxwell was determined that

Patrick Colquhoun's confidence in him would not be misplaced.

It was only that certain things, experienced unexpectedly and without warning—the acrid smell of gunpowder, or the loud report of a firearm close at hand—recalled the chaotic retreat to his mind so vividly that it might have taken place yesterday, instead of almost nine months ago.

In the present instance, he had left the Bow Street Public Office a few hours earlier and had headed west along the Strand, only to come upon the near-collision of a peddler's wagon with a cumbersome landau. While the drivers of the two vehicles had exchanged pleasantries (most of which were unfit to be spoken in mixed company, let alone on a public thoroughfare), the spooked horses had added their own terrified contributions to the conversation. It had all come rushing back: the shouts and the curses, the shrieking, sweating horses, the stench of gunpowder and blood, the screams of men falling around him, never to rise again...

He could not face an empty house, with only the ghosts for company. For here was the great irony: While he had survived on that cold day in January, his wife had not. Instead, poor Sally had succumbed to an attack of influenza at roughly the same time that he'd been dragging himself aboard a British transport ship for evacuation back to England. To England, and London, and an empty house...

No, he could not face that house, not tonight. He'd made straight for the nearest tavern, and there he remained. He raised the glass to his lips and discovered that it was empty. Perhaps he should order a fourth; the brew was clearly not doing its job, for it seemed he could still hear the confusion of the disordered retreat.

Gradually he realized that the noise was not some trick of memory, but of a loud commotion in the street. Even as the recognition registered, he heard a shout, followed by the hollow *clack-clack-clack* of the watchman's wooden rattle. The ghosts vanished as he, along with every other man in the place, jumped up and hurried from the premises to join in the hue and cry.

Three men—no, he amended mentally, two men and a youth—had just emerged into the street through the gaping door of Number 59, and now ran eastward along the Strand. One of the men paused in his flight and turned back just long enough to throw something at the pursuing watchman, who fell with a scream that ended, sickeningly, in a gurgle.

Maxwell had seen enough men bayoneted to recognize the sound, and to know there was nothing that could be done for the poor fellow. Instead, he turned his attention to the escaping felons, leaving his fellow public-house patrons to administer whatever comfort they could to the dying, or dead, watchman.

But he missed his footing in the uncertain light of the gas lamps. As he stepped off the curb, pain shot up his injured leg and he fell sprawling into the street. Clutching his throbbing knee, he looked up at the fleeing robbers just as something fell from the youth's hand. The boy would have turned back to retrieve it, but one of the men, the one who had thrown the knife, grabbed him by the arm with a curse and dragged him away.

As they fled, however, the boy looked back at whatever it was that he'd dropped, and the yellow light from the nearby streetlamp fell full onto his face.

Maxwell, staring after him, breathed, "Well, I'll be damned!"

* * *

"Bradley never stood a chance, poor devil," concluded Maxwell, having reported the incident to the magistrate the following morning. "The knife caught him in the throat. He apparently surprised a group of men in the act of robbing Number 59. That would be the bank, sir—Thomas Coutts and Company."

Scowling fiercely beneath bushy white eyebrows, Patrick Colquhoun examined the knife that Maxwell had retrieved from the scene of the crime. It was cheap as such weapons went, and had been repaired at least once, when the blade had apparently separated from the haft. Still, it had been honed to razor sharpness, as Mr. Colquhoun discovered when he tapped its point and a bead of bright red blood appeared on the tip of his finger. He wiped it away with his thumb and addressed his newest Runner. "And the man who threw it?"

Maxwell sighed. "Escaped, I'm afraid. I stumbled and fell, and between half of the witnesses stopping to see to Bradley and the other half stopping to see to me, the robbers got clean away, headed north on Bedford Street."

Mr. Colquhoun nodded in resignation. "Toward the rookeries of St. Giles and Seven Dials, no doubt."

Maxwell didn't have to ask for an explanation. The twisting, narrow streets north of Covent Garden were a regular rabbit warren, offering bolt-holes sufficient for sheltering the practitioners of every sort of vice. And the watchmen were utterly ineffective as a deterrent. They were elderly men— former soldiers, most of them—who had been given the position as a supplement to pensions that amounted to little more than a pittance. God knew they needed something; unlike the officers who commanded them, the enlisted men had no commissions to sell in order to fund their retirement.

Unfortunately, what had sounded good in theory was less so in practice: Most of them, perhaps feeling they had already done their bit in the wars of the last century, were content to doze peacefully in their watchmen's boxes with a bottle of gin for company. And perhaps they had the right of it; Bradley had apparently been more conscientious than most, and look what that had got him.

"Did you see anything else?" the magistrate was asking. "I realize it was dark, but anything at all might be useful."

With an effort, Maxwell dragged his attention back to the present. "I can tell you there were three of them, and they were all male, but other than that—" he broke off with a shrug.

"The inquest will no doubt bring in a verdict of willful murder by person or persons unknown. In the meantime, you might begin with this," Mr. Colquhoun said, handing the knife over the railing that separated his bench from the rest of the room. "If you can find the shop where it was repaired, they might be able to tell you who brought it in. God knows it's little enough to go on, but it appears to be all we have."

"There is one other thing, sir," Maxwell began hesitantly.

"Yes?" prompted the magistrate. "What is it?"

"One of the gang of robbers—well, sir, I thought he was a youth—twelve or thirteen years old—but then he turned back, and I realized he was only a child. He'd dropped this."

He handed something across the railing, and Mr. Colquhoun took and examined it. It was no weapon, this, but a toy soldier made of metal. It was something between two and three inches tall, and its uniform depicted that worn a quarter-century earlier, as well as he could tell, given that the paint was so chipped as to be almost nonexistent, and at some point the bayonet had snapped off the end of its tiny musket.

Mr. Colquhoun could recall his own son having once owned an entire set of similar soldiers—a set which, his wife might have told him, still resided in the attic of his Mayfair residence, where his grandchildren might play with them whenever they came to visit. Mr. Colquhoun had seen too much of the world to cherish many illusions, but he found something rather poignant about a child young enough to play with toys being put to work robbing banks instead.

"It's unfortunate, Mr. Maxwell, but not uncommon," he acknowledged with a sigh. "A child can get into places a grown man can't—through windows, gaps in the walls, even down chimneys, if he's small enough."

"Yes, sir, but this child—" He broke off frowning.

"Well?" prompted the magistrate, when his principal officer seemed disinclined to continue. "What of him?"

"This child—the light from the gas lamp was shining on him, you understand, and I got a good look at his face."

"Yes, Mr. Maxwell?" Mr. Colquhoun's voice held an edge of impatience. "What of it?"

Maxwell took a deep breath. "He looked just like Mr. Pickett."

2

*In Which John Pickett's Character
Is More than Once Called into Question*

M r. Colquhoun scowled at him over bushy white brows. "Just what are you implying, Mr. Maxwell?"

"I'm not implying anything, sir. It just seemed to me that if some by-blow of Mr. Pickett's is going about robbing banks, then he might ought to know about it."

"I can assure you, Mr. Maxwell, whoever that child may have been, he is no by-blow of Mr. Pickett's."

The magistrate's tone left no room for argument, but Maxwell could not be entirely satisfied. "I tell you, sir, the resemblance was remarkable—staggering, even."

Mr. Colquhoun drummed his fingers on the bench for a long moment before asking, "And how old would you say this child was?"

Maxwell frowned thoughtfully. "I expect he must have been around ten years old. He was tall for his age, though, so I mistook him at first for older." After a discreet pause, he added, "Then, too, Mr. Pickett is quite tall, is he not?"

"Ten years," echoed Mr. Colquhoun thoughtfully. "You realize that for it to be as you say, Mr. Pickett must have fathered a child at the age of fourteen?"

"I realize, of course, that he must have been very young," said Maxwell, readily conceding the point, "but I don't see that youth alone eliminates him. He's a good-looking lad, and, well, God knows young men of the poorest classes have little enough else to look forward to."

Mr. Colquhoun emitted a low growl, and for a moment Maxwell feared he had overstepped in referring to John Pickett's criminal past—a past widely known at Bow Street, but rarely mentioned outright, at least not by those with an eye to their careers. A man more familiar with the magistrate's moods—a man, in fact, such as the one currently under discussion—might have assured him that the sound was indicative of nothing more ominous than deep concentration.

Ten years, Mr. Colquhoun thought. Which meant he would have been born in 1799... And Pickett Senior had been transported in 1798... Yes, it was just within the realm of possibility...

"The coroner's inquest is scheduled for tomorrow morning," he said briskly, giving Mr. Maxwell to understand that no further speculations were to be made regarding his fellow principal officer. "Until then, see what you can discover about that knife. Oh, and when Mr. Pickett comes in, tell him I want a word with him."

* * *

Meanwhile, the subject of this discussion sat on an

uncomfortable wooden chair while the governor of no less venerable an institution than the Bank of England addressed him in placating tones and studiously avoided looking him in the eye.

"I'm sorry, Mr. Pickett, but I'm afraid we haven't a place for you," said Mr. John Whitmore. He picked up the quill pen lying on his desk, then looked at it as if surprised to find it in his hand, and put it down again.

"Oh?" John Pickett fumbled in the inside pocket of his tailcoat (the plum-colored one, fashionable enough to suggest prosperity and yet sufficiently sober in hue to escape the censure of even the staidest banker) and fished out the rectangle of paper he'd cut from the *Times* just that morning. "It says here—"

"Yes, I know what it says," Mr. Whitmore said hastily. "I wrote out the advertisement myself."

Pickett read it aloud nonetheless. " 'Clerk wanted. Young man of good character with strong ciphering skills and neat penmanship.' " He glanced down at the desk, and the sheet of paper where he had demonstrated these abilities. "Were my calculations not correct?"

"They were," Mr. Whitmore conceded the point, albeit reluctantly. In fact, they had been accurate down to the last farthing, including the one designed to trip up all but the most careful applicants.

"Has the position already been filled?"

"It has not," the bank's governor confessed somewhat sheepishly.

"I can only assume, then, that the sticking point is the

matter of my character," Pickett said with great dignity. "In fact, you don't trust me to keep my hand out of the till."

"It isn't that." Somehow Mr. Whitmore's objection had the effect of confirming Pickett's suspicions rather than allaying them. "But, well, one never knows what latent tendencies one might possess until actually faced with temptation. And you, with your, er, background, might be, let us say, more susceptible than most."

"Let me remind you, sir, that I have been employed by Bow Street since I was nineteen years old. During that time, I have handled not only large sums of money, but jewelry and other valuables as well—and I returned every last farthing to its rightful owner, whether that rightful owner was the victim of a theft or the magistrate himself. If I had any 'latent tendencies' toward theft, don't you think they would have shown themselves by now?"

"And yet, you have a criminal record, Mr. Pickett."

"Yes—as a fourteen-year-old boy, trying to survive any way I could! But I made a vow to the man who rescued me, a vow I've kept for more than ten years. Even if I were tempted—which I beg leave to doubt—I would resist it out of loyalty to him."

"And this would be"—he looked at the letter of recommendation Pickett had supplied—"Major James Pennington of Norwood Green in Somersetshire?"

"No. Patrick Colquhoun, the magistrate who oversees my work at Bow Street."

"And yet you bring me no endorsement from him, Mr. Pickett. Why is that?"

For the first time in the interview, Pickett's air of confidence faltered. "He—he doesn't know I'm looking for a new position." Neither did Major James Pennington, for that matter, and the major was his brother-in-law. But Pickett would cross that bridge when he came to it—an event that would *not* take place today, given the governor's unenthusiastic response to his application.

"Oh?" Mr. Whitmore frowned. "And just why *are* you looking for a new position, given your apparently successful career at Bow Street?"

"It—it has recently been brought home to me that I could be putting my wife in danger," Pickett said, choosing his words with care. "For her sake, I thought it was time I sought out a safer line of work."

"I see." Mr. Whitmore was silent for a long moment, during which he studied Pickett thoughtfully. "Mr. Pickett, if it were entirely up to me, I would be sorely tempted to engage you, at least on a trial basis. But I have the shareholders to answer to, you know. If I were to take such a chance, and be mistaken in you—"

"You wouldn't be, sir, I assure you," Pickett insisted.

"So you say. And you may be telling the truth, or at least believe you are. And as I say, if it were only my own funds at risk—" He broke off with a dismissive shake of his head. "But I don't have the right to take such a chance with other people's money, Mr. Pickett. I wish you all the best, truly I do, but I can do nothing for you. I hope you understand."

Oh, I understand, all right, Pickett thought bitterly, pushing back his chair with a screech of wood on marble-tiled floor. *I understand that no matter what I do, no matter what I may accomplish, I'll never be anything more than a pickpocket.*

Ignoring Mr. Whitmore's proffered handshake, he turned and left the governor's office without a backward glance. He strode through the large room where dozens of clerks bent over their work, carrying out the drudgery on which the Empire was built. High over their heads, the caryatids supporting the domed skylight seemed to look down on Pickett with scorn, or perhaps pity; he wasn't sure which would be worse.

He passed through the door at the opposite end of this room, resisting the urge to slam it shut behind him, and entered another room where the bank's clients conducted their business. A few of these, as well as the clerks assisting them, cast curious glances at the well-dressed young man in a clear state of agitation before turning their attention back to their own concerns.

Pickett could not recall passing through such a room upon his arrival; clearly, he had taken a wrong turn upon leaving the governor's office. He retraced his steps, and was thankful to see that the governor had already closed the door behind him. It would be too humiliating to admit that not only was he unqualified to hold a position there, he couldn't even find his way out of the building.

Or perhaps, he considered with growing certainty, that closed door had not been the one to the governor's office at all. For now he found himself standing in a long corridor that stretched away to both the right and the left, its walls broken at intervals by narrow arched doorways or wider, grander openings flanked with columns and crowned with triangular pediments. He knew there existed a passage leading from Lothbury Street to somewhere deep within the bank's three-acre complex, through which wagons would come to be loaded with the gold that financed England's war with Bonaparte. But this could not possibly be it. Could it? Surely this was too narrow to accommodate any such vehicle. And even if it were not, even if it were wide enough, who would want wagon wheels—to say nothing of horses' hooves!—trundling up and down floors that appeared to be made of marble. No, this could not possibly be the passage that would lead him to the Lothbury entrance.

But it might very well lead him to an entrance; it didn't matter which one. He chose a direction at random and set off with what he hoped was the air of a man who knew exactly where he was going and what he intended to do when he got there. This direction, as it soon proved, turned out to be the wrong one, for it decanted Pickett, not into any of the streets surrounding the bank, but into a circular chamber too small to be the great rotunda easily accessed from the main entrance on Threadneedle Street. He thought it a great pity that there were no compass points set into its domed skylight by which he might judge his direction, as there were in the larger rotunda just off the paved court that made up the bank's impressive main entrance. Of course, it was quite possible that a compass would have been no help to him in any case; still, it could not have left him any more completely lost than he already was.

He turned to make his way back down the long passage to the other end, but before he reached it, he was drawn up short by a glimpse of sunlight. He took two steps backward and, yes, there it was: a shaft of sunlight streaming through tall, arched windows. He had not realized he was so near the outside wall; he'd imagined himself to be somewhere deep within the sprawling edifice.

Alas, before he could locate the door through which he could make his escape, a man—one of the bank's officers, Pickett thought, if the man's sober clothing and air of offended dignity were anything to judge by—stepped squarely into his path.

"Here now, you can't come in here! Move along, if you please."

Too late, Pickett realized that what he'd thought was open air was actually one of several enclosed courtyards built into the bank in order to incorporate more windows into the design; after all, the Bank of England did not attain its present status by being profligate with candles.

"I—I'm looking for a way out," Pickett confessed. "I seem to have got lost."

"You'll have to go back the way you came," the man informed him without sympathy. "No one is allowed through here."

As if to make a liar of him, at that very moment the door of a wide arched bay set into the opposite wall of the courtyard opened, and a man stepped out into the sunlight.

Pickett resisted the urge to point this out, saying instead, "If you can tell me how to get back to the street—"

"I suppose you'd better come through here after all," the bank's officer conceded grudgingly. "Straight through that door is the Pay Hall. Step lively, now, and no loitering!"

"I'm obliged to you," Pickett said, adding mentally, *Although why you think I should want to loiter about a place I hope never to set foot in again—*

In fact, so eager was he to escape the scene of his humiliation that he darted through the doorway into the Pay Hall and ran full tilt into a man approaching from the other direction, a tall, lean man who seemed in imminent danger of falling over backwards. Pickett grabbed the sleeve of the fellow's shabby coat to steady him, thinking it curious that anyone wearing such worn and threadbare clothing should have business with the Bank of England. Then again, there were men who squeezed every penny until it screamed for mercy, men whom no one would suspect of having great wealth until they died, leaving vast sums to their stunned and gratified heirs. No doubt Mr. Whitmore and his cronies would welcome this fellow with open arms, while John Pickett, clothed in all the finery of Mr. Meyer of Conduit Street, was held in such low regard that no one could be bothered even to show him the door.

He muttered a disjointed apology (which received no answer beyond a glare from cold eyes of so pale a blue that they might have been carved from ice), then flung himself through the massive outer doors and into the paved courtyard abutting Threadneedle Street. Here he stopped and took a deep, steadying breath, struggling to gain control of himself before returning to Bow Street.

22

For, having endured the humiliating interview, he now had to pretend, first to his magistrate and, later, to his wife, that it had never happened.

* * *

Pickett entered the Bow Street Public Office a short time later, having taken advantage of the walk from Threadneedle Street to compose his thoughts—and a very good thing, too, as he was met with the information that Mr. Colquhoun was in his office and wanted a word with him. Pickett thanked Maxwell for the information, then strode across the room to the closed door of the magistrate's *sanctum sanctorum*. As he knocked on the wooden panel, he glanced back and found Maxwell regarding him with a thoughtful frown.

"Is anything the matter?" Pickett asked, when his colleague offered no explanation for this sudden interest.

"No, nothing—that is, I'm sure Mr. Colquhoun will—" Maxwell broke off abruptly as the door swung open and a pronounced Scots burr bade Pickett enter.

"Mr. Maxwell said you wanted to see me, sir," Pickett said as Mr. Colquhoun closed the door behind them.

"Yes. Tell me, John, what do you make of this?"

He picked up a small object lying on his desk and handed it to Pickett, who turned it over in his hands. It was a toy soldier, and it was at least twenty years old, if its painted uniform was anything to judge by. Pickett made this observation aloud, concluding with, "I would lay you odds that some mudlark found it along the foreshore."

"Oh? What makes you say so?"

"It's worn so smooth," Pickett answered, running his

finger up and down the length of molded metal. "Then, too, the paint is intact on the front, but almost completely worn away on the back. I should say this poor fellow has been lying face-down in the mud for a long time—and if I'd found something like him when I was a lad, Da would never have had him to sell for scrap metal! I'd have hidden him under my pillow and taken him out to play with after I was supposed to be asleep. But how came you to have him, sir?"

"He—it—was left behind last night at the scene of a botched robbery." Keen blue eyes, previously fixed on the toy soldier, now looked up to regard Pickett. "I expect you've heard about what happened to Bradley, poor devil."

"Er, no, sir," confessed Pickett, painfully aware of the fact that had he not been away from Bow Street for most of the morning pursuing his own ends, he would have very likely heard the news from some obliging member of the Foot Patrol, if not from the magistrate himself.

Briefly, Mr. Colquhoun recounted the story as he'd had it from Maxwell, pausing at the end of his recital to sink heavily into the chair behind his desk. "Between Bradley's catching a knife in the throat and Maxwell's taking a tumble off the curb, the miscreants were able to make their escape."

"I see," Pickett said thoughtfully. "Am I to understand that you want me to take the case, sir? I should have thought Maxwell—"

"Since Mr. Maxwell was on the scene at the time, I think it only makes sense for him to continue with the investigation, don't you?"

"Yes, sir." After a brief, awkward pause, Pickett asked,

"What, then—?" He broke off, not quite sure how to ask why, if he were not to be given the case, the magistrate had made a point of spelling out the details to him.

Mr. Colquhoun, for his part, was strangely reluctant to enlighten him; it had occurred to the magistrate that there was no tactful way that one could ask a man, even one whom he had known since boyhood, if he had not, after all, gone to his marriage bed as pure (so to speak) as the driven snow.

But it would not do to be sentimental where the lad was concerned. Clearly, John Pickett had been no saint, as evidenced by the fact that he had first come to Mr. Colquhoun's attention fresh from stealing an apple from the market at Covent Garden. And he was, as Mr. Maxwell had pointed out, a good-looking lad—and had very likely been even more so, before an overeager member of the Foot Patrol had taken it upon himself to rearrange young John Pickett's nose.

Now that Mr. Colquhoun thought of it, it was quite possible that the chagrin Pickett had suffered in the wake of his accidental marriage and the ensuing annulment procedure was not that of a chaste young man embarrassed at his own lack of experience, but of one obliged to refute previously proven capabilities at the behest of a powerful family who numbered amongst its members the lady with whom Pickett had fallen in love—the lady who was now Mrs. John Pickett.

No, it would not do to build up a romanticized picture which bore no resemblance to any living human being, least of all the one who now stood before him. Mr. Colquhoun scowled fiercely, and addressed his youngest Runner in formal terms jarringly at odds with the intimate subject he was obliged to broach.

"I want you to cast your mind back, Mr. Pickett," he said sternly, "back to the time before you came to Bow Street, before you went to work for Elias Granger."

Good God, he thought with some dismay, *is it possible that he and Sophy Granger—?* He scowled all the more fiercely at the thought of having to break the news to Elias Granger that he had a grandson running amok in the rookeries of London, sired by the same apprentice that he himself had foisted upon his old friend.

"Yes, sir, what of it?" Pickett asked, momentarily startling Mr. Colquhoun with his air of indifference, until the magistrate recalled that he had not, as yet, voiced Maxwell's suspicions aloud.

"Is it possible that during those days—say, eleven years ago—that you and—you and some obliging damsel—that is—" He realized he was trying to blame some unknown female for any straying on young John Pickett's part from the path of righteousness, and broke off abruptly. "Oh, the devil! Is it possible that in your misspent youth, you got some girl in the family way?"

Pickett could only stare at him, and will himself not to blush. "No, sir!"

"You're sure of that?"

Pickett's efforts at composure failed, and he flushed crimson. "Quite—quite sure."

His blushes told Mr. Colquhoun more than his words ever could, and the magistrate nodded, relieved at having his previous assumptions so clearly confirmed. "That's all right, then. What of your father? Is it possible that he left some woman with a pudding in the oven?"

Pickett cast his mind back to the days before his father had been transported to Botany Bay, to the nights of awakening from a deep sleep to hear sounds emitting from the tiny bedroom his father had shared with Moll—sounds of Moll in a rage, of his father's impatient replies—and other sounds, meaningless at the time, but now, in retrospect...

"I suppose it's possible. In fact," he added, recalling an encounter only a few months earlier with a young pickpocket, "I'd say it was quite likely."

"Oh? What makes you say so?"

"I think I may have met him once, when he tried to pick my pocket." His infrequent grin flashed briefly. "How's that for irony?"

"You didn't place him under arrest?"

"No." In fact, he'd made a few suggestions as to how the young thief might improve his technique, but he doubted the magistrate would approve this course of action. "It occurred to me at the time that he might have been me some years earlier—I suppose that was why I was so lenient with him— but I had other things on my mind, and beyond noticing a certain superficial resemblance, I didn't give it—or him— another thought. But why this sudden interest? If you don't mind my asking," he added hastily.

The magistrate sighed. "I told you about the murder of Bradley, and the three robbers who escaped. What I did *not* tell you was that one of them was a child who, according to

Maxwell, bore a striking resemblance to you."

"And so, naturally, he assumed the boy must be a bastard of mine!" Pickett said indignantly, recalling Maxwell's speculative gaze upon him. "I must remember to thank him!"

"Come down off your high ropes," Mr. Colquhoun chided him. "Recall that until this past January, Maxwell was with the army in Spain. He took part in the retreat from Corunna; he's seen firsthand what unsupervised young men are capable of, and he doesn't yet know you well enough to make exceptions for you."

" 'Yet,' " Pickett echoed, picking up on the single word. "Am I to understand that you expect him to know me better in the near future?"

"You are quick, aren't you?" The question was purely rhetorical, as Mr. Colquhoun regarded his protégé with an almost fatherly pride.

"You want me to assist Maxwell, then?" Pickett, who had successfully conducted more than one investigation on his own, was not quite sure how he felt about being reduced to the rôle of assistant to someone else, especially when the man under whose supervision he would be working had considerably less experience than he did himself.

"Er, not exactly," Mr. Colquhoun said. "Mr. Maxwell saw three people rob Coutts bank; he is now charged with finding them and bringing them to justice. Let me remind you that Bradley, the watchman, was killed during their escape. Therefore, what would have been a charge of robbery becomes one of murder. 'Justice,' then, is not transportation, as punishment for a simple robbery might be, but execution by hanging. And as all three are accomplices to the crime, that sentence would apply to all three, regardless of which one actually threw the knife."

Pickett nodded. "I see."

Mr. Colquhoun continued as if he had not spoken. "Given that the lad is very likely your half-brother, it occurs to me that you might want to get in, find him, and get him out."

"In fact," Pickett said thoughtfully, "you want me to attach myself to Maxwell's investigation, and throw a spanner into the works."

The magistrate's bushy white eyebrows arched toward his hairline. "I never said any such thing!"

"You didn't have to. Assuming, for the moment, that I'm successful, what am I to do with the boy once I've got him?"

Mr. Colquhoun leaned back in his chair with the air of one who, having fulfilled his obligation, has washed his hands of the matter. "That, Mr. Pickett, is entirely up to you."

* * *

In quite a different part of London, a stout man in a shabby coat and a knitted woolen cap entered a small, sparsely furnished room and closed the door firmly behind him before collapsing, puffing slightly, onto a rickety wooden armchair. Three faces regarded him expectantly: a tall, lean man with something of the look of a whippet about him, who idly picked his teeth with the tip of a knife blade as he studied the new arrival with narrowed eyes; a pretty young woman whose thin cotton dress, inadequate to staving off the crisp autumn air, was supplemented by a threadbare shawl draped across her shoulders and knotted over her chest; and a ragged boy kneeling on the floor and crumbling bread into a small metal cage in which a tiny goldfinch hopped about, a boy whose tear-stained face wore an expression more indicative of hostility than sadness.

"It wasn't there," the stout man said, with all the misery of one who knows his report to be unsatisfactory.

The tall, thin man muttered a curse under his breath. "You're sure, Jud?"

The stout fellow pulled off the cap and twisted it in his hands. "I looked as careful as I dared, without attracting no unwanted attention," he insisted. "I tell you, Roger, it wasn't there!"

"Taken as evidence, likely as not," grumbled the tall man, the one called Roger. He wheeled to face the boy, one arm raised to strike. "You see what you've done, you and your—"

"Don't, Roger!" beseeched the young woman, clutching at his sleeve. "You're upset because all your plans came to naught last night, but there's no reason to take it out on a helpless child."

But the "helpless child," no stranger to the back of Roger's hand, had hardly even flinched. "Leastways you can't take it away from me no more," he said, with a defiance in his brown eyes and a firmness in the set of his jaw that contrasted sharply with the tears drying on his cheeks. "You said you'd give it back if I helped you get into the bank. Well, I helped you, and I got you in, for all the good it did you. But you can't take it away from me no more, so I don't got to help you no more." The goldfinch added its own contribution to this speech, a full-throated song that seemed to express agreement with the boy's claims.

"Oh, no?" Roger retorted, his earlier anger giving way to scornful amusement. "What do you think you'll do, then—go home to your mum? I gave her two quid for you. What makes you think she'll want you back?"

The boy swallowed hard, then gave voice to something he'd never spoken aloud before, something he wasn't even supposed to know. "I have a b-brother," he said defiantly. "He'll come get me, and when he does, he'll—he'll darken your daylights!"

"Ooh, I'm *sooo scaaared!*" The stout man, Jud, made a show of knocking his knees together and biting his dirt-encrusted fingernails, then abandoned all pretense of fear. "You really think Roger's afraid of some brat?"

"He's not a boy—he's a man. And when he comes, he'll draw Roger's cork—and yours, too!" the boy added with relish.

Roger grinned at him. "So, why haven't we seen him? Where is he, this brother of yours?"

The air of bravado faltered and the child turned back to the bird in the cage, mumbling something as he stuck his finger between the bars. With a flurry of yellow wings, the goldfinch landed on this new perch and began picking at the crumbs that clung to it.

"What was that?" Roger asked sharply.

"I said *I don't know!*"

This was true; in fact, he wouldn't have known about his

brother at all, had his mother not mentioned him once when she'd had too much gin. She'd said something about Gentleman Jack—that was his father, he knew, who had been sent to Botany Bay before he was born—and then something about someone called John. It soon became clear that John was also a son of Gentleman Jack, but when he'd asked her about John the next morning, when she was sober, she'd boxed his ears and ordered him never again to speak that name in her hearing, not if he knew what was good for him. Having learned, often the hard way, what was good for him, he had obeyed this command.

Still, Mum couldn't stop him from *thinking*, and he'd never stopped thinking about the older brother who had, somehow, got away. When he'd found the toy soldier half-buried in the mud along the river's edge, he hadn't turned it over to Mum to be sold as scrap metal. Instead, he'd kept it. Sometimes the small painted figure was a soldier, as his creator had intended, fighting Bonaparte; other times, he was a bold explorer searching for the source of the Nile—that was a river in Africa, one even longer than the Thames. He'd seen it in a book once, when he'd briefly gone to school. But whatever daring deeds his imagination contrived for the toy soldier, one thing was constant: His name was always John—John Pickett, after the elder brother who'd got away.

And now the soldier, too, was gone. Although he hated himself for showing any sign of weakness in front of Roger or Jud, he couldn't hold back the tear that escaped at the thought and ran down the salty track that had dried on his cheek.

"Never mind it, lad." Roger's voice was almost gentle,

as he reached out a hand to rumple the boy's dirty brown curls. "We pull off this next job, and you can have a whole army of the things, bought brand-new from the toy shop."

"What's that, Roger? Another job?" Jud asked eagerly, sitting forward in his chair. "What is it?"

"Why should we waste our time on Coutts when there are bigger fish to be fried?" Roger asked, grinning broadly.

"You mean—?" Jud could imagine only one fish bigger than Thomas Coutts and Company, and the thought of it made the breath catch in his throat.

"I mean the Old Lady of Threadneedle Street. About time somebody got up the old girl's skirts," he added, pulling the young woman to him with one arm about her waist while he thrust his other hand beneath the hem of her dress, presumably by way of a demonstration.

"Stop it, Roger," she chided, pushing herself away and straightening her clothing as she rolled her eyes in the boy's direction. "Little pitchers have big ears. Eyes too, come to that."

"You really think we can rob the Bank of England?" Jud's eyes bulged with the enormity of the undertaking.

"We've got to," Roger said simply. "Coutts is right out— they'll have the watch, maybe even the Runners, keeping an eye on the place now. And after what happened last night," he added, his voice hardening, "we've got to get away before they take us in, not just for robbery, but for murder. It takes money to book passage to Amsterdam—aye, and even more to grease the fist of the ship's captain, who wouldn't think twice about selling us to Bow Street—and if we had that kind of money, we wouldn't be robbing banks, now, would we?"

"And the boy?" the young woman asked.

Roger cast a menacing look at the boy, who met his gaze with wide brown eyes that couldn't quite conceal the fear behind them. "He'll do what we tell him to, if he don't want his neck stretched."

The boy looked back down at the bird, surely no less a prisoner than he was himself. *Please come and get me,* he silently pleaded with a man somewhere too far away to hear him. *Please come...John.*

3

*In Which John Pickett Visits Another Bank
on Very Different Business*

His interview with the magistrate being at an end, Pickett left Mr. Colquhoun's office and approached Maxwell with what he hoped was an air of nonchalance.

"I hear you had a bit of excitement last night," he remarked.

Maxwell looked up from perusing an issue of the *Hue and Cry*, one of a stack of similar periodicals at his elbow. "You could say so." He folded the paper, set it aside, and picked up another from the top of the stack.

"Looking for anything in particular?" Pickett asked, trying another approach.

"I'm looking for other robberies with a similar pattern."

"Oh? What pattern is that?"

Maxwell gave a little sigh of annoyance, and Pickett realized his persistence was doing nothing to endear him to his colleague. "I'm wondering about other robberies in which the building has been breached through a small window or a vent too small for a grown man."

"Breached by my bastard son, you mean." Pickett grinned, letting the former military man know that he bore him no ill will.

"I meant no offense—" Maxwell began.

"And I took none," Pickett assured him. "There was very little moon, and God knows the street lamps aren't much help. If you saw the boy in daylight, you would very likely find no resemblance at all."

"Possibly," Maxwell agreed, albeit without much conviction.

"It's an interesting approach," Pickett said, nodding at the stack of periodicals. "Looking for similar cases, I mean. I'm not sure I would have thought of it."

Maxwell gave a grunt that might have meant anything from "I'm so glad you approve" to "go away and leave me alone." Pickett rather suspected it was the latter; clearly, bootlicking would not inspire the man to confide in him.

"I'll leave you to it, then, and hope for your sake that something useful turns up," he said, giving Maxwell a pitying glance. "It looks like a tedious task."

Receiving no reply, he betook himself from the Bow Street Public Office, quite as if it didn't matter at all.

A short walk brought him to Thomas Coutts and Company at 59 Strand. The attempted robbery had apparently left the establishment undaunted, for in spite of the affront to its hallowed walls, it was once again open for business. Like most of the buildings in this part of London, it was fronted with a low wrought iron railing that protected the unwary from tumbling into the stairwell that led to a basement and coal cellar below street level. Pickett peered into the shadowy depths and saw that the basement level was lit, at least partially, by a small window through which a little sunlight might enter, at least at certain times of the day—most likely early morning, and that only during the summer months.

At the moment, however, sunlight was not the only thing that could enter: The glass had been broken out, leaving a gaping hole large enough for a child to pass through— provided that the child had some means of reaching a hole that was fully seven feet above the foot of the stairs.

Pickett did not hesitate. He followed the wrought iron railing to its open end, where a locked gate no higher than the railing barred access to the staircase. This, however, offered no real barrier to a tall man, nor, Pickett suspected, a determined one. Gripping the top of the gate, he swung one long leg over it and then the other, then swiftly descended the stairs to the lower level. He glanced quickly up toward the street to ensure that no curious passersby had stepped up to the railing to watch, and, assured that he was alone, turned his attention to the window just above his head. He reached up and brushed the sill clean of any shards of broken glass, then grasped it and hefted himself up to peer inside.

Most of the basement was lost in darkness, but he could see tiny points of light winking on and off as the shadow cast by his own head and shoulders blocked the light from illuminating the fragments of glass littering the floor. Yes, the window had certainly been broken from the outside, although he could see no sign of what had been used to shatter it. The knife, perhaps, the one that had only a short time later been thrown at Bradley, the hapless watchman who had sounded the alarm. Even a man's fist could have done the job, provided it was wrapped sufficiently to prevent him from cutting himself to ribbons in the process. Pickett looked down at the sill beneath his hands (which was now right under his nose) and found no sign of blood.

And after the window had been broken out, then…what? The resulting opening was not large, even for a child to go through. He doubted his own shoulders would fit. It was quite possible—he would even venture to say it was probable—that the boy's adult cohorts were not feeding him sufficiently, in order to keep him small enough to serve their purposes. But sooner or later, nature would have its way, and the child would grow to a size where he would no longer be of use to them, at least not as a little snakesman. What would happen to him then? Pickett knew from bitter experience that life in the rookeries of London was a constant fight for survival—and woe to the one who could no longer pull his own weight.

An angry voice suddenly interrupted his thoughts, banishing the sordid images, real and imagined, that crowded his brain. "Here now, fellow! Get away from there!"

The shout, coming from directly over his head made Pickett lose his grip. He dropped to his feet, then turned to identify the source of the sound. A man in an outmoded wig and a sober black cutaway coat stood glaring at him over the wrought iron railing.

"I—I beg your pardon—" Pickett began.

"As well you might! What the devil are you doing down there? But I think I need not ask! It's a bold fellow who'll attempt a robbery in broad daylight—finishing the task he began last night, no doubt!"

"This is not what it seems," Pickett insisted, dusting his hands clean of any minuscule splinters of glass that might have lodged there. Seeing the man was not convinced, he hurried up the stairs, climbed back over the gate—an operation conducted with such ease that it served to confirm rather than allay the suspicions of his fiercely scowling accuser—and groped in the inside pocket of his coat for a card.

"John Pickett, of Bow Street," he said, offering his card as proof of his identification. He couldn't help wondering what he would do once he could no longer claim this particular form of address. Of course, it was to be assumed that he would also no longer have reason to peer through broken windows or otherwise trespass in places where he had no business being. Then again, given his young brother's unique skill set, that assumption might well be misplaced; in spite of his question to the magistrate as to what he might do with the boy, he had a very good idea of what the end result would be.

"Bow Street?" echoed the man, clearly skeptical of this claim. "We've had a Runner here already, looking the place over."

"Yes—that would be Mr. Maxwell," Pickett agreed, improvising rapidly. "A good man, but new to investigative work. Only a year ago he was in Spain, fighting Boney on the

Peninsula. I would be obliged if you don't mention to him that we're checking up on him—he'd very likely take offense—I know I would have, when I first joined the Bow Street force—and if you should happen to catch sight of me at the inquest tomorrow morning, just act as if you've never seen me before, there's a good fellow."

His accuser's ire wilted in the face of this burst of eloquence. "Yes, of course. That is—allow me to introduce myself," he said, offering his hand. "Jeremiah Davidson, at your service. You must forgive me. I have been employed by Thomas Coutts and Co. for more than thirty years, since I came here as a clerk at very nearly your own age. I now have the honor of being one of its officers, albeit in a junior capacity. And in all that time, nothing like this has ever happened before. Thank God they failed in their attempt to open the safe! Had they not—" He broke off and groped in his coat pocket for a handkerchief and mopped his brow, which was glistening with perspiration in spite of the autumnal chill in the air.

Pickett nodded. "I understand. Now that I've seen how the miscreants gained access, I should like to have a look inside. I must say," he added, glancing down into the stairwell at the opening left by the broken window, "it seems a very tight squeeze. I know I should not like to attempt it."

"Yes, well, the other Runner, Mr.—Maxwell, you said?—he was having a pint at the public house across the street, and he claims one of the three was a child."

"No!" breathed Pickett in a voice that clearly communicated his willingness to hear more.

"Aye, and this child must have been lifted up to the window—I don't see how else he could have climbed in, do you?—and then, after he'd got inside, he unlocked the door for the others. For it was unlocked, you know, the back door that gives access to William Street."

Pickett expressed an interest in seeing this door for himself, and Mr. Davidson, now all eagerness to make amends for his earlier hostility, was quick to offer to show it to him. Pickett, nothing loth, agreed with alacrity, and was led inside the bank with all the obsequiousness usually reserved for a client who wished to deposit a very large sum of money.

Unlike the Neoclassical behemoth from which he had been so unceremoniously dismissed earlier that morning, the premises of Thomas Coutts and Co. were so discreet that one might pass by on the street without ever noticing the establishment at all. Pickett, observing the clients conducting their business with the assistance of some half-dozen soberly dressed men behind the long counter, all of them speaking in the hushed tones one might find in a church, wondered wistfully if this bank might have any need for additional clerks.

Alas, the inspection told him very little that he did not already know. The door opening onto the narrow passage known as William Street bore no scratch marks nor any other signs of its lock having been forced. The banker's assumption (Pickett wondered if it had been Maxwell who had first suggested it) that the door must have been unlocked from someone inside would appear to be confirmed. The safe, however, was another matter entirely. Having got inside through the unlocked back door, at least one member of the trio had clearly made an attempt at opening the safe, for its heavy iron door was scored with scratches.

"And these?" Pickett asked, tracing one long mark with his finger. "Were they there before last night?"

"No, they were most certainly not!" responded the indignant banker. "But if that watchman, poor blighter, hadn't come along when he did—" He shook his head, apparently finding such a conclusion too terrible to contemplate.

Privately, Pickett thought it unlikely they could have breached the safe even with unlimited time to complete the task. Any cracksman worthy of the name would have been able to open the lock without leaving any indication of his having been there at all. Whoever they were, this gang with whom the boy had cast his lot, their ambition must have outstripped their skills, at least this once. Far from being reassured by this discovery, Pickett found it rather ominous. For the less accomplished the criminal, the greater his chances of being discovered—and, after that, of being arrested, tried, convicted...and executed.

If he had any hope of finding the boy and extricating him from the criminal gang before Maxwell arrested the lot of them, it clearly behooved Pickett to attend the inquest into Bradley's death. Granted, the purpose of the coroner's inquest was to determine the cause of death, and with an entire pub full of witnesses who had seen it happen, there was no doubt of the jury's bringing in a verdict of willful murder. Little would be said about who had committed that murder, much less any speculation as to where that person or persons had gone to ground. Still, Maxwell was, as Pickett had said, new to investigative work; perhaps he might let something slip, something that might provide a possible lead. Or perhaps one or more of the pub's customers might be unfamiliar with the limitations of a coroner's inquest, and would offer some pertinent information. Pickett could only hope so; if he were forced to wait until Maxwell chose to confide in him, he feared he would be waiting a very long time.

In the meantime, there was one other thing he had to do. And so, after leaving the banking establishment, he did not turn to the northeast and Bow Street, but westward into Mayfair, and thence to 22 Curzon Street.

"Julia," he began, after greeting his wife with a lingering kiss, "how would you feel about taking in a pickpocket?"

SHERI COBB SOUTH

4

*In Which John Pickett Proposes a Change
in the Pickett Household*

W hat? Another one?" she asked, smiling coyly up at
him.

She had known about his disreputable past long before
they were wed, having been informed of his history by his
magistrate—who had then (and practically in the same breath)
warned her to keep her distance from the handsome and
impressionable young man who was taking, in Mr.
Colquhoun's opinion, far too keen an interest in a lady far
above his touch. It was rarely spoken of these days, not
because it was too delicate a subject to broach without cause,
but because it had very little to do with their present-day lives.
With the birth of their first child only three months away, the
future was far more interesting than the past. Her reference to
it now had more to do with flirtation than remonstrance. She
was more than a little surprised, then, when he failed to take
the bait.

"Actually, I suppose it would be more accurate to say he's a snakesman, and at least one amongst his present company is on the glazier-lay, using him to get inside and crack the peter so they can pike the ready."

Julia's playful smile faded, to be replaced with a look of blank bewilderment. "It's truly amazing how one can recognize all the words—well, almost all the words—and yet fail to understand anything that has just been said! John, darling, what are you talking about?"

"I'm sorry—I suppose this has brought it all back. Thieves' cant, I mean."

She nodded knowingly. "Yes, I had gathered as much. But since I'm reasonably certain that no other old habits have reasserted themselves, I can't help wondering: What, pray, has 'brought it all back'?"

He took a deep breath and blew it out. "Sweetheart, I have a brother. Half-brother, actually, sired by my father just before he was transported to Botany Bay. He—my brother, that is, not my father—he seems to have got himself in a bad way, you see, and—"

In fact, Julia did *not* see, but of one thing, at least, she was certain: the coming discussion, the subject of which appeared to be a matter of some delicacy, should not take place with the participants standing right inside the door, where anyone passing by in the street might be made privy to it. "Perhaps we would do better to discuss it in the drawing room," she suggested, taking his arm and gently steering him in the proper direction. "Shall I ring for tea?"

He shook his head. "I can't stay. I just wanted to warn

you of what's in the wind. I'll need to get back—"

"Nonsense! You have to eat sometime, so you might as well do it here, in the company of your wife."

With this declaration, she gave a tug to the bellpull, and conversation was temporarily suspended while she gave instructions to the footman. It was not until the tea tray had been brought and they were settled side by side on the drawing room sofa that she picked up the thread of their interrupted discussion.

"And so, you have a half-brother," she said, dispensing two cups of tea while he filled a small plate from an assortment of sweets and savories. "I take it his existence came as a surprise to you."

"Yes, although perhaps it shouldn't have. But that's not the half of it. He appears to have fallen in with a gang of thieves. They tried to rob Thomas Coutts and Co. last night, and although they managed to show the watchman a clean pair of heels, the poor fellow was murdered when one of the three threw a knife that caught him in the throat." Upon seeing Julia wince at the mental picture this description evoked, Pickett was filled with remorse. "I'm sorry—I shouldn't burden you with such things—"

"Nonsense! I'm quite all right," Julia insisted, fortifying herself with a long pull from her teacup nevertheless. "But the boy—your brother, I should say—he was unharmed?"

Pickett nodded. "He was. He won't be for long, though, not if he's arrested as an accessory. In that case, he'll be dancing Jack Ketch's jig."

No knowledge of thieves' cant was needed to understand

that Pickett referred to execution by hanging. "But John, if he is truly your father's son, then he can't be more than ten years old!"

"I'm afraid age doesn't matter, not when it comes to murder. And when the murdered man happens to be an officer of the law, even an incompetent one—" He shrugged, giving Julia to understand that the younger Pickett's fate would be sealed. She had no cause to doubt it; had she been arrested for the murder of her first husband, a powerful and influential aristocrat, she would have met a similar end. The fact that she had not could be credited entirely to the efforts of the man seated beside her.

"Perhaps they won't be discovered," she suggested, her loyalties now fully ranged on the side of the criminals, rather than the law her husband was charged with upholding.

"Perhaps," he echoed doubtfully. "Maxwell is on the case, since he happened to be at the pub across the street when the crime was committed. He's new, but he seems to have a good head on his shoulders, and of course he's eager to prove himself. In fact, it's due to him that I know about the boy. Maxwell got a good look at him as they made their escape, and he told Mr. Colquhoun the boy looked just like me." A fleeting smile temporarily lightened his bleak expression. "In fact, he thought I might have a by-blow running amok."

"Hmm." Regarding him through narrowed eyes, Julia made a mockingly threatening sound. In fact, she had absolutely no doubts on that head; no man with any experience in that area could have been quite so adorably incompetent as he had been on the night they had consummated the marriage

47

by declaration they had accidentally formed in Scotland.

"Anyway," Pickett continued, "Mr. Colquhoun 'suggested' that I might want to get in ahead of Maxwell and extricate the boy."

"That's the third time you've called him 'the boy,' " she observed. "Does this brother of yours have a name?"

"I suppose he must, but I don't know what it is."

"But if you do as Mr. Colquhoun suggests, doesn't that make you guilty of—I don't know—obstructing justice? Or, at the very least, wouldn't you be an accessory after the fact?"

"Very likely," Pickett conceded with a sigh. "Which is why, if I make the attempt, I'd better succeed."

"And if you do—succeed, that is—what happens to the boy then?"

Pickett shrugged. "I suppose I'm left with him."

"Yes, that's where we started, is it not? With your asking me how I would feel about taking in a pickpocket."

"I hate to ask such a thing of you," he said apologetically. "Especially considering that most of the burden would fall on you, since I would be at—at work," he concluded feebly, having caught himself up just before saying "at Bow Street."

She regarded him thoughtfully. "You sound as if you don't really want to take him in."

Having just taken a bite of poppy seed cake, Pickett held up one finger, giving Julia to understand that she was to wait upon a reply until after he'd swallowed the morsel in his mouth. "I'll admit, I'm not exactly champing at the bit," he confessed at last. "I suppose I owe him something—he is family, after all—but he's still a stranger to me, even though we have the same father."

"Yes, but do you? Have the same father, I mean. The likeness this Mr. Maxwell claims to have seen might be no more than a coincidence. In fact," she added, warming to this theme, "it might not even exist at all, were he to see the child in the light of day."

"I shall have to make sure, of course—I suppose that means a visit to Moll," he concluded with a marked lack of enthusiasm. "Maybe I can learn enough at the inquest tomorrow to spare me that, at least."

"Oh, is the inquest tomorrow, then? Shall I come with you?" she asked, brightening.

He stared at her in mock horror. "What a bloodthirsty woman I've married!"

"You must admit, John, they can be rather interesting—provided, of course, that one is not obliged to give evidence."

Pickett hesitated. On the one hand, allowing her to take an interest in the case might help her feel as if she had a personal stake in the boy's rescue, making him more of a family member and less of an interloper. On the other hand, her presence could not help but attract a degree of attention which he would prefer to avoid.

"If you really want to attend, I suppose I can't stop you," he conceded. "After all, they are public procedures. But I would prefer not to let Maxwell know I'm there. At best, he would think I was checking up on him, as if I didn't trust him to investigate the case on his own; at worst, he would realize I'm trying to thrust a spoke in his wheel. Either way, it's hard to be inconspicuous when one is sitting next to the most beautiful woman in London."

"John Pickett!" she scolded. "That is the most gratifying snub I've ever heard! Very well, I shan't tease you to take me to the inquest. But what of this Moll?"

"What of her?"

"Who is she?"

"Moll is the mother of my half-brother. She calls herself my stepmother, although if she and my father ever married, it's news to me."

"But if his mother is still living, then surely the boy is her responsibility, not yours!"

"You would think so," Pickett said slowly, "but given the fact that she turned me out of the house before my father's ship had even cleared the Pool—"

"John!" Julia cried indignantly. "She didn't!"

"She did. Actually, it makes sense now, in a way that it didn't before. If she knew, or at least suspected, that she'd 'sprained her ankle,' as the saying goes, she'd want to find a new cull quickly enough to convince the poor sap that he was the father. A fourteen-year-old 'stepson' in the house would only be in the way."

"She sounds delightful," Julia said in a tone that conveyed quite the opposite. "And this is the woman whose child you are proposing to take in? Could you not—I don't know—make him an allowance instead?"

Pickett shook his head. "Moll would only drink it."

"Drink—?" Julia echoed in bewilderment.

"She has a weakness for Blue Ruin—cheap gin."

Julia nodded in resigned understanding. "Then of course

you must—you must not send him back to her. How long do we—that is, when do you think—?"

"I wish I knew," Pickett said with a sigh. "It would help if I knew whether Maxwell suspects anyone in particular, and if so, where the thieves' den is located, but he's keeping his tongue between his teeth. In fact, he—what? What's so funny?"

"I'm sorry," she said, choking back her laughter. "It's just that you, of all people, should complain about anyone else's lack of communication!"

His answering grin was somewhat sheepish, in view of the fact that he had not yet told her of his decision to leave Bow Street, but when he spoke again, his tone was serious. "It's not just on Maxwell's word, you know. I think—I'm almost certain I've run across the boy myself once, maybe twice."

"Oh? When was that?"

"The first time was when I was recovering from the business at Drury Lane Theatre, and he—or at least, someone—tried to break into Mrs. Catchpole's shop."

"I remember that," Julia said thoughtfully. "As I recall, you opened the window directly above and, in spite of your injuries, jumped out and landed on top of him."

"And if I hadn't been such a cursed weakling, he wouldn't have got away, and we might have settled the matter then and there," Pickett recollected bitterly.

"But you said you'd run across him twice. When was the second time?"

The second"—he let out a long breath—"the second was

51

while I was investigating the Washbourn case, and I'd just returned from Croydon. I walked down to the river and a boy tried to pick my pocket. I caught him in the act—as they say, 'set a thief to catch a thief'—and although it was almost dark by that time, it occurred to me that he might have been me fifteen years earlier."

"It was almost dark by that time," echoed Julia, brushing the crumbs from her hands so that she might lace her fingers through his, "and yet the stagecoach from Croydon had arrived earlier that evening. I know, because I sent Thomas to inquire. John, why did you go to the river that night?"

Pickett's gaze slid away from hers, to fasten instead on their clasped hands. "I thought I'd lost you. I couldn't go home, so"—he shrugged—"I went to the river."

"And what did you intend to do when you got there?"

"I—I don't exactly know."

"I think I can guess. Shall I tell you what I think?"

"I don't—"

She continued as if he had not spoken. "I think you went to the river intending to make a hole in it. But then a boy tried to pick your pocket, and something about that encounter made you change your mind."

Actually, the event she described had taken place before he had reached the river. And it had not been petty larceny, but pouring rain—as if a bit more water would have made a difference to one about to drown himself!—that had made him abandon the notion and go instead to his magistrate's house. But if the boy had not delayed him—what then? He would never know. And that was probably a good thing.

"Find your brother and bring him home," Julia said, leaning over to kiss his cheek. "I shall be glad to welcome him. After all, I owe him a debt I can never repay."

5

In Which Julia Confesses to More than a Few Qualms

The trouble with having more than two dozen witnesses to a crime, Pickett reflected at the inquest the following morning, was that one had more than two dozen opinions as to what had happened when, and to whom. Of the persons who had been present at the pub across the street at the time of the attempted robbery and the murder that had followed, four had recalled seeing three men fleeing from the scene, while three had been certain there had only been two, and one held firmly to the conviction that there had been four. Seven stated that they had seen one of the three (or two, or four, depending on the person speaking) throw a knife at the pursuing watchman, although when pressed for details, most had confessed that they had not actually known it was a knife at the time, for not until Bradley had fallen did they recognize the weapon for what it was.

Maxwell, Pickett had to admit, was acquitting himself

well. He gave his evidence with none of the lurid relish displayed by his fellows, and what information he offered was backed up, more often than not, with specific details that, while less thrilling than the recollections of his fellows, gave added weight to his testimony.

"And so, Mr. Maxwell," the coroner continued, "these three men you saw—"

"Begging your pardon," Maxwell interrupted, "but I never said there were three men."

The coroner scowled and turned to address the clerk who was charged with taking down the words of the various witnesses. "Read back, if you will, Mr. Maxwell's testimony, beginning with the part just after he left the pub."

The clerk cleared his throat and began to read. " 'I saw three people run out the front door of Thomas Coutts and Co. and into the Strand. As the watchman pursued—"

"That will be sufficient. Well, Mr. Maxwell?"

Pickett, slumped in his chair at the back of the room in order to avoid his colleague's eye, did not have to see the coroner's face to recognize the smugness in his voice.

"I said there were three people," pointed out Maxwell, undaunted. "I never said they were all men."

Here it comes, thought Pickett, shifting uncomfortably in his seat.

"Do you really mean to suggest that one of the three was a woman?" demanded the coroner impatiently.

"Not at all," replied Maxwell. "I only mean that one of them was a child. But he was not a very young child, and was fairly tall, so I can see how the fact escaped the notice of most of these good people who have testified. It wasn't until the lad dropped something and turned back to retrieve it that I got a good look at his face in the light of the street lamp and realized that he was much younger than I had first surmised."

"You say he dropped something?" The coroner's voice had grown sharp, and every trace of mockery had vanished. "Did you see what it was?"

Maxwell nodded. "I did, sir."

"And?"

"It was a metal figure of a soldier, of the type commonly played with by children."

"Do you mean to tell me that it was a *toy?*" demanded the coroner, as if half-suspecting that the witness—and he a Bow Street man!—was making a May game of him.

Again that dispassionate nod. "I do." Apparently feeling some further comment was called for, he added, "It's not so unusual, you know, for criminal gangs to use a child as a little snakesman, one who can gain access to a locked building by squirming through tight spaces too small for grown man."

"Yes, well, be that as it may, it seems a damned odd thing to take a toy soldier along on a robbery. Do you have any proof of this claim?"

Maxwell's cool self-confidence faltered somewhat. "I do, sir, but I don't have it with me. I took it in as evidence and gave it to the magistrate at the Bow Street Public Office. It'll be locked up in the safe there."

Pickett's hand went instinctively to the inside pocket of his coat, where the small pewter figure rested. He was glad he'd had the forethought to ask Mr. Colquhoun if he could keep it; he would, after all, have to gain the trust of a younger brother who was no doubt as ignorant of Pickett's existence as Pickett had been of his. Returning what was clearly a treasured object might go some little way toward establishing that trust. In any case, it wasn't needed here, for the coroner's jury had already heard more than enough eyewitness testimony to bring in a verdict of willful murder without his surrendering the purloined plaything; clearly, his own need was the greater.

It soon appeared, however, that greater trials were in store. For the man who testified after Maxwell reiterated that he had indeed seen three men running out of the banking establishment at Number 59, and then interrupted himself to point straight at Pickett and exclaim, "There's one of the fellows there!"

Immediately, all eyes turned in his direction, but Pickett noticed only Maxwell, regarding him with a narrowed and none too friendly gaze.

"Let me remind the witness," the coroner said sternly, raising his voice to be heard over the buzz of speculation that followed this pronouncement, "that the purpose of this inquest is not to point the finger at any person or persons, but merely to establish the cause of death."

But the damage was done. Pickett had intended to slip away after the last witness had given his testimony, without staying to hear the jury's verdict. He had, after all, attended the inquest purely to discover what he could about where the gang, and thus his brother, might have run to ground. Not only had he discovered no pertinent information—alas, even the most determined of the pursuers had been given the slip by the time they reached Long Acre—but now he found himself in the uncomfortable position of being the prime, indeed at this point the *only*, suspect. If he were to leave now, it would no doubt be seen as the attempt of a guilty party to flee. And so, although he had hoped to make his escape before Maxwell had noticed his presence—a lost cause now, in any case—he was obliged to remain in his seat at the back of the room until the jury returned the utterly unsurprising verdict of willful murder.

Upon seeing that the morning's entertainment was over, the various witnesses and interested spectators filed out of the room, several of them casting uncertain glances in Pickett's direction as they passed. Eventually he was able to make his own exit, but he had not gone far before a hand fell heavily upon his shoulder.

"Well, Mr. Pickett?" It was more a challenge than a question. "I trust my testimony met with your approval."

"I thought you did very well," Pickett said, aware that his assurances sounded condescending, but uncertain how else he could answer. "I'll admit, I'm curious about this lad who seems to look like me. It appears you weren't the only one who noticed a resemblance. I confess, I was hoping to discover where I might get a look at him, but everyone seems to have stopped to tend to Bradley or—to tend to Bradley," he finished lamely, realizing too late that Maxwell would not welcome any references to an old injury he went to great pains to conceal. "So I guess I'll never know."

"I'm flattered by your faith in me, Mr. Pickett," Maxwell

said dryly.

Pickett mentally cursed himself. Why could he never open his mouth in Maxwell's presence without putting his foot in it?

"I didn't mean it that way," he said quickly. "I have every confidence in your—but how did your search go? Did you find any leads in the *Hue and Cry*, then?"

Maxwell shrugged. "Possibilities, but nothing definite. I've taken a few issues home to examine more closely."

Which meant that Pickett himself would be obliged to have a look at those issues for himself, although how he was to do so when Maxwell had taken them home was anyone's guess. In any case, he hadn't the luxury of waiting upon Maxwell's convenience, for there was something else he had to do first.

He would go to the rookery of St. Giles, and for the first time in more than ten years he would face the woman who had turned him out onto the streets.

* * *

"What a big girl you're getting to be!" cooed Julia, lifting three-month-old Lady Iphigenia Dunnington from her crib and raising her high enough to free the baby's long skirts from the bulge of her own abdomen.

"Isn't she, though?" agreed little Lady Genie's proud mama, Emily, Lady Dunnington. "And she has her father securely wrapped about her little finger! Why, just yesterday Dunnington was saying he would have to keep his dueling pistols cleaned in anticipation of the day he will be obliged to hold would-be suitors at bay." Receiving no response to this sally, she lapsed into silence and watched in quiet understanding as Julia nestled the baby against her shoulder, turning her head to press her lips against the soft plump cheek. "Patience, my dear! Not much longer before you'll be hearing the pitter-patter of little feet in your own nursery."

Julia sighed. "In fact, it may be even sooner than you think. Although I'm not sure how 'little' the feet in question will be."

"Julia?" Emily regarded her in utter bewilderment. "What are you talking about?"

"It seems John has a younger brother—half-brother, actually—who has fallen in with a gang of thieves. He'll be coming to live with us—provided, of course, that John can find him before the law does."

"And you're not pleased about that," Emily observed.

"About taking a complete stranger into my home? How can I be?"

"Isn't it a bit late to be thinking of that?" Emily asked, gesturing toward Julia's middle.

"Yes, but you must admit that this is a bit different! The baby will be a stranger, but at least it will be *ours*. This child— why, I don't know anything about him! He must be ten years old, or very near it, and his character already formed. And with *such* a background! What if he turns out to be perfectly beastly?"

Emily shrugged. "It seems to me that your Mr. Pickett came from a very similar background, and you seem pleased enough with the way he turned out."

"Yes, but John is—John," Julia replied with unassailable

logic. "There can't possibly be another like him."

"If he were as wonderful as all that, he wouldn't be bringing a little criminal into the household against your will," pointed out Emily, unimpressed.

"It wasn't against my will," Julia protested. "At least, not exactly. He did ask for my opinion, and if I had raised any objection, I have no doubt he would have made some other arrangements for the boy."

"Well, then—"

"But Emily, how could I do anything but agree? I'll admit, at first I thought we might reach an acceptable compromise—pay the boy's mother an allowance for his upkeep, perhaps—"

"Well, then—" Emily said again.

"But John says she would only drink it, which I take to mean that she's a bit too fond of the bottle. In any case, John is quite certain the child would never see a farthing of it. So you see how it must be."

"Well, then—"

"And John asks so little of me, bless him. How could I possible refuse him in this?"

Privately, Lady Dunnington considered that to ask a lady to marry beneath her, knowing full well that the marriage would result in her being ostracized from all good society, was to ask a very great deal indeed. But they had debated this point more than once already, and while Julia readily conceded the point that few of her old acquaintances would send her an invitation to their next ball or rout-party (and none of these would ever dream of inviting her husband), she refused to consider the withdrawal of their society as any real loss. And Emily had to own that, in the six months since her marriage to her Bow Street Runner, there had been a glow about Julia that had less to do with her pregnancy than it had to do with happiness, a happiness Emily had not seen on her friend's face since she had first come to London as Lord Fieldhurst's not yet disillusioned bride.

"Well, then—"

"Yes, you're quite right," Julia said decisively. "There is nothing for it but to put on a brave face and make the best of things." With a sigh of resigned acceptance, she turned her attention back to the baby in her arms.

"I'm so glad to be of assistance," Emily said dryly.

Julia, however, was oblivious to irony. "But except for a few weeks in Scotland with George's three sons, I know nothing of small boys! What does one *do* with them?"

"Preventing them from killing themselves or each other is half the battle," Emily assured her. "You managed to achieve that, while at the same time getting yourself accidentally married to your Mr. Pickett. Quite a notable accomplishment, really."

"The best thing I ever did," Julia put in emphatically.

"Preventing George's sons from killing each other?" asked Emily, deliberately obtuse.

"Marrying John. Although I can't be sorry about the boys, either. The eldest, Harold, appears to be thriving in the Navy, and we get a letter from him whenever his ship is in port. Robert, too, seems quite happy at Eton, for he is of a scholarly disposition. I'm not quite certain about the youngest, for Edward is a poor correspondent, I fear, and his infrequent letters are very nearly illegible, and so liberally spattered with ink that I'm sure he must be the despair of his penmanship instructor." She frowned as a new and unwelcome thought occurred to her. "I suppose we shall have to see to this boy's education."

"There you are, then!" declared Emily. "Put him in a good boarding school, and you can rid your household of him with a clear conscience."

"A *good* boarding school? We shall be fortunate to find any school to take him at all! I don't even know if the child is literate."

"In that case, you shall hire a tutor to bring him up to snuff. It's done in the best families, I assure you! By the time the boy is able to meet the academic standards of any reputable institution, your Mr. Pickett will have been made a magistrate, and be as respectable as anyone could wish." Seeing Julia answer this sally with a rather perfunctory smile, she added in a more serious vein, "I know it must seem rather overwhelming—with an infant, at least, one is able to make one's early mistakes before the child is old enough to notice!—but if it's true that George's sons write affectionate letters to you after only a few weeks' acquaintance in Scotland, then you must have done something right."

"Only because I pitied them, George having treated them and their mother so shabbily," protested Julia.

"There you are, then," Emily pronounced. "If you can't love this child, perhaps you can pity him. It cannot have been an easy life, I should think, being dependent upon the whims of a gang of criminals. Or of a drunken mama, for that matter."

"Yes," Julia said, embracing her future rôle with, if not enthusiasm, at least determined acceptance. Yes, she could, she *would* pity this child whose fate had not been so fortunate as his elder brother's, whose own life had been difficult enough. She would do it for love of that elder brother, and someday, if she were lucky, she might perhaps grow to love the boy for his own sake.

Perhaps.

If she were lucky.

6

Which Features a Family Reunion, of Sorts

The inquest having produced no information worthy of note, Pickett returned to the Curzon Street town house to prepare for his confrontation with his "stepmother." He went upstairs to change his clothes, but sought in vain for his brown serge coat. This garment had until quite recently been his preferred workday costume; although he owned better clothing, thanks to his wife's machinations, he had been reluctant to flaunt these before his less sartorially splendid colleagues at Bow Street. The cat was out of the bag now, however, thanks to a protracted journey in company with Harry Carson of the Horse Patrol, and Pickett had been so peppered with questions as to the veracity of Carson's claims regarding his wardrobe that he had been obliged to put an end to the pretense and satisfy everyone's curiosity by displaying his finery. But it appeared that now, when he needed to return to a humbler style of dress, the old familiar garment was nowhere to be found.

"Julia?" he called, going to the top of the stairs and leaning over the railing clad in his oldest breeches, a shirt badly in need of laundering, and a faded waistcoat that predated his marriage by several years. "Sweetheart, have you seen my brown coat?"

Julia, having only that moment returned from her visit with Lady Dunnington, surrendered her bonnet, gloves, and pelisse to the butler and looked up at him. "You gave it to Thomas," she reminded him. "I daresay he has sold it to the rag man by now. If you'll recall, it has a bullet hole in the shoulder, and you bled all down one sleeve."

"Better and better!" pronounced Pickett, brightening. "I only hope he hasn't got rid of it yet. Thomas! Oh, there you are," he said, moderating his tone as his valet emerged from the jib door that concealed the servants' stair. "What have you done with my brown serge coat?"

"Why, it's in the bag for the rag-and-bone man," Thomas said, taken aback by this request. "I'm afraid I never even tried to get the bloodstains out of the sleeve, for there was still the hole where the ball went in, and—"

"Never mind that," Pickett interrupted, cutting off what appeared to be a lengthy attempt at self-exoneration. "Go and fetch it for me, will you?"

"Should I at least sponge it and iron it first, sir?"

"Don't you dare! The more disreputable it looks, the better."

Thomas glanced uncertainly toward Julia, climbing the stairs to join them. Seeing that she seemed to notice nothing unusual in this request, he merely said, "Very good, sir," and went off on his errand.

Once they were alone, however, Julia was rather less accepting of her husband's sudden preference for his old garments. "John, why do you want it? What is—*this*—all about?" Her gesture took in the dingy shirt, breeches worn threadbare at the knees, and darned stockings. These last she recognized at once, for she had mended them with her own hands, while he had lain unconscious and she had struggled with the dilemma of making an unequal marriage or giving him up forever. She'd chosen the former and never looked back.

"I didn't learn anything at the inquest as to where I might look for this brother of mine—if he's a brother of mine at all. The only alternative is to go straight to the source."

"Meaning?" prompted Julia.

"I'm going to ask Moll to her face if she had a child after Da was transported."

"And you mean to dress for the company you keep? I should have thought you would want to show her that you'd managed to succeed in spite of her."

"It's tempting," he said with a sigh. "But I don't want her to know about you. If she ever discovers I've come into money, we'll never be rid of her."

"Nonsense! What could she possibly do?"

"You don't know Moll. If nothing else, she would blackmail me, threatening to become an embarrassment to us—to you, especially—if I didn't pay…and pay…and pay. Once you pay a blackmailer, you're never free of them."

"Then we simply don't pay," Julia pointed out reasonably.

"Believe me, I would pay quite a bit to spare you any more embarrassment than you've already suffered! Do you think I haven't noticed the way people ignore you when they see you at the theatre, the way ladies draw their skirts aside when they pass you in church, as if they feared contamination? Well, I have, and I won't subject you to the likes of Moll, were she to bleed me dry for it!"

"I have never been embarrassed to be your wife, John," she said softly. "I never could be."

Whatever Pickett might have said in answer to this was destined to remain unspoken, for Thomas returned at that moment with the brown serge coat. Several weeks' residence in the rag-and-bone man's bag had done nothing to improve it, but Pickett did not seem to mind. He shrugged his arms into the sleeves with the ease of long familiarity, and for one moment Julia was so forcibly reminded of the young Bow Street Runner as she had first known him that her breath caught in her throat, and she clung to his arm in spite of the rust-colored stains on his sleeve.

"You will be careful, won't you?"

"I have a lifetime of experience in being careful around Moll," he assured her. "But I'm a big boy now, and I don't have to fear her anymore."

He punctuated this statement with a kiss, but as she watched him descend the stairs and exit the house, it occurred to Julia to wonder whether this reassurance was for her, or for himself.

* * *

The walk from Mayfair to Seven Dials was scarcely more than a mile and a half, but anyone plucked willy-nilly from one location and set down in the other might have supposed himself to have been transported to a different world. The genteel streets and elegantly appointed squares of Mayfair, laid out in the previous century, hardly seemed to belong to the same city as the squalid environs of St. Giles. Here, one building in every four housed a pub in which blowsy women were as readily available for purchase as was the cheap gin known as Blue Ruin, denounced by more than one frustrated magistrate as the scourge of the lower classes.

As he approached the dwelling where he had once lived with his father and his father's common-law wife, it occurred to Pickett that Moll might no longer be found there. She might have moved in with some new man. She might even be dead; life was cheap in the rookeries of London, and those denizens who avoided being murdered for their meager possessions frequently succumbed to disease, often before they reached their fortieth year—by which time they had begat a new generation to inherit the birthright of misery. Yes, Moll might well be dead; in fact, that might go some way toward explaining how his young half-brother had fallen in with a gang of murderers and thieves.

But no. The same tattered curtains still hung in the window, and these would certainly have been claimed by some enterprising soul, quite possibly with the body still laid out on the bed for burial, to be sold for a few pence before they could be claimed by the undertaker as payment for services rendered. Suppressing a sigh, Pickett strode up to the door (which appeared to have not been painted since he had been thrown out on his ear more than ten years earlier) and knocked.

"What do you—?" The woman who opened it broke off abruptly, her pale blue eyes blinking in disbelief. "Jack? Jack Pickett?"

"Close, but no," Pickett said. "Try 'John.' "

"And the very image of your father, I'll be bound," she breathed, staring at him as if confronted with a ghost.

"So I've been told." He supposed she must have been pretty once, he acknowledged, determined to give the woman her due. Certainly his father, whose sobriquet of "Gentleman Jack" had testified as to his appreciation of feminine beauty, would not otherwise have given her a second glance. But years of poverty and an affinity for strong drink had robbed her of any beauty she might once have had. Her wide blue eyes were already bloodshot, although the hour had not yet reached three o'clock in the afternoon, and her nose and cheeks were latticed with fine red lines, the broken blood vessels of the alcoholic. Her improbably yellow hair was no doubt a feeble attempt to reclaim the blonde ringlets of which she had once been perhaps justifiably proud. "It's been a long time, Moll. May I come in?"

"Aye, that it has," agreed Moll, giving him an appraising look as she stepped aside to allow him to enter. "Ten years, at least."

"Eleven," Pickett said, glancing about the familiar room. It was essentially unchanged, except for the fact that still more plaster had crumbled from the ceiling, exposing the beams that supported the floor above, and the paper covering the walls had peeled in places to reveal patches of a still older paper patterned with faded cabbage roses. The furniture was just as he remembered it, and an open bottle, half empty, stood upon the table, confirming his theory as to Moll's drinking. He noticed that no glass accompanied it; apparently Moll held no truck with such elegancies, but drank the noxious stuff straight from the bottle.

It soon became clear that while Pickett had been examining the ramshackle room, Moll had been examining him. "You were a boy when you left here, and now look at you, a man grown!"

"No thanks to you."

"Now, now, let's not hold grudges," she chided. "I always did have a soft spot for you, you know." In demonstration of this rather questionable pronouncement, she stepped nearer and slid one chapped red hand through the crook of his elbow.

"Did you?" asked Pickett with mild interest. "You'll forgive me for saying you had a strange way of showing it."

"Now, now," she said again, moving closer in such a way that her ample bosom was pressed against him, "is that any way to talk to one who always had your best interests at heart?"

"My 'best interests'?" Pickett echoed in astonishment, trying without success to put some distance between himself and Moll's determined breasts. "I fail to see how throwing me out of the house could possibly be considered acting in my best interests!"

"Oh, but just look at what a fine fellow you've turned out to be," she insisted. "You could come back home now, since Dick Robbins—him that took you in such dislike, you know—has gone to his eternal reward—and may he find it a deal too hot for his liking, him going off like that and leaving me with not even a ha'penny for the undertaker! But that's neither here nor there. Now that you're all grown up, you could come back here to live, and I could take care of you, just like I used to take care of your poor father."

If Pickett had any doubts as to what form of "care" she had in mind, these would have been laid to rest (not unlike the recently departed Dick Robbins) by the arms that stretched upward, no longer to box his ears as in times past, but in an attempt to entwine themselves about his neck.

"Not a chance," Pickett declared in no uncertain terms, detaching himself from her embrace and stepping back far enough to prevent a second attempt. "Even if I were tempted—which I'm not!—do you honestly think I could consider for one moment such an arrangement with a woman who put me out on the streets to fend for myself, and me only fourteen years old?"

"But, Jack—John, that is, although you look so much like your poor father that I'm sure—but that's neither here nor there! Think of me, of the quandary I was in, with my cull sent halfway 'round the world and me with a belly full of marrow. I had to find a new cull quick-like, so he'd think the little bastard was his! It wouldn't have been that hard, for Dick Robbins had always had an eye to me, but no man wants a great hulking lad under the same roof, eating his head off and outgrowing his clothes every new moon."

"And did you?" Pickett asked, seeing an opportunity to steer the conversation toward the purpose for which he'd come. "Convince him the child was his, I mean?"

"Aye, at first I did. Until the little whoreson started growing into the spitting image of his father," she grumbled, as if the child had chosen to resemble his father just to spite her. "Beat me black and blue, old Dick did, saying either the brat went, or he would."

"I take it 'the brat' went," was Pickett's dry observation.

"Aye. And so did Dick, scarcely more than a fortnight ago, so I got the last laugh in the end."

"And the brat? What did he get?"

Moll shrugged, and her stained and threadbare gown slipped off one shoulder, exposing the dirty shift beneath. "Lud, how should I know?"

"You don't know where the child is?"

"No, for I gave him to a fellow who promised to set him up in a trade."

"You gave away your own son?" demanded Pickett, appalled though hardly surprised.

"Lud, no! D'you think I'm such an unnatural mother that I'd give away my own flesh and blood?" retorted Moll, bristling. "I got two quid for him."

"You sold—" Pickett broke off, shaking his head. There was no point in chiding Moll for what was already done, and she'd done nothing that nine out of every ten women in St. Giles wouldn't have done, given half a chance. "Who was this fellow?"

"How should I know?"

"Where does he live, then?" Pickett asked with growing impatience. "What sort of trade did he have in mind?"

"He didn't say."

"You might have asked! Good God, Moll, we're talking about your son, your own flesh and blood!"

"I figure once he'd paid me for the boy, it was no business of mine what he did with him."

"Well, he's my half-brother, and I intend to make it my business," declared Pickett.

"Suit yourself," Moll said, clearly washing her hands of the matter. "It'll cost you, though. He'll never give the brat up, not after paying good money for him."

"Look here, does this boy have a name? Or do you not know that, either?"

"Of course he has a name! Do you think I'm such an unnatural mother that I'd—"

"We're not discussing your capabilities as a mother," Pickett interrupted, thinking that any analysis of Moll's maternal instincts must be a very short conversation. "What is the boy's name?"

"He's called Kit."

"Kit?"

"Short for Christopher," she explained. "I'd thought to name him after his father, but you were already named John. So I named him after St. Christopher instead, thinking he was the patron saint of thieves such as your father was. Only it turns out to be no such thing, and St. Christopher is only the patron saint of travelers and bachelors—not that that don't fit your father, too, damn his eyes," she added darkly, and spat onto the floor in a manner that suggested she would have liked to do the same to the elder Pickett's face.

"And you have no idea where he might be?" asked Pickett the Younger, dragging her attention back to the matter at hand.

Moll gave another shrug, and the sleeve of her shift followed that of her gown, leaving one shoulder bare and her right breast in imminent danger of exposure. "Far as I know, he's still at Botany Bay."

"Not my father," he said impatiently. "The fellow who took the boy."

"How should I know?" asked Moll, not for the first time.

"Then I suppose I'll be on my way," Pickett said, and started for the door.

"What?" Moll's voice rose to a beggar's whine. "Not a penny, not even a farthing, for one who loved you like a mother?"

Having been spurned as a potential lover, Moll had apparently reverted back to role of loving stepmother. But since leaving her house, Pickett had come to know what love was, both the giving and the receiving of it, and nothing Moll might offer could even come close.

"Not a farthing," he agreed, and the screech of the rusty hinges seemed to echo her protests as he opened the ill-fitting door.

"Not even if I can tell you where to find his dolly-mop?"

Pickett paused in midstride and turned, pulling the

groaning door closed behind him. "You know where the fellow's mistress is?"

Moll said nothing, but held up one cupped palm. Pickett fumbled in the pocket of his coat for his coin purse (grateful that he'd had the forethought to empty this of anything that might betray his newfound prosperity), and withdrew a single silver coin, which he dropped into Moll's waiting hand.

"Only a measly half a crown?" she complained.

"There'll be another if I find you've told me the truth," he promised.

"You'll find her selling cabbages in Covent Garden," Moll said. "Yaller-haired girl called Jenny. She's held to be a pretty piece, not but what I couldn't have given her a run for her money in my younger days! Why, I remember one time—"

"Thank you," Pickett said, and made his escape.

7

In Which John Pickett Pursues a Beautiful Cabbage-Seller

B y the time he left Moll's house, Pickett decided, it was too late to search for the beauteous Jenny. The vegetable sellers of Covent Garden would be eager to unload their remaining inventory before yielding their places to the flower sellers who hawked their wares to those gentlefolk attending the nearby theatres at Covent Garden or perhaps Drury Lane, in the days before that edifice had burned to the ground. Jenny would no doubt have little patience with anyone hindering her trade by plaguing her with questions about her lover. As for the possibility of returning to Bow Street, Pickett rejected the idea out of hand. To appear there with a bullet hole in the shoulder of his coat and bloodstains down one sleeve would attract just the sort of attention he most wished to avoid.

And so, resigning himself to the fact that there was nothing more he could accomplish that day, he returned to his home in Curzon Street, where he found Julia in consultation with the cook regarding meals for the week. Upon his entrance, she dismissed the woman with a nod and turned to greet him with a kiss.

"Back so soon?"

"Afraid so," he said with a sigh.

"You needn't sound quite so thrilled about it," she chided him.

"It isn't that," he assured her hastily. "Moll wasn't quite as helpful as I'd hoped. Although you'll be pleased to know that, should you ever tire of me, my loving 'stepmother' will be happy to 'take care' of me. And yes," he added as her eyes widened, "she meant that in exactly the way you're thinking."

"And after treating you so shockingly when you were a child! What a horrible woman!" Julia exclaimed indignantly.

"You, my lady, are an excellent judge of character." He punctuated this statement by dropping a kiss onto the tip of her nose.

"You usually tell me I'm a poor one," she reminded him.

"Because you married me, when you could have done so much better. If you'll excuse me, I'll go upstairs and change. I doubt you want to look at bloodstains and bullet holes the rest of the evening."

"Only one bullet hole, and the worst of the bloodstains are inside, on the lining. Besides, I want to look at *you*—I'll take you any way I can get you."

Nevertheless, she tucked her hand into the curve of his arm and accompanied him upstairs to the bedroom; it was more tactful to choose his clothes herself than to point out that he had not yet mastered the intricacies of dressing for dinner.

Upon reaching the bedroom, he rang for Thomas, and once his valet had arrived, stripped off the offending garment and handed it to him. "I've changed my mind, Thomas," he said. "I'll need you to do something with this, after all. I know the bloodstains won't come out completely, but do what you can." Seeing bewilderment writ large upon his wife's countenance, he added, with a hint of mischief in his eyes, "I need to make myself agreeable to an attractive young woman."

"John!" Julia exclaimed. "Not Moll, surely!"

"Moll is no longer young, and although she must have once been attractive, that ship has long since sailed—carried away on a sea of gin, most likely. No, the object of my attentions is a cabbage seller named Jenny."

"Then there really is a young woman?" Julia asked as Thomas received the soiled tailcoat from his master and quitted the room. "I thought you must be roasting me!"

"No, Jenny is real enough. At least, I don't *think* Moll was having me on," he added, frowning at the thought of this new and unwelcome possibility.

"But who is she?"

"A seller of cabbages, just as I said. She also happens to be the mistress of the fellow who paid Moll for my brother."

"There can be no doubt, then, that he *is* your brother?" Julia asked wistfully, seeing her last, best hope go up in smoke.

"None at all. Moll readily admits to being in the family way when my father was transported—in fact, she gave it as her excuse for putting me out on the streets—and says she sold him to a man who offered to teach him a trade."

"It can't be as bad as it sounds, then, can it?" asked Julia, grasping at straws. "If she saw an opportunity for the boy to learn a trade—"

"Julia, I'll lay you all Lombard Street to a China orange that the man was the leader of this criminal gang, and that the 'trade' he had in mind was thievery of one sort or another."

"But surely Moll wouldn't—her own son—"

"For two quid? She wouldn't be able to resist! And she never even asked the fellow's name, much less what trade he planned to teach him. She was too eager to get the money, to say nothing of the boy—whose name is Kit, by the way, short for Christopher—off her hands."

"But where does this Jenny fit in?"

"Moll doesn't know—or says she doesn't know—where I might look for the man, but told me—for a price—where I could find his mistress." Seeing that Julia looked less than delighted with this plan, he added, "I promise, sweetheart, you have nothing to fear from this Jenny or any other female. You have my whole heart. It's been yours from the moment we met."

"I know," she sighed, placing a hand on the bulge of her abdomen. "But I might feel better about the business if I didn't look such a positive fright! I don't know how you can bear to look at me, much less—" She made a helpless little gesture toward the bed.

"Is it possible," Pickett said slowly, staring at her, "that you *don't know?*"

"Don't know what?" she asked, bewildered.

In answer, he sat on the nearest of the two wing chairs positioned before the fireplace, and pulled her down onto his knee. "Don't know that when I see you going about the house looking like a ripe peach, and realize that I'm the one responsible, it makes me want to—I don't know—go out and slay dragons for you."

"There aren't any more dragons, John," she said, leaning into his embrace until her forehead rested against his, the tips of their noses touching. "You've already slain them all."

* * *

In Pickett's opinion, there was still one rather large dragon running amok, and not only had he not slain it, he hadn't even found it. Thus, with this end in view, he approached the Covent Garden market where he had once pinched an apple and, in the process (although he could not have known it at the time), changed the trajectory of his life. With some vague feeling of making amends, he sought out a costermonger presiding over a large wicker basket piled high with rosy red apples. He selected one of these, and when the apple seller held out a chapped hand for payment, dropped a large copper coin into her hand and turned away, sinking his teeth into the juicy flesh of the fruit.

"Lookee here, sir, you've give me a cartwheel," the woman called after him. "You don't owe me naught but a ha'penny."

Pickett shook his head. "Keep it. It'll be harder to lose."

She cackled with laughter, revealing a gap-toothed smile. "Aye, that it will. God bless you, sir."

This exchange attracted the attention of another seller, a

very fat woman with a long wooden pole from which hung braided ropes of onions.

"Jack?" she asked incredulously. "Jack Pickett?"

"Now, Bess!" Pickett chided. "Don't tell me you've forgot me!"

"*Johnny?* Bless my soul if it ain't little Johnny Pickett, all grown up! Come and give Stout Bess a kiss, do!"

Pickett was quick to obey, ducking beneath the swaying garlands of onions and planting a hearty smack on one plump cheek.

"Lud, I haven't seen you this age! Not since your father left, I'll be bound. Where've you been keeping yourself?"

Pickett, fully aware that the mention of Bow Street was not always welcome amongst the lower classes, neatly sidestepped the question by asking one of his own. "You should talk! I thought you'd gone to live with your daughter in—Islington, was it?" he asked, knowing quite well that it was Shoreditch.

"No, Polly and her brood live in Shoreditch, and while I don't mind going up for a visit now and again, I'm never happy but what I'm in the City." She expounded on this theme at some length, and just when Pickett was congratulating himself for successfully avoiding the subject of his profession, she asked abruptly, "And what are you doing with yourself these days?"

"I—I can usually be found at Bow Street," he said with perfect, if incomplete, truth.

She laughed heartily at this. "Aye, I don't doubt it, for you always were your father's son. What'd they take you up for?"

"Actually, I—I have a position there," he confessed somewhat sheepishly. "I'm a principal officer."

Her bright, birdlike eyes grew round. "Never say you've turned Runner! Lud, what your father would say to that—!"

"Yes, well, he's not here, and a fellow has to put food in his belly some way," he answered evasively, then added, "In fact, I wonder if you might help me."

Her whole demeanor changed, her eyes narrowing to slits in the fleshy face. "If you're thinking to make me rat on anybody—"

"No, nothing like that," Pickett assured her hastily. "It's just that—well, I'm looking for a young woman named Jenny. I believe she sells cabbages here?"

Bess's suspicions were banished, and she gave a hearty laugh. "O-ho, so it's Jenny, is it? You young men are all alike!"

Pickett blushed, and would have hastily denied that his interest in Jenny was of an amorous nature, then changed his mind; Stout Bess would very likely be more willing to lend her aid to a romantic pursuit than a criminal one. "You know her, then?"

"Aye, I know her, all right. You'd best have a care, though," she added, lowering her voice to a conspiratorial near-whisper. "She's got a man already, and he's as mean a bastard as ever there was."

"I'll be careful," he promised. "But what about her? Is she here?"

Bess cast a quick glance around the piazza. "If she's not

yet, she soon will be. Usually sets up on the east side, she does, opposite the church."

Pickett thanked her for the information and then, aware that he was hindering the cause of commerce, moved away, surveying the crowd for an attractive young woman selling cabbages. He traversed the length and breadth of the piazza from St. Paul's church to Russel Street and back again, declining invitations to "Come and buy!" from purveyors of such hothouse treats as lemons and oranges to humbler fare such as turnips and potatoes, but saw no sign of a cabbage seller, at least not one who would fit Moll's description. For if Moll, still vain about the looks that she had long since lost, described the girl as a "pretty piece," then the unknown Jenny, Pickett reasoned, must be a diamond of the first water. Hoping to obtain a better view from a higher vantage point, he stepped up onto the wide, shallow portico of the church and climbed onto the plinth of one of its four Doric columns.

And then he saw her. That it must be her, he had no doubt, although it could not be said that she was selling cabbages, at least not at that moment. In fact, she appeared to be struggling with a wooden wheelbarrow which she attempted to steer through the press of buyers and sellers, and although Pickett could not say for certain that her barrow contained cabbages, he could trace her progress (or lack thereof) by the annoyed faces of those persons who were bumped by the forward edge of the vehicle, or whose feet were run over by its wheel.

Having found what (or rather, who) he had come for, Pickett leapt down from the plinth of the column and pushed and squeezed his way through the crowd until he drew up beside the young woman with the wheelbarrow. Sure enough, it was full of cabbages.

"Excuse me," he said, "but you appear to be having some difficulty. May I push your wheelbarrow for you?"

She looked up at him with large, leaf-green eyes in which gratitude and suspicion fought for prominence. Suspicion won, however, and she shook her head, dislodging a tress of white-blonde hair that slipped out from beneath her bonnet. She pushed it out of her face with one lace-mittened hand. "I'm obliged to you, sir, but I don't want to put you to any trouble." Her voice was soft, but her tone did not invite persistence.

"It's no trouble at all," declared Pickett, deliberately obtuse.

She had been obliged to release one handle of the wheelbarrow in order to brush the hair from her eyes, and the barrow, deprived of this support, wobbled in a manner most threatening to the cabbages that comprised its contents. Pickett, seeing his opportunity, did not hesitate. He seized the handle and steadied the vehicle, and by the time Jenny had secured her hair, she discovered that he had somehow contrived to obtain sole possession of the barrow.

"You really shouldn't—"

"Nonsense! You wouldn't deprive me of my chance to rescue a damsel in distress, would you? Now, where are we going?"

Yielding to the inevitable, Jenny smiled shyly at him, exposing a dimple in her left cheek. "I reckon if I were to try to take it back by main force, it would only cause a scene."

"That it would," he agreed. "So you might as well say 'thank you kindly, sir,' and tell me where you want me to take this thing."

"Thank you kindly, sir," she echoed meekly, her dimple peeping. "If you can push it over there"—she pointed to a spot farther down the piazza—"next to the tall woman with the turnips, I would be much obliged to you."

It took a great many "excuse me's" and not a few "coming through, please's," and once he was obliged to drive the front edge of the barrow squarely into the legs of a man who seemed determined to ignore all more courteous entreaties, but at last they reached the point she had indicated.

"I'm obliged to you, sir," she said as he set the legs of the wheelbarrow down upon the cobblestones. "I'm usually here before it gets so crowded, but—" She broke off with a helpless little shrug.

"The pleasure was all mine," he assured her, all the while wondering what had made her late that day. One more mouth to feed, perhaps?

"I didn't mean to sound ungrateful," she continued, taking another swipe at the errant lock of hair that had once more escaped its confinement. "It's just that, well, my Roger don't half like it when other men try to make up to me."

At any other time, Pickett might have been quick to deny that he had been "making up to" Jenny or any other female except his own wife; at the moment, however, he was thinking that now he had a name: *Roger*. But Roger who? And where, exactly, might this Roger be found?

"I can't say I blame him," he said, with what he hoped might be construed as regretful admiration. "But—Roger, you say? I think I may know him. Tall, wiry fellow, is he, with black hair?"

It was a pity that the description Maxwell had given Mr. Colquhoun was so vague, but to do the fellow justice, he'd seen the man only briefly, and by the light of a single gas lamp plus whatever additional illumination might have reached the fellow from the windows of the pub across the street. Still, it seemed to stir a cord of memory, as if he himself had seen just such a man, and quite recently, at that. Then again, he probably had, and very likely more than once; it would no doubt fit hundreds, if not thousands, of London's one million residents.

"Aye, that's my Roger," Jenny said with simple pride. Pickett did not wonder at it; any man who would kill as readily as Roger had slain the watchman would be respected, even feared, in the unsavory environs of St. Giles. To be under the protection of such a man would be no small thing for a woman.

"I haven't seen Roger since I don't know when," Pickett said with perfect truth. "Where is he keeping himself these days?"

All her earlier suspicions returned, suddenly and in full force. "I see what it is! You're only being kind to me so I'll tell you where Roger is!"

"I wasn't—" Pickett protested, recognizing even as he spoke the words that they were a lie.

"You're no better than that other fellow, coming here

nosing around and asking questions—"

"What—what 'other fellow'?" Pickett asked. "Did he give his name?"

"No—but I wouldn't tell you even if he had!" she retorted.

"About forty years old?" persisted Pickett, ignoring this rider. "Perhaps walked with a slight limp, but with a military bearing?"

This last had the effect of making her forget her anger, at least for the moment. "He wasn't marching, if that's what you mean."

"No, of course not. By military bearing, I mean he stood very straight—rather as if he had a ramrod shoved up his arse."

This description drew a reluctant giggle. "Aye, that's him to the life!"

Maxwell, then, thought Pickett. *Although I'd give a lot to know how he got here ahead of me.* Aloud, he said, "So, he was asking where to find Roger, too? I hope you didn't tell him!"

The green eyes opened wide. "Then—then you're not looking to turn him in and claim the reward? He's worth forty pounds now, you know," she added, with again that note of pride, as if Roger had accomplished an exemplary feat in having such a price upon his head.

Pickett placed a hand on his heart and said, with all the sincerity he could muster, "Believe me, the last thing I want to do is see Roger arrested." *At least until I have young Kit well away,* he added mentally. *Then they can string Roger up with my blessing.*

It was a master stroke. All her suspicions were put to rest, for this young man was clearly on Roger's side. "No, I didn't tell him nothing. Lud, Roger would've beat me black and blue for it!"

"Good girl!" Pickett said, and was rewarded with another glimpse of the dimple.

His thoughts, however, were elsewhere. It was clear that Maxwell had made more progress on the case than he'd given the fellow credit for. How? Pickett remembered those issues of the *Hue and Cry* that Maxwell had taken home to study. Had he returned them yet? Pickett rather hoped not; if he could ascertain the dates of those issues, he could perhaps borrow them from one of the other, less well-known police offices dotting the Metropolis and discover what Maxwell had found so interesting in them. On the other hand, if Maxwell had already returned them, finding the pertinent information would be more difficult and a lot more tedious.

He returned to Bow Street, but any hope of slipping in unnoticed, obtaining the desired information, and slipping out again died almost as soon as he crossed the threshold.

"My, how the mighty are fallen," Harry Carson called in mock sympathy, the buckles on his spurs jingling faintly as he crossed the room to greet his erstwhile colleague. "What happened to all your finery?"

Too late, Pickett remembered that he was still wearing his old brown serge coat. Thomas had patched the bullet hole so neatly that it was almost invisible (in this, he'd had more than a little help from Julia's lady's maid), but just as he'd predicted, the rusty stains on the sleeve had not yielded, even though Thomas had tried every cleaning method at his disposal, from soap and water to fuller's earth.

"I, um, I had business in St. Giles," Pickett said. "I didn't want my pockets picked—which certainly would have happened if I'd shown my face there looking like a Bond Street beau."

"St. Giles?" Maxwell looked up from the periodical he was reading. Pickett felt a sudden urge to snatch it out of his hands, until he realized that it was not the *Hue and Cry*, but a publication of particular interest to military men. "Have you taken on a case there?"

Or are you merely following me to check up on me? Granted, he hadn't spoken the words, but Pickett heard them nevertheless. On this occasion, at least, he had a ready answer. "I had to pay a call on my stepmother," he said. It was perfectly true, if one overlooked the fact that his visit to Moll had taken place the previous day.

Maxwell apparently found this explanation acceptable, for he gave a grunt of acknowledgement and turned his attention back to his journal.

"Does that fellow never leave the office?" Pickett grumbled under his breath.

"Who, Maxwell?" In a rare act of discretion, Carson, evidently sensing the need for privacy, lowered his voice to match Pickett's. "What have you got against him?"

"Nothing," Pickett said, perhaps a bit too hastily. "He appears to be a very capable officer. But he's taken a few issues of the *Cry* home to study at his leisure. I should like to know which ones, so I can have a look at them myself, but I don't want him to know I'm interested. He seems to think I don't trust his handling of the case as it is."

"Do you?" asked Carson, scenting a mystery. "Trust him, I mean."

"Let's just say I'm pursuing a line of inquiry closely related to the case he's working—the attempted robbery at Coutts and the murder of the watchman, that is."

Carson's gaze shifted to the magistrate's bench and back again. "Does Mr. Colquhoun know?"

Pickett gave him a rather pained smile. "Who do you think put me on to it?"

"Oh. Well, if you're needing Maxwell to be absent for a few minutes, all you have to do is wait until four o'clock."

"Four o'clock? Why four?"

"Because at four o'clock, the actors at Covent Garden"— Carson gave a nod in the direction of the theatre adjacent to the Bow Street Public Office—"arrive to prepare for the night's performance."

"I didn't know Maxwell had any particular interest in the theatre."

Carson gave a shrug. "He may not, for all I know."

"Well, then—"

"But he does have a very particular interest in Mrs. Cummings."

"Mrs. Cummings?" Pickett darted a quick glance at Maxwell, still intent upon his reading. "The actress, Mrs. Cummings?"

"If there's another Mrs. Cummings, I'm not aware of

her."

"Well, I'm dashed," Pickett marveled, trying without success to imagine his fellow principal officer in this new and unexpected light. "Maxwell, the original 'stiff upper lip,' pining after an actress."

Carson's faintly mocking blue eyes grew larger as the significance of Pickett's reaction became clear. "Don't tell me that you, Mr. Colquhoun's wonder boy, hadn't noticed how Maxwell always contrives to be standing on the portico blowing a cloud when Mrs. Cummings arrives at the theatre!"

"How do you know?" retorted Pickett, nettled. "You're supposed to be off somewhere on horseback, patrolling the roads leading into Town!"

"Observation, my lad," Carson said, tapping the side of his head near the corner of his eye. "All part and parcel of being a Bow Street man. Perhaps you've heard of us."

Pickett gave him a withering look and turned away.

But he watched the clock for the hour of four, nevertheless.

8

In Which John Pickett Indulges in a Bit of Light Reading

However insulting his manner, Pickett could find no fault with Carson's observations. At exactly four o'clock, Maxwell stood up and stretched, then reached into the inside breast pocket of his coat and withdrew one of the slim brown *cigarillos* which so many soldiers had brought back from Spain. He exited the Bow Street Public Office without preamble, and when Pickett discreetly withdrew to the front window a few minutes later, he saw his fellow principal officer leaning against one of the pillars that supported the portico. His back was turned toward Pickett, for he faced the theatre which dominated the north end of Bow Street, but the feathery trail of smoke whisked away on the sharp breeze indicated that he was indeed "blowing a cloud," just as Carson had said.

Never having formed that particular habit, Pickett had no idea how long Maxwell would be absent. He lost no time, therefore, in striding over to the cabinet where the back issues of the *Hue and Cry* were kept, opening the drawer, and rifling through the newspapers. Since he had reason to believe that he had encountered his young half-brother in early June, at which time the lad was apparently free to roam the streets at will, he saw no reason to examine the publications before the first of that month. No, he decided, he would go back to the beginning of May instead, just in case his memory was faulty.

He withdrew the small occurrence book and pencil from the pocket of his coat, in order to mark down the dates of any issues of the weekly periodical that were missing. Of course, there might be other issues absent, having been taken by other officers, or misfiled, or simply lost, but he could do nothing about that. Better, he reasoned, to assume that Maxwell had taken them and examine too many rather than too few.

By the time Maxwell reentered the Bow Street office fifteen minutes later, a list comprising some half-dozen dates resided in the pocket of Pickett's coat, a list covering dates from 17 June 1809—a mere fortnight after his own encounter with the lad, if memory served, right after he'd solved the Washbourn case, but not without coming perilously close to wrecking his marriage in the process—to the most recent issue, dated 9 September and printed too late, alas, to contain any description of the attempted robbery at Coutts and the murder of the watchman.

Pickett was disappointed at this last; Maxwell would have been the source of most of the information cited in any such article, and it might have been helpful to have an account that had not come at second hand from Mr. Colquhoun. Then, too, there might have been some mention of Jenny as a person of interest, along with some clue as to what had put Maxwell onto her trail. In the absence of any such information, Pickett could only think the fellow's methods were much too thorough for his own peace of mind.

After a low-voiced conference with Mr. Colquhoun, during which he informed the magistrate of his next move and received in return some very sound advice, Pickett hailed a hackney and was soon set down in front of the police office in Queens Square, where Mr. Colquhoun had served as magistrate for several years and was still highly regarded—a fact of which Pickett made full use. He left the police office a short time later bearing six issues of the Hue and Cry in a bundle under his arm.

"A little light reading," he explained to Julia upon his return to Curzon Street. "Maxwell took a few issues of the *Cry* home to study—the *Hue and Cry*, that is. It's a police gazette that details unsolved crimes in the hopes that anyone at the other police offices with pertinent information might come forward. With a little help from Mr. Colquhoun and Harry Carson, of all people, I was able to discover which issues Maxwell had taken, and procure copies of them from the Queens Square office."

"That Mr. Colquhoun would offer assistance doesn't surprise me," she said, standing on tiptoe to greet him with a kiss. "Harry Carson, on the other hand, does. I thought you disliked Mr. Carson intensely."

"I hope I'm not such a fool as to allow my personal opinions to get in the way of an investigation," Pickett objected. "Say what you will about Harry—and I could say quite a lot—he does seem to have a gift for discovering the very thing one most wants to keep secret."

"And what secrets, pray, might you be hiding?" she asked, her eyes narrowing in mock suspicion.

Pickett shook his head, then turned away to set down his burden and divest himself of hat and gloves. "Not me—at least, not this time. It turns out that Maxwell has been wearing the willow for one of the actresses at Covent Garden."

"Has he?" asked Julia, slipping her hand through his arm and guiding him in the direction of the dining room. "But what does his unrequited *tendre* have to do with your search for your brother?"

"I needed a few minutes to identify the missing issues without him knowing of it. I've rather got off on the wrong foot with Maxwell, I'm afraid, and he seems to think I'm checking up on him. Which I am, of course, but not for the reason he thinks. Anyway, Harry told me Maxwell always contrives to be standing outside at four o'clock in order to watch for Mrs. Cummings to arrive at the theatre. And he was right."

"Oh, so it's Mrs. Cummings, is it?" Julia's ears pricked up at the name.

"You know her?"

"I've seen her perform, of course. Mr. Maxwell has good taste; she is both beautiful and talented."

"Is she?" Pickett asked in mild surprise. "I hadn't noticed."

Julia patted his arm. "You, my dear, are a very wise

man."

It was a very pleasant dinner, during which, by tacit agreement, they abandoned all discussions of Pickett's doings at Bow Street in favor of such domestic trivialities as the letter that had arrived that morning from Julia's mother, the shocking price the cook had been obliged to pay for the veal cutlets that now adorned their plates, and the desirability of having the chimneys cleaned before winter. The subject of Pickett's search was not raised again until they had repaired to the drawing room, at which time Pickett heaved a sigh and untied the string holding the roll of newspapers together.

"I suppose there's no putting it off any longer," he said, smoothing the roll flat and picking up the topmost publication from the stack.

"Can I help?" Julia asked somewhat mechanically. In fact, she was so accustomed to having her offers of help declined (albeit always gently, and with thanks) that she was somewhat taken aback when he picked up the next periodical, the one dated 2 September, and handed it to her.

"Thank you," he said with real gratitude. "I'm obliged to you."

"What am I looking for?" she asked, pleased as always to be given some part, however small, in his work.

"Any crime that seems to resemble the recent burglary at Coutts."

"Resemble in what way?"

"Anything. The method of entry, the number of persons, or, especially, the possibility of a child, or an undersized individual who might have been a child, involved."

Julia entered eagerly into the spirit of the thing, but her help was not an unmixed blessing. She paused often, interrupting Pickett to read aloud to him the details of some particularly shocking, bizarre, or even amusing crime.

"—And the cow," she concluded between gales of laughter, "—was later discovered roaming about Clerkenwell!"

"Sweetheart," he said at last, interrupting her account of two drovers whose dispute over the possession of the aforementioned cow had led one to assault the other before abandoning his remaining livestock and fleeing to parts unknown, "I'm sure that's all very amusing, but what it might have to do with the whereabouts of my brother, I'm at a loss to understand."

"No, of course not," she agreed readily. "But it's all so *interesting!* John, darling, were any of these cases yours? I had no idea!"

"I'm glad you approve," he said with a hint of a smile. "But since I need to return these to Queens Square as soon as possible, perhaps we'd better concentrate on those crimes that might have some bearing on the matter at hand."

"I'm sorry," she said, looking so contrite that Pickett felt guilty for spoiling her enjoyment. "I promise, I won't be distracted again."

However well-meaning her promise, the faint gasps and stifled giggles that occasionally broke the silence indicated that she was not entirely successful in keeping it. She did not interrupt him again, however, and by the time Pickett folded the last of the periodicals and laid it aside, they had compiled a rough calendar of sorts, delineating similar crimes occurring at somewhat regular intervals from the end of June to the most recent attempt at Coutts.

"They're getting bolder. Look at this." He slid off the sofa and began crawling about on the floor, spreading the pertinent pages in chronological order from left to right. "On the seventeenth of June, two men and a boy were seen fleeing a pub in St. Giles after rifling the cash drawer and nicking the contents. Two other pubs in the area were robbed that same night, and although no one was seen in either case, it seems likely that all three crimes were committed by the same gang of robbers. In all three instances, a window opening onto the cellar was either prized open or broken out completely."

"Just like the cellar window at Coutts," Julia observed, leaning forward to peer over his shoulder.

"Exactly. Then, a fortnight later"—Pickett indicated the periodical dated 1 July—"a linen-draper's shop in Soho was robbed. Again, the cash drawer was forced open and the contents stolen. No one saw the thieves, but the method was the same as the St. Giles pub robberies. A se'ennight after that, on the sixth of July, a milliner's shop was breached, once again through the cellar window. Here our criminals were out of luck, for the owner had taken the week's receipts to the bank that afternoon, the next day being Saturday, and there was nothing left in the cash drawer but a few shillings. But the milliner has two apprentices who live in the attic, and one of the girls says she was awakened by a noise like shattering glass. She ran to her window, which looks out onto a narrow alley giving access to the rear of the building, and saw two men assisting a third to climb through the window into the cellar."

"John! Did she go downstairs and confront them?"

"No, for—I'm quoting here—'I was afeared they would murder me, and me in my nightrail!' "

"I suppose it is important to be properly dressed for one's murder," Julia conceded. "Still, it seems a pity that she stayed cowering in the attic while they robbed her mistress."

"Considering what they did to that poor watchman— assuming it was the same men—she was probably wise," Pickett pointed out. "Depend upon it, her sex wouldn't have protected her any more than his age did him. To her credit, she did summon the watch as soon as she judged it safe, but by that time it was too late, of course. Unfortunately, they left behind no clues as to where they might have gone to ground. I would lay you any odds that it's somewhere in St. Giles, but that's not much help. The place is a regular rabbit-warren."

"What did they do next?" Julia asked. "After robbing the milliner's shop, I mean."

"For the last couple of months, they've seemed to target the more prosperous shops. It's interesting that there are no more pub robberies that match the pattern, not after that one night in June. It appears that, having perfected their method, they've moved on to bigger and better things."

"Like Coutts, you mean," Julia put in.

Pickett nodded. "Coutts, and just before that, a jeweler in Piccadilly. But here's a curious thing: in that case, they stole only the cash in the drawer. The jewels themselves don't seem to have been touched."

"How very odd! Do you suppose they didn't realize what they were worth?"

"No, for I don't think the jewels *were* worth anything— not to them. The only way they might profit from a jewel theft would be in selling their haul for whatever they could get. I think they didn't want to run the risk of the gems being recognized, or of having to explain how the stuff had come into their possession." He frowned thoughtfully. "But they're definitely getting more ambitious. They're working up to something, something big. And that might be the thing that sends them to the gallows; as they say, the bigger the risk, the bigger the reward. I only hope I can get young Kit well away before they make the attempt."

He leaned back against the sofa as he spoke, and she stroked his brown curls with loving fingers. "You'll do it," she said bracingly, determined not to betray her own ambivalence on the subject.

"Are you ready for bed?" He collected the periodicals into a single stack, then rose to his feet and held out his hand to her. "I think we've done all we can do here."

"I'm sorry," Julia said as they climbed the stairs toward the bedchamber. "I'm sorry you didn't find anything more helpful."

He gave a resigned shrug. "Oh well, if they've been breaking and entering at will for almost three months, perhaps they can continue to evade Maxwell long enough for me to find the boy and spirit him away. But it's the devil of a position to be in, having to work against one of my colleagues."

Julia offered no answer, but gave his arm a squeeze and leaned her head against his shoulder. He responded by extricating his arm from hers so that he might put it about her waist and draw her closer to his side. Once they reached the door to the bedchamber, however, he stopped abruptly.

"Look at this," he said, eyeing the tastefully appointed room with disfavor. "I'm living in the lap of luxury, while somewhere out there"—he made a restless gesture toward the window—"my ten-year-old brother is at the mercy of a gang of cutthroats."

"Perhaps you'll discover something useful from this girl," Julia suggested, steeling herself—not for the first time—to welcome the child for her husband's sake. "The cabbage seller, I mean. What was her name again?"

"Jenny. But I don't think there's anything else to be had from her. Between first Maxwell and then me asking questions, she's got the wind up."

"But she can't stay in Covent Garden forever, surely. Couldn't you follow her, and discover where she goes?"

Pickett frowned thoughtfully. "I suppose I could try, but it won't be easy. By the time she packs up shop in the evening, the crowd in the market has thinned. It'll be a challenge not to be noticed." He glanced down uncertainly at Julia. "I may be obliged to play the determined suitor. Will you mind?"

"Hmm." Julia pretended to ponder the question for a long moment. "I can't say I'm thrilled at the prospect, but I can't argue, since I was the one who suggested you follow her home. I only hope you don't decide you prefer the woman who sells cabbages to the woman who looks as if she swallowed one," she added, putting a hand to her belly.

"I'll let you know," he promised, and together they went into the bedroom and closed the door. And although Julia knew his young half-brother was never far from his thoughts, she made sure he did not dwell on the boy's plight.

At least, not until morning.

9

In Which Is Revealed Maxwell's Source of Information

While Pickett visited the police office at Queens Square, Jenny pushed her pale hair back up under her cap, bade her fellow vendors goodbye, and pushed her wheelbarrow (empty now save for a few wilted and drooping cabbage leaves) through the streets leading from Covent Garden into St. Giles. From James Street, she crossed Long Acre and soon turned east into Castle Street, tracing the perimeter of Seven Dials until she came to the dark, narrow passage called Nottingham Court. She turned into this, recalling as she did so that a former beau, a soldier who had seen action in France, had once told her that the French word for such blind alleys was *cul-de-sac*, meaning "bottom of the bag." And so it was, she reflected, in more ways than one. She stopped before the third door from the end and fumbled at her bodice for the key, which she wore on a string around her neck. She bent low to enable her to insert the key into the lock without being obliged to pull it over her head, and a moment later she pushed the door open. At the same moment, a second door opened, this one leading to a room at the back of the house.

"About time," grumbled Jud, emerging from this back room just as Jenny closed and locked the door behind her. "Find the brat something to eat, will you? He'll be waking up soon."

"Later, Jud." Roger had been leaning back against the wall and smoking a pipe, his chair balanced on two legs, but he sat up straight at her entrance. "How'd you do, Jenny-love?"

"See for yourself, Roger," she said. "I think you'll be pleased."

She reached into her bodice and pulled out the coin purse tucked into the top of her stays. Roger snatched it from her hand and tugged open the drawstring, then dumped the contents onto a scarred table.

"Two shillings ninepence," he announced, having sorted and counted the coins. "It'll have to do, I reckon."

Jenny's face fell. "I sold all my cabbages, Roger. I can buy more in the morning with this, and if I sell all of them—"

" '*If!*' " Roger echoed bitterly, bringing his fist down on the table hard enough to topple the little stack of coins. "I'm sick of 'ifs' and 'whens' and 'somedays'!"

"You're the one who's holding us back, Rog'," Jud pointed out sullenly. "I was ready to do the thing last night, but no, you wouldn't hear of it."

"You keep a still tongue in your head!" retorted Roger, wheeling to confront him. "We'll do it when I say we will, and not one minute before. You understand?"

"Stop it, both of you," Jenny said wearily, struggling to position the wheelbarrow in the corner where it would take up the least room. One didn't leave anything outside on the street, not if one expected to find it there in the morning. Neither of the two men glaring at one another made any attempt to help her, and she found herself thinking rather wistfully of the young man who had pushed it across the piazza for her that morning. "He has a point, Roger. The money's almost gone."

"D'you think I don't know how much we've got, down to the last farthing?" Roger snapped. He grabbed her arm and pulled her onto his lap, a gesture so abrupt that she cried out before she could stop herself. "If it's not enough to suit you, I guess you'll have to find something else to sell, won't you? I know a couple of 'cabbages' that might be worth a shilling or two." In case she missed his point, he thrust his hand down her bodice and squeezed.

"I'm sorry, Roger," she said placatingly, her voice low and coaxing. He'd been in an ugly mood ever since the botched business at Coutts, quick to fire up at any slight, real or imagined. She felt as if she'd spent the last two days walking on eggshells. "I guess I'm just a little on edge. A man was asking about you today, Roger."

"Another one?" Roger asked sharply. "What did he want with me?"

"He didn't say. He seemed to know you, and wanted to know where you'd been keeping yourself."

"You never told him!"

"No, of course not," she assured him hastily, then added, "I—I don't think he means you any harm. Said the last thing he wanted was for you to be arrested."

"He knows there's a price on my head, then?"

Jenny ventured a smile. "Is there anybody in London who *doesn't* know that, Roger?"

Roger was silent for a long moment, as if he were deciding whether or not to take offense. Finally, seeing no implied criticism, he nodded. "All right, then. This one last job, and we'll be set for life. But after what happened at Coutts, I'm taking no chances, d'you hear? I haven't yet made up my mind as to how we'll do the thing, and until I decide for sure, we're biding our time." Roger traced the string at Jenny's bosom, then hooked it with one quick twist and pulled out the key. "After that, we'll sail for Amsterdam, and I'll set you up as a lady. We'll trade this thing for a necklace of gold and diamonds. You'd like that, wouldn't you, Jenny-love?"

"And what about the boy?" Jud asked, not entirely convinced by this rosy picture of the future. "Does he sail, too?"

"Of course he does," answered Roger, then grinned. "Haven't you ever heard of the River Styx?"

"There's something else you should know, Roger," Jenny insisted. "This young man who was asking about you—"

"Oh, so he was a *young* man, was he? Should I be jealous?"

His tone was teasing, almost playful, but she blushed

nonetheless at having her thoughts so easily read and, ignoring a charge that came much too close to the truth for her peace of mind, came straight to the point. "He looked just like the boy."

Roger's sudden good humor evaporated, and he swore fluently. "But the brat has no other family! The slattern who sold him to me swore it!"

"She lied to you," Jud said, shrugging as if this should have been obvious to the meanest intelligence. "She wanted the two quid, so she lied to you."

"Was he the boy's father, d'you think?" Roger demanded of Jenny.

"I—I don't think so," she said, considering the matter carefully. "I think he was too young for that."

"I have a brother," announced a new voice, half defiant and half frightened. The boy stood in the doorway of the back room. "I said so, didn't I? Maybe now you'll believe me."

"And maybe now," said Jud, advancing menacingly on him, "you'll shut your mummer before I fill it with Blue Ruin again."

"Stop it, Jud," chided Jenny, sliding off Roger's lap and turning to address the boy. "So you're awake, are you? Come sit down, and I'll fetch you something to eat." She grabbed a dull kitchen knife and began sawing slices of stale bread off what remained of a loaf.

Roger snatched up the largest piece and tore it in half, then gave the smaller of the two halves to the boy. "Who d'you think you're feeding, the Lord Mayor?"

"He's a child, Roger," Jenny pointed out. "Children need

plenty to eat."

"Well, this child can grow on his own time. He's mine, at least for now, and I won't have you fattening him up until he can't fit through windows no more. Y'hear that?" he demanded, turning his attention to the boy, who was stuffing bread into his mouth as if he hadn't eaten in days. "You belong to me, just like the clothes on your back and the food in your belly. If you know what's good for you, you'll make sure you're useful to me. If you're no longer pulling your own weight, why, who knows what other arrangements I might have to make?" He picked up the knife Jenny had used to cut the bread, and idly tapped his forefinger against the point of the blade, as if testing its sharpness.

"Never you mind Roger," Jenny told the boy in an undervoice, tousling his dirty brown curls with a gentle hand. "He just likes to frighten people. You be a good lad, and you've nothing to fear, you understand?"

"My brother will come for me." He glared at Roger, but spoke too softly for anyone but Jenny to hear.

"Maybe he will, and maybe he won't," Jenny said noncommittally. "But maybe you'd best keep that to yourself."

Already she regretted telling Roger about the young man she'd met at the market, and his uncanny resemblance to Roger's little snakesman. For one thing was certain: Whether he was any relation to the boy or not, nothing good could come of him entering Roger's orbit.

* * *

The following morning, Maxwell arose very early, left

his lodgings, and hailed a hackney, pretending it did not pain him at all to hoist himself up into the carriage on his injured leg. He acknowledged that hiring a vehicle to convey him the short distance from Red Lion Square to the market at Covent Garden seemed an appalling waste of money; since joining the Bow Street force, however, he never knew how many miles he would be obliged to cover on foot. It was better, surely, to spare his leg this little distance in order to appear hale and hearty before his counterparts at the Bow Street Public Office—to say nothing of the magistrate, who had only engaged him after being given his word that the old injury would not hinder him in the performance of his duty.

No, it was best to spare himself when he could, and be grateful that the careful housewifery of his poor Betsy—God rest her soul—had left him sufficient savings with which to fund these little luxuries, at least until he began to receive the sort of commissions that would allow him to pay for them out of his earnings.

As he had hoped, the costermongers who hawked their wares in Covent Garden were still setting up their stalls for the day; neither the crush of shoppers nor the multitude of petty thieves and pickpockets who moved among them had yet descended upon the piazza. On the portico of St. Paul's church, however, one man had taken up a position from which he would not move until that evening after the shoppers had returned to their homes, the vendors taken down their stalls, and the pickpockets turned their attention to the well-dressed ladies and gentlemen on their way to the theatre. It was this man for whom Maxwell sought, and at the sight of him, the

Runner's pace quickened.

" 'Morning, Bailey," Maxwell said, lowering himself to sit beside him. He was careful to suppress the groan that tended to accompany such movements; he could not see the younger man's breeches, carefully rolled and pinned closed just below the left knee, without thinking that his own injuries were so slight as to be almost nonexistent.

"Sergeant." Bailey acknowledged the greeting, then moved his tin cup (still empty, so early in the day) and shifted to give his compatriot more room.

"No, don't trouble yourself," Maxwell said hastily, but the deed was already done.

"No trouble, sir," his subordinate assured him. "But tell me: was I right?"

"Quite right." As the younger man grinned, Maxwell added, "Unfortunately, she won't talk."

"She'll come around, sir," Bailey predicted confidently. "As they say, faint heart ne'er won fair lady."

"She's too young for me," Maxwell protested with a chuckle. "There is another who may have an interest there, though, and if he gets wind of her—" He broke off, frowning.

"Who's that, sir?"

Maxwell did not answer, at least not directly. "Tell me, do you know of a fellow named Pickett? I believe he grew up not far from here."

Bailey considered the matter for a long moment. "I've heard of one called Gentleman Jack Pickett, but I don't think he can be the one you're looking for. He'd be forty years old, at least, and was sent to Botany Bay years ago, what's more—

and left a lot of women behind to mourn him, if rumor don't lie."

"A rare one for the ladies, was he?"

Bailey lifted one shoulder. "So they say."

"He must have left more than a few bastards behind, then," Maxwell observed.

"I've only ever heard mention of one, sir. A boy, although I suppose he would be a man grown by this time."

"Whatever became of him? Do you know?"

Bailey shook his head. "Nobody seems to know what happened to him after his father was transported. Some say he may have stowed away on his father's ship, but others say they saw him in the rookery not long after."

"Consoling his father's women, no doubt," Maxwell drawled.

"No, sir, not that I've ever heard tell of."

Maxwell gave a noncommittal grunt that Pickett would have instantly recognized, but offered no opinion. The magistrate had seemed quite certain that Mr. Pickett could not have sired a bastard at the tender age of fourteen, but Maxwell was not entirely convinced. His years in the army had given him considerable experience of very young men, and he thought it not unlikely that a lad of fourteen, having lost his father to transportation, might turn to a female for comfort—a female, moreover, who might have her own ideas as to the best way to offer comfort to a personable lad on the threshold of manhood. More to the point, neither Mr. Colquhoun nor Bailey had seen the child fleeing from Coutts that night; he had, and there was no mistaking the resemblance.

But there was someone who might know the truth, someone that Pickett himself had mentioned.

"I believe the younger Pickett has a stepmother living not far from here," Maxwell said. "St. Giles, in fact. Have you any idea where I might find her?"

"No, but you shouldn't have to look far to find someone who does." He gave a discreet cough. "She's known to do a bit of whoring occasionally, when needs must."

Far from being shocked by this revelation, Maxwell merely nodded. "It's the way of the world, Bailey. Men steal to put food in their belly; women whore for the same reason. Life in the rookery is ugly, isn't it? Perhaps it's a mercy that it's usually short." Too late, he realized that Bailey, a soldier reduced to begging for his bread, might take exception to this tactless observation. "Still, I should have thought her stepson would have intervened before she reached such dire straits as that. What's her name? Do you know?"

Bailey shrugged. "She's called Moll. I've never heard a surname."

Maxwell frowned. "I should have thought it was Pickett."

"Only if he married her, and—well, with a reputation like Gentleman Jack's, I'd think it was unlikely."

"Yes, I see your point."

Bailey shifted, and Maxwell wondered if he was troubled by phantom pains; he'd heard that those who had lost a limb sometimes felt pain where the injured limb had once been, as if it were still there. Then again, all of the men who had seen action at Corunna suffered from phantom pains, although not necessarily the physical kind.

"Begging your pardon, sir, but—what's it all about? I thought you said it was a boy involved in the robbery at Coutts. Was this Pickett fellow in on it, too?"

"No—well, at least, not directly," Maxwell amended. "It may surprise you to know that Gentleman Jack's son works for Bow Street, and he seems to be taking an uncommon interest in my investigation."

"The veteran's mistrust of the raw recruit, sir?" suggested Bailey with a grin.

"I suppose it could be," Maxwell conceded without much conviction. "He's considered something of a prodigy at Bow Street, so there is that. But I can't get past his likeness to the boy I saw fleeing from Coutts. If I find he's trying to protect his by-blow by throwing a spanner into the works, I'll—"

He broke off abruptly. He didn't like the idea of sending a child to the gallows any more than the next man, and yet, what else could he do? Laws, like military orders, were meant to be obeyed. He was the king's agent to enforce those laws; he didn't have the luxury of choosing which to follow and which to ignore. And while a jury might have taken pity on a youngster involved in a simple robbery and sentenced him to transportation, the murder of the watchman put paid to any chance of clemency.

"Anyway," he said, rising somewhat stiffly to his feet, "if you hear anything else about any of these people—anything at all, no matter how trivial it may seem—you send word to me at Bow Street, do you understand?"

"Yes, sir!" Grinning broadly, Bailey snapped his right

hand smartly to his forehead in a salute.

It was not until his sergeant had walked away that Bailey glanced down at his tin cup, then snatched it up for a closer look. Where it had been empty before, it now held a folded one-pound note.

10

In Which Are Seen Further Complications for John Pickett

As Bailey had predicted, it wasn't difficult to find someone to tell him where to find Moll, nominal stepmother of John Pickett. Maxwell rapped on the door, and it was soon opened by a blowsy woman who appeared to be in a rather advanced state of inebriation in spite of the fact that the hour was not yet noon. Once again, he was taken aback by the realization that his Bow Street colleague had apparently done nothing to relieve the financial distress of the woman who had seemingly raised him.

"Er, Mrs. Pickett?" he asked, trying without much success to imagine this woman having charge of his reserved Bow Street colleague during that young man's formative years.

"That I'm not," she slurred, adding resentfully, "not but what I cooked and cleaned and reared his brats much as any lawful wedded wife would have."

Maxwell had to wonder at Moll's idea of the duties of a lawfully wedded wife. The house, or what he could see of it over her shoulder, looked like it hadn't been cleaned in months, if not years, while as for cooking—well, he would have to be hungry to the point of starvation before he would willingly partake of anything that came from this woman's kitchen.

"Robert Maxwell of the Bow Street Public Office," he said by way of introduction. "I have a few questions I should like to ask you. May I come in?"

"I ain't done nothin' 'gainst the law," she said, bristling.

"My good woman, I never said you had," he had meant to reassure her, but could not quite keep the impatience out of his voice. "Now, may I come in, or would you prefer to discuss it on the front stoop, for all the neighbors to hear?"

Not, he thought, that any of the neighbors were likely to be any more sober than she was. Still, his words seemed to have the desired effect, for she took an unsteady step backwards and made a sweeping motion with one arm that appeared to indicate invitation. In any case, he chose to interpret it that way, stepping over the threshold before she could protest and gently but firmly closing the door behind him.

"I'd offer you a drop of gin, but it's all gone," she said, glancing back rather wistfully at the empty bottle that stood on the table.

"That's quite all right," Maxwell assured her, removing his hat. "I won't trespass on your hospitality. I only want to ask you a few questions."

SHERI COBB SOUTH

Moll regarded him warily. "Aye, so you said. What was
it you was wanting to know?"

"Tell me, Mrs.—er, Moll, do you have a grandson living
here in London?"

Intoxicated she might be, but Moll was not so drunk that
she didn't recognize an insult when one was offered. "Just
how old d'you think I am?" she demanded.

"I neither know nor care," Maxwell informed her. "Just
answer the question, if you please. You are, I believe the
stepmother of John Pickett, my colleague at Bow Street?"

"Aye, that I—" Moll broke off abruptly, shocked into a
state approaching sobriety as the significance of his words
penetrated her gin-soaked brain. "Bow Street, did you say?"

Maxwell nodded. "Mr. Pickett has been a principal
officer—a Runner, as you might say—for the past two years,
but I believe he has been with Bow Street since he was
nineteen. I am trying to determine if he fathered a child, a boy,
some years before, when he was much younger."

Moll, it soon became clear, was less disturbed by her
stepson's youthful peccadilloes than she was by his present
career path. "Bow Street, you say! Why, how could he do such
a thing when he knows it must fair break his father's heart if
he ever came to learn of it!"

"About this boy, Mrs.—er, Moll—" prodded Maxwell,
trying without success to steer the conversation back to the
topic which had brought him to St. Giles. "If your stepson is
indeed the father, then he must have been little more than a
child himself at the time the boy was conceived. Tell me, had
he, er, discovered the fair sex by the time he was, say, thirteen

to fifteen years old?"

He might have saved his breath. Moll, having got the bit between her teeth, ignored the question, electing instead to unburden herself of a comprehensive catalog of her stepson's failings, which were apparently many. "—And now," she concluded, having come at last to the end of this recital, "after making my life such a misery that I was obliged to deny him the house, what does he do but turn his back on his poor father and me by going to work for the very man who was responsible for my Jack's being sent across the sea, and me in the pudding-club, although I wasn't yet aware of it. It's a slap in the face, I tell you. A slap in the face, that's what it is, to one who cared for him as well as any natural-born mother might have!"

"The pudding-club?" Maxwell asked sharply. "Do you mean to say you bore a child after your husband—that is, after Jack sailed for Botany Bay?"

"Aye, seven months after his ship sailed. Another boy." She heaved the world-weary sigh of one upon whose shoulders had been placed a burden too heavy to bear. "And after I'd just got rid of t'other one!"

"And what of this second son?" Maxwell asked. "Did you, er, 'get rid of' him, too?" In fact, he was rapidly revising his earlier opinion. Far from feeling any obligation to support the woman who claimed to have reared him, young Mr. Pickett very likely thought he'd made a lucky escape.

"Aye, that I did, though not before time. I bound him over as an apprentice only a few months ago to a man who promised to teach him a trade."

"Did you indeed? What is the man's name? What is his trade?"

"Lud, you sound just like John," she grumbled. "I'll tell you what I told him, no more and no less. After the fellow gave me two quid for the brat, I figure it's his own business what he does with him. You want any more than that, you'll have to ask that fancy-piece of his what sells cabbages in Covent Garden."

"So I sound 'just like John,' do I? Has Mr. Pickett been asking after the boy, then?"

" 'Mr. Pickett,' " she echoed bitterly. "There's naught but one 'Mr. Pickett' in my book, and him a better man than that whelp of his'll ever be!"

"Your stepson, then," Maxwell amended, fairly certain that this unflattering description was not intended to refer to her own son. "He's taking an interest in his half-brother's apprenticeship?"

"Aye, although what business it is of his, I'd like to know. If he wanted the little bastard, why didn't *he* cough up two quid for him?"

Maxwell suspected that he could have enlightened her, but judged it best to keep a still tongue in his head. In fact, he was beginning to feel a new respect for his meddlesome colleague; it was nothing short of miraculous that anyone reared by such a woman could turn out as well as he had. "I am obliged to you, Mrs.—er, Moll." He set his hat on his head and strode toward the door.

"Here now, there's no need to go haring off back to Bow Street," protested Moll, laying a hand on his arm and moving so close to him that the smell of liquor on her breath almost overpowered him. "It's been a long time since I've had a fine man like you under my roof. If you'd like to stay, I'm sure I could think of some way to make it worth your while."

Maxwell gently but firmly extricated his arm from her grasp. "I am obliged to you, ma'am, but no," he said in a voice that brooked no argument, and quitted the house, leaving a sullen Moll behind to ponder the many ways in which she had been wronged.

* * *

Maxwell's visit proved to be the beginning of a busy day for Moll. The Bow Street Runner had not been gone long before another rap fell on her door, this one harder and more urgent than the first. Moll had been preparing to go out and replenish her supply of gin, but at this summons, she heaved a sigh, tossed her threadbare cloak over the back of an upholstered armchair that had long since lost its stuffing, and started toward the door. It flew open before she reached it, and her son's new master strode uninvited into the room.

"I've got a thing or two to say to you," he said, his tone indicating that Moll was unlikely to enjoy the exchange.

This threat, however, left Moll unmoved. "If you're thinking to return that brat of mine, you're out of luck," she retorted, not without satisfaction. "We've done shook hands on it, and as they say, a bargain's a bargain. Besides, I've already spent the money, so I couldn't pay you back even if I wanted to. He's your problem now, so you'll just have to make the best of—"

"You told me you and he was all alone in the world!"

Roger interrupted, his face reddening with rage. "You said he had no other family but yourself, that there was no one else to know or care what became of him!"

Moll, still stinging from Maxwell's revelations, was quick to defend herself against the implication, wholly unjust, that she had deliberately misled him as to the boy's family situation. "And nor was there, for all I knew at the time. But if you're afraid I'm going to cut up stiff or anything—"

Roger gave a short, ugly laugh that held nothing of humor. "That'll be the day, when I'm 'afraid' of anything you may do to me! But if the little bastard is so all alone in the world, then maybe you'll tell me why a fellow who looks just like him has been sniffing around my Jenny."

"That's John all right, damn his eyes," Moll grumbled, her gaze sliding guiltily away from Roger's. "As like their father as peas in a pod, both of 'em."

"So you knew about this fellow, and didn't tell me!"

Moll was quick to deny this charge. "I'll swear I never did! It's been more than ten years since I've laid eyes on him! For all I knew, he was dead—in fact, when he never came back home begging me to take him in, I thought he must be! How was I to know he'd become a damned thief-taker instead? And what his poor father would say, if he knew—"

But Roger seemed uninterested in the opinions of the elder Pickett. Instead, his heightened color ebbed away, leaving him deathly pale and so still that he might have been transformed into a marble statue. "Do you mean to tell me," he said softly, through clenched teeth, "that this fellow is a *Bow Street Runner?*"

Moll beheld the change in her visitor's demeanor and felt a sudden chill. "I'm sure I never said so," she insisted in placating tones. "It was that other fellow who told me, the one who was here just ahead of you, and who knows but what he was having me on?" Without being aware of doing so, she took a step backward, and then another, until she bumped into a rickety straight chair, setting it rocking on two spindly legs.

The movement, or perhaps the noise that accompanied it, had the effect of breaking Roger out of his stupor. "You'd better hope so," he said, his voice still low and menacing. "Aye, you'd really better hope so."

And with this threat, he left the house as abruptly as he'd entered it.

* * *

John Pickett, of course, knew nothing about any of this. He arrived at Covent Garden later than usual, the better to avoid being seen by Jenny, and thus was unaware that Maxwell had been there that very morning, just as he was unaware that the crippled young soldier occupying one end of the portico of St. Paul's Church was anything else than one more unfortunate reduced to begging in the greatest city in the world. He dropped a silver shilling into the soldier's tin cup as he passed, cringing a little at the clink of metal on metal. He need not have worried; the market was as noisy and crowded as ever—perhaps even more so, now that the more prosperous customers of the morning (those who wanted first choice of the produce on offer, and who could afford to pay for it) had yielded their places to those less affluent folk who were compelled to wait until late afternoon, when the vendors might be willing to lower their prices in the hopes of selling the last of their no longer fresh wares.

By taking up a position behind a wagon, Pickett was able to keep an eye on Jenny without being seen—at least, by anyone except the driver of the wagon, whose expression as the day wore on hardened from mildly curious to highly suspicious, as if he suspected Pickett of planning to make off with the empty sacks in the back of the vehicle.

Pickett, recalling the incognito he had suggested to Julia, sought recourse to it now. "The girl with the cabbages," he said *sotto voce*, jerking his thumb in Jenny's direction, "who is she? Do you know?"

"Oh, aye." Pickett had to admit that the ploy had worked, insofar as it banished the suspicion from the man's eyes; unfortunately, he now had to contend with the fellow's knowing grin. "That'll be Jenny Lovett. Taking little thing, she be, but I'd tread wary, if I were you. Her man's Roger Thorne, and he don't take kindly to other men trying to poach on his preserves. Yessir, I'd tread wary."

Pickett offered no response to this warning, but his gambit had produced the desired effect. He was not challenged again, at least not until late in the afternoon, when the bulk of St. Paul's Church cast much of the piazza into shadow, and Jenny grasped the handles of her wheelbarrow and began making her way through the maze of vendors lining the northeastern perimeter of the piazza. Pickett, doing his best to look like a timid lover, gave a tug to his waistcoat, ran a finger beneath his cravat as if it suddenly felt too tight, and prepared to emerge from the shelter of the wagon.

"Good luck to you, then, lad," said its grinning driver. "But don't say I didn't warn you."

Pickett acknowledged this caveat with a nervous nod that was only half feigned, then set out in pursuit, being careful to stay a safe distance back. He saw her turn into James Street, halfway down the length of the piazza, and was obliged to pick up his pace in order to see which direction she took upon reaching Long Acre. He was considerably hampered by the crush of vendors, but upon reaching the corner of James Street, he had the satisfaction of seeing Jenny's slender form some distance ahead, still pushing her wheelbarrow.

The streets of London were never really silent, but the sounds grew more muted after they left the bustling market, and eventually Pickett was able to hear, very faintly, the creak of the barrow's single wheel turning on its axle. He breathed a sigh of relief at the realization that his task had just become a great deal easier. He need not follow Jenny closely enough to risk being seen; in fact, he need not keep her in sight at all, so long as he had the sound of that creaking wheel to serve as a guide.

Almost as soon as his brain had formed the thought, it was proven wrong. For at some distance ahead and around the corner, the sound had come to an abrupt halt: Jenny had stopped. *What happened?* Pickett wondered. Had she known, or at least suspected, that she was being followed? It certainly appeared so, for a moment later the creak of the wheel began again, only this time the noise came at much shorter intervals, as if Jenny were walking faster, perhaps even running. Away from him, Pickett thought, or was she fleeing some nearer, more immediate danger?

The loud cries that now came from that direction, drowning the sound of the creaky wheel, seemed to indicate the latter. He picked up his pace and chased after the sound, reaching the corner just in time to see the barrow disappear into another street some little distance ahead. Only now it was not Jenny pushing it, but a scrawny youth of about twelve. Nor did it contain cabbages; instead, three or four urchins appeared to have piled into its bowl, whooping with delight at this novel form of conveyance.

"Hey! Bring that back!"

Pickett's voice was all but drowned by the shouts of the barrow's new burden, and he was obliged to pursue it, albeit not without wondering fleetingly where Jenny had disappeared to. But he would think about that later. His first priority was recovering her property; perhaps the act of returning it to her would serve to establish a bond of trust—and, consequently, loosen her tongue as to her lover's whereabouts.

Ordinarily, Pickett might have been hard pressed to chase down a street urchin half his age, but he was aided by the fact that this particular urchin had the added burden of a wooden wheelbarrow loaded down with passengers. However scrawny these might be as individuals, their combined weight, especially when added to that of a sturdy wooden vehicle, must surely be considerable. In any case, it was not long before Pickett cornered them at the end of a blind alley off Denmark Court.

"Caught you!" he said, not without satisfaction. "Now, I

suggest you return this thing"—his gesture indicated the wheelbarrow, from whose bowl three rather sheepish-looking lads were scrambling—"to its rightful owner."

"We ain't done nuffink wrong!" insisted the eldest of the group, to whom had fallen the task of conveying his juniors.

Pickett was unconvinced. "Surely you must know this thing doesn't belong to you."

The biggest of the barrow's three passengers spat on the ground. "Oh, aye. Everybody knows that."

"B'longs to a coster-mort named Jenny," said the eldest, adding. " 'Er wot sells cabbages in th'market."

"She said we could play with it," the smallest piped up, determined not to be left out of the conversation. He opened one grimy fist to reveal an even grimier coin. "She give us a ha'penny each and told us to lose the bloke wot was tailin' 'er."

"Then—you didn't steal it," said Pickett, feeling rather as if the ground were giving way beneath his feet.

" 'ell no! 'er cull, Roger, wouldn't 'alf 'ave our 'eads if we did such a thing."

Two small heads bobbed in agreement. "Us nor nobody else," agreed a third, raking his hand through dirty blond hair that was badly in need of trimming. "That careful of Jenny, he is."

"I see," said Pickett, improvising rapidly. "Still, she'll need it tomorrow morning. Why don't we all take it to her? Climb in, all of you, and I'll push."

The smallest boy clambered over the rim of the bowl with a cry of delight, but his companions were more skeptical.

"And 'ow," asked the eldest, regarding Pickett through eyes narrowed in suspicion, "are we to know you aren't the cove she were tryin' to escape from?"

"There you have me," Pickett said, trying not to sound as frustrated as he felt. "For that matter, how am I to know the four of you won't lead me into some cutthroat's lair? I suppose"—he threw in a careless shrug for good measure—"we'll just have to trust each other."

The eldest of the urchins shook his head. "Not a chance. We weren't born yestiddy, y'know—although Benny 'ere comes pretty close." He cuffed the youngest, clearly his brother, on the ear. Benny began to howl, so that he was obliged to raise his voice to be heard. "Jenny tole us wot to do wi' 'er barrow when we'd done wi' it, and she didn't say nuffink about the likes of you."

Pickett stifled a sigh. Clearly, he had lived too long in Mayfair; easy living was making him soft. Childlike trust didn't exist in this part of London, as he had reason to know—or, if it did, it didn't last long. He considered fleetingly the possibility of lurking in some doorway or alley and watching to see what the boys did with the wheelbarrow, but rejected the idea at once. Their suspicions were well and truly roused, and they—at least, the elder boys—would be watching for any such action on his part. There was nothing more he could do here, at least not until the morrow.

And then, he decided, it was time to confront Jenny with what he knew, and give her two choices: she could cooperate, or she could be charged as an accomplice.

11

In Which Roger Eliminates a Threat

B y the time she hurried into Nottingham Court and stopped before her own door, Jenny was panting and out of breath. She'd dared not look back to see if she was being followed, but now that both Roger and Jud were within shouting distance, she could risk watching the open end of the alley for the appearance of a tall young man with curling brown hair. When no such person emerged, she began to breathe easier, both literally and figuratively. It would not do to have Roger see her breathless and flustered; it was bad enough that she must think of some story to account for the absence of her wheelbarrow. She supposed she must be the one to open the door to the boys when they returned it, lest Roger interrogate them and they, all unknowing, blurt out the truth: She was being followed by the same young man who had shown her such flattering attention the day before, and she'd recruited their help in giving him the slip.

She wasn't quite sure why it was so important that Roger remain unaware of his continuing interest in her; one would think it would be quite the opposite, and Roger, as her protector, would be the one to send the fellow off with such a flea in his ear that she would never be troubled by him again.

Confess it, she scolded herself. *You don't want Roger to frighten him off. You* want *to see him again, and if Roger were to learn of your interest in him, it would be very much the worse for you.*

And all for what? Gratifying as she found it to be pursued by a personable young man, she was almost certain that his pursuit was *not* inspired by admiration of her person. False modesty aside, she knew what it was to be desired by a man; more than one young tradesman or apprentice had demonstrated a marked preference for her company, until Roger had staked his claim and even the most devoted of her admirers had decided it was healthier to ignore her existence. For all this new fellow's persistence, the questions he asked were not those of a lover trying to fix his interest with the object of his desire.

One thing was certain: She was unlikely to find any answers standing outside in the gathering dusk. Heaving a sigh, she fumbled at her bodice for the key hanging from its string, then let herself into the house.

It was much too quiet; she noticed that at once. Jud sat at the table, taking a long pull from a tall black bottle. Of Roger, and of the boy, there was no sign.

"Where's Roger?" she asked without preamble, closing the door behind her and turning the key in the lock.

"Gone to see Moll."

"Moll?" she echoed.

"Boy's mum."

"What for?"

Jud shrugged. "Ask him, why don't you? Rog' never tells me nothing."

He never told her much, either. It was odd, in a way, how she shared Roger's bed every night, and yet knew so little about him, aside from his quick temper and how best to avoid rousing it. Still, that was none of Jud's affair. "And the boy?" she asked.

Jud set the bottle back on the table and jerked his thumb in the direction of the back room. "Asleep."

She frowned. "You mean you pumped him full of Blue Ruin again."

"Not this time, I didn't," Jud insisted, lifting wide, almost childlike blue eyes to hers. "He's just sleeping natural-like."

She planted her hands on her hips and regarded him skeptically. "A healthy boy, fast asleep at four o'clock in the afternoon? Tell me another one, why don't you?"

Jud spread his hands in a gesture of helplessness. "Is it my fault the whelp worked himself up into such a state that he wore himself out?"

"Worked himself up into—over what, pray? Have you been teasing him again?"

"I didn't do him any harm. He just needed bringing down a peg or two, going on about that brother of his like he was a cross between King George, Father Christmas, and Jesus Christ. Tell you the truth, I think he's just having us on. I don't believe any such person exists."

Whatever she might have said to this was forgotten as the doorknob rattled. Clearly, Roger had returned. Jenny and Jud exchanged looks, temporarily unified by a single thought: *Pray God he's in a good mood.*

"Well?" Roger demanded, opening the door at that moment to find two faces regarding him with identical expressions of anticipation and fear. "What are you staring at me for?"

"Sit down and let me get you something to eat," Jenny said quickly, moving toward the pantry.

"How'd it go?" Jud asked, taking another pull from the bottle. "Find out anything useful from Moll?"

"I found out something, all right." His eyes were locked on Jenny, but it was to Jud that he addressed himself. "Go fetch the barrow, Jud."

So the boys have returned it, Jenny thought. She'd given them specific instructions as to where to leave it, near enough that it could be reclaimed before someone stole it, but not so near as to give any clue as to where she, and thus Roger, might be found. Roger had clearly seen it, though, and she had yet to invent an excuse as to its being there. But Roger didn't question her on the subject, just stared at her with a feverish glitter in his eyes as Jud regretfully put down his bottle and rose to carry out Roger's command. *I wonder,* she thought irrelevantly, *what Roger would say if we ever told him 'no'?*

As the door closed behind Jud, Roger advanced upon her. It was not unheard of for him to send Jud off on some errand when he didn't want to wait until Jud retired for the night to take her. Still, there was an ugly look in his eyes that she could not like. *He's going to want it rough*, she thought, resigning herself to bruised flesh and aching bones in the morning.

"What—what did the boy's mother have to say?" she asked, taking a pewter plate down from the shelf and setting it on the table along with a mismatched fork and spoon.

"She said a lot." Roger's voice was low, and Jenny, accustomed to seeing him in a towering rage, began to lower her guard—which made it all the more unexpected when he pinned her against the wall with enough force to crack her head against the flaking plaster. "You slut! So eager for another man in your bed that you'd spread your legs for anything in breeches, so long as he paid you a few pretty compliments first!"

"What?—But—Roger—*no*—!" This last was cut off abruptly as his hand went to her throat and pressed against her windpipe.

"You stupid cow, you've got a damned Bow Street Runner on our tail!"

Dimly, through the roaring in her ears, Jenny heard the door to the back room open, and a child's voice shouting, "Stop it! *Stop it!*" and the goldfinch flinging itself against the bars of its cage and shrieking in agitation. Suddenly two small hands had locked themselves around Roger's arm and were tugging for all they were worth. Roger backhanded the boy as easily as he might swat at a gnat. Jenny felt rather than saw the small body slam into the floor, heard the crack as his head made contact.

But in that split second when Roger's grip was loosened,

she lunged for the fork on the table, the only weapon within reach. It was too little, too late. Roger grabbed at her, and although he missed her neck, his fingers found the string showing at the edge of her bodice. He snatched it up and pulled, twisting it so tightly that the key bit into the soft flesh of her throat. Her splayed hand groped in vain for the fork; the room was growing strangely dark, and she could no longer see it. The days were growing so much shorter now, as autumn succumbed to winter. She ought to light the lamp—it would be full dark soon—but she couldn't breathe, and her legs were weak, so very weak that they could no longer support her weight...

She slid down the wall until she landed in a heap on the floor. An unnatural silence filled the room, a silence broken only by the rasp of Roger's heavy breathing and the quiet sobs of a child with hands pressed to his face in an effort to blot out the sight of Jenny's bulging eyes and outthrust tongue.

* * *

The creak of the wheelbarrow announced Jud's return long before the door opened and he stood on the threshold, staring in bewilderment from Roger to the heap of tangled limbs, faded skirts, and disheveled hair that had once been a living, breathing person.

"Jenny?" Jud's gaze swiveled from the body on the floor to Roger. "Is she—?"

"Dead," Roger said curtly. "You'll have to get rid of the body, but not until sometime after midnight."

Jud didn't dare ask the question uppermost in his mind, so he settled instead on a secondary concern. "*Me?* Why me?

134

Seems to me it's a job for both of us."

Roger scowled at the door to the back room, where a series of thumps and howls emitting from the other side suggested that the boy had been locked in. "One of us has to make sure the brat don't escape."

Jud cast an uneasy glance at the body. While arguing the point with Roger, he'd advanced farther into the center of the room, and from this angle it was possible to see the bulging eyes, the gaping mouth. "If she's going to be lying there 'til midnight, can't we at least cover her up? Seeing her like that gives me the creeps."

Roger threw him a contemptuous glance. "I never knew you were so squeamish. If you want to sacrifice your blanket to the cause, be my guest."

Jud considered it for a moment, then nodded. "After all, it's not like she'll get blood all over it, is it?"

He stumped up the stairs to his own room, directly above the one where the boy was kept, and returned a moment later with a threadbare blanket so faded that it was impossible to tell what its original color had been. He unfurled it over Jenny's body and let it settle to the floor. One of her hands jutted from beneath the folds, fingers splayed as if she were trying to claw her way out, but at least those staring eyes no longer reproached him. Freed from the silent accusation, he returned to the subject at hand.

"Why can't *I* stay with the brat while *you* get rid of Jen— er—the body? After all— " He broke off abruptly, afraid to finish the thought.

Roger bristled in indignation. "What? After all, I killed

her? Damn right I did! I only wish I'd done it sooner, before she set a bloody Bow Street Runner on my tail!"

"A *Bow Street*—" Jud tore his gaze from the blanket-covered heap on the floor to stare at Roger, his eyes wide with alarm. "How do you know?"

"Brat's mum said so. And his name is John, so it looks like the little bastard wasn't lying when he said he had a brother. Pity he didn't see fit to mention that the fellow was a bloody copper." His eyebrows drew together as he considered this curious omission. "Unless the brat didn't know it himself."

Jud muttered a curse under his breath. "So, what'll we do now?"

"First, you get rid of the body. Take the wheelbarrow and dump her somewhere that won't lead any Nosey Parker from Bow Street straight to our door."

Jud cast a dubious glance at the blanket-draped lump. "I'll do it, but you'll have to pick her up and put her into the barrow." He shuddered. "Face down, if you don't mind."

Roger gave a contemptuous huff. "All right, then, since you're so nice in your sensibilities. And then"—his pale eyes narrowed, and his jaw set—"since Brother John seems so set on finding me, I think it's time I made his acquaintance. But I'll do it on my turf, and on my terms."

* * *

Although there were few still awake to hear it, the clock in the bell tower of St. Giles-in-the-Fields struck the hour of two. Some distance away in Nottingham Court, a door slowly opened, and a bulky figure in a dark cloak peered out. The hood of his cloak was pulled forward, casting his face into shadow, but the turn of his head, first in one direction and then in the other, indicated a careful survey of his surroundings. Apparently he was satisfied with what he saw, for the head was drawn back into the house only to emerge a moment later with the rest of his person, pushing a heavily laden wheelbarrow before him. He closed the door behind him and steered his burden up the short length of the court to Castle Street. For a long time after, there was no sound but the huff of his labored breathing and the creak of the barrow's wheel as he pushed the vehicle up street and down alley until he reached the agreed-upon destination, a short alley off the Vinegar Yard just north of the St. Giles workhouse—near enough that he could trudge there and back in a short space of time, yet not so near that anyone would connect the body of a young woman discovered there with a dilapidated house in Nottingham Court.

Having reached this insalubrious location, he pushed the barrow into the farthest corner of the alley and tipped the vehicle forward until its burden slid out and landed in a heap on the ground with a soft noise that sounded almost like a sigh. His task complete, the figure turned and made his way back up the alley and into the mews, willing himself not to run. The return trip was faster, given the lighter weight of the barrow, and a short time later he turned into Nottingham Court and let himself back into the house, releasing a long breath as he locked the door behind him.

Somewhere in the distance, the clock in the bell tower of St. Giles-in-the-Fields chimed the half-hour.

12

In Which John Pickett Makes a Shocking Discovery

"What are your plans for the day?" Julia asked, facing her husband across the breakfast table. "Are you still pursuing the beautiful cabbage-seller?"

Pickett swallowed a mouthful of buttered eggs and heaved the exaggerated sigh of the thwarted lover. "I'm afraid not. I seem to have offended the lady, and now she has nothing more to say to me." Dropping the pretense of unsuccessful suitor, he added, "I showed my hand a bit too plainly yesterday, and now she's got the wind up. Today I'm more likely to grab her and shake her until her teeth rattle," he concluded grimly.

Julia, fully aware that he would never treat a woman so roughly, no matter how great the provocation, thought nevertheless that the fact he would voice such a threat spoke volumes about his frustration. Perhaps, she decided, a slight change of subject was in order.

"It occurs to me that we have no place to put this child when you find him," she said. "I thought we might put him in the largest of the rooms on the second floor, but first we'll need to furnish it. I intend to go shopping today, if you have no objection."

He laid his fork down so abruptly that it clattered against his plate. "Sweetheart, you don't have to ask my permission to spend your own money!"

"Very true. But now it's *your* money, according to the law," she pointed out with unassailable logic.

"According to the law, maybe. But you and I both know better."

"Yes, and if it weren't for you, I would be too dead to spend any of it." She held out her hand to him. "Shall we compromise and call it *our* money?"

Even after six months of marriage, it still seemed like a miracle that this woman had, somehow, chosen *him*. He took her proffered hand and pressed it to his lips. "I like the way you think, Mrs. Pickett."

Having finished their morning meal, they rose from the table and made their way to the foyer, where the butler, Rogers, had left Pickett's hat and gloves on a small side table in readiness for his departure. Before donning them, Pickett took Julia in his arms and kissed her with a thoroughness that left her breathless.

"Why, John!" she exclaimed, panting slightly, when at last he released her. "What brought *that* on?"

"Just a little something on account," he promised, and began tugging on his gloves. "In case you have any concerns about beautiful cabbage-sellers."

"It seems almost a pity to admit that she doesn't worry me at all."

She handed him his hat, and he put it on. He had one hand on the doorknob when a thought suddenly occurred to him, inspired by the small object residing in his coat pocket. He turned back to his wife.

"About this shopping trip of yours—I do have one request."

"Oh?" His tone was quite different from a moment earlier, when he'd teased her about beautiful cabbage-sellers, and her curiosity was fully roused. "What is it?"

"Buy him a set of toy soldiers, will you?"

"Of course, if you wish it. But why toy soldiers, pray?"

"I just think he would like them, that's all."

"Very well, then." She smiled mischievously up at him. "Although I know you only want an excuse to sprawl out on the floor with this brother of yours and re-enact the Battle of Corunna, or some such thing."

"Guilty as charged," he confessed cheerfully. "Between the two of us, maybe we can pull the thing off without being mortally wounded like poor Sir John Moore."

It was not until after he'd gone that Julia considered this last statement and wondered if he had unconsciously betrayed some fear that he, or his young half-brother, or perhaps both, might be killed in the course of his investigation.

"Nonsense!" she chided herself. "He has no more expectation in being killed in the performance of his duty than he does of being seduced by beautiful cabbage-sellers. You are making a great to-do over nothing."

But she could not quite make herself believe it.

* * *

As for Pickett, the exchange, playful as it was, raised a concern he had not considered before. Although Julia's jesting accusation suggested that he and his young half-brother would interact as equals, the truth of the matter was that he, at five-and-twenty the elder by fifteen years, would be more father than brother to the boy. He'd thought to have some time—ten years, to be exact—to learn how to do the thing before becoming father to a ten-year-old child. An infant would, presumably, be oblivious to his more glaring errors; not so a boy of ten, least of all one whose formative years had been spent in the rookeries of London—as he, of all people, had cause to know.

So troubling was this thought that it was almost a relief to step into the Bow Street Public Office and discover a more immediate concern: Maxwell had pinned a large map of the City and its environs to the wall and was now engaged in marking, by means of a system of pins tagged with colored paper, the very same robberies he had noted in certain issues of the *Hue and Cry*. Pickett didn't know why he was surprised; after all, he would never have consulted those particular periodicals, had Maxwell not shown an interest in them first. He noted with some satisfaction that his colleague seemed to have missed the robbery of the jewelry store in Piccadilly, but this was short-lived; even as his brain formed the thought, Maxwell pushed a pin into the map at a location that Pickett recognized, even at this distance, as the

SHERI COBB SOUTH

fashionable shopping district.

Seeing Mr. Colquhoun attempting to catch his eye, he approached the magistrate's bench at a leisurely pace so as not to attract Maxwell's notice.

"Mr. Maxwell appears to be making some progress," the magistrate informed him without preamble, pitching his voice low enough that none of the other men milling about the office could hear. "If you've located the lad, I suggest you lose no time in extricating him, before Maxwell beats you to the post."

Pickett sighed. "There's the trouble, sir. He always seems to be one step ahead of me, and by the time I catch up, he's thoroughly poisoned the waters. I asked Moll—she calls herself my stepmother, you know, but only when it suits her—anyway, I asked her about the man who holds the boy's indenture. She said she didn't know his name, or where to find him, but she did tell me where I could find the fellow's lover. She's a young woman who sells cabbages in Covent Garden. But by the time I got there, Maxwell had been there first—I have no idea where he got the information—and I couldn't persuade her to talk. I tried following her yesterday when she left the market, but she appears to have seen me—or perhaps she suspected I might try some such thing. In any case, she gave me the slip."

"I believe there is a crippled soldier who begs in the piazza; according to Maxwell, he is a very useful source of information. Then, too, I daresay it makes him feel useful, being able to offer some service in exchange for coin in his cup."

"Yes, I've seen him," said Pickett, much struck. "I

wonder if he would be interested in playing both sides against the middle—for a price, of course."

Mr. Colquhoun could not be optimistic. "I suppose you could ask, but I wouldn't put all my eggs in that particular basket if I were you. I believe a certain sense of brotherhood exists between men who have seen military service, whether or not they actually fought side by side. Mr. Maxwell and the cripple in Covent Garden are both members of that brotherhood; you, on the other hand are not."

Pickett sighed. "No, sir."

"But about this lass with the cabbages: it appears you are slipping, Mr. Pickett. You seem to be losing your touch with the fairer sex."

"Begging your pardon, sir, but Mrs. Pickett might disagree," Pickett said, not without a hint of smugness in his voice.

The magistrate gave a bark of laughter that caused several of the men, Maxwell among them, to look their way. "I'm pleased to hear it! How is your lady wife, by the bye?"

"Very well, sir, thank you."

"And what does she think of opening her home to this brother of yours?" asked Mr. Colquhoun, lowering his voice once more.

Pickett considered the question thoughtfully. "I suspect she isn't quite as delighted as she lets on—well, and how could she be?—but she hasn't uttered a word against the scheme, God bless her."

Mr. Colquhoun nodded. "I suppose that is the best one can hope for, at least for the nonce. Perhaps she'll discover that the lad grows on her. After all," he added with a mischievous twinkle in his eye, "his brother appears to have done."

"For which I am profoundly thankful," Pickett agreed. In a more serious vein, he added, "There is one thing that troubles me, sir."

"And that is?" prompted the magistrate.

"This boy—I suppose I'll be more father than brother to him, even though I'm only fifteen years older than he is."

Mr. Colquhoun nodded. "I should say you have the right of it."

"Yes, sir, but—well—how is it *done?* I'd thought to have some time—ten years, to be exact—before becoming father to a ten-year-old child!"

"I hate to disappoint you, John," said the magistrate, leaning back in his chair, "but there is no big secret, no magic words. In fact, I should say ninety percent of fatherhood consists of making it up as you go along."

"Begging your pardon, sir, but—is that supposed to make me feel better?"

The magistrate chuckled. "Look at it this way: you can't possibly make a worse job of it than what the lad has had heretofore."

"There is that," Pickett conceded. Between the pair of them, a drunken mother and a criminal master had set the bar extremely low. After a moment's hesitation, he added, "Then, too, I have had the advantage of learning from the best."

"Faugh!" scoffed the magistrate. "If that's what you think, I can only say that your memories of your father are vastly different from mine!"

"I—er—I wasn't thinking of my father," Pickett said. It occurred to him just how much he would miss working with Mr. Colquhoun every day, once he'd extracted his brother from the criminal gang who held him, and resigned his position at Bow Street.

"Ah, well, lingering about the office isn't going to find the lad," pointed out Mr. Colquhoun, uncomfortable, as always, with any suggestion of sentiment. "Have you any other plans?"

"I'm going back to Covent Garden," Pickett said. "I'm going to confront Jenny again—she's the girl with the cabbages—and if she still won't talk, I'll threaten to have her arrested as an accomplice." He sighed. "If that doesn't do the trick, then I don't know what will."

* * *

Unfortunately, Pickett's plans suffered a check when he arrived at Covent Garden and found no sign of Jenny among the many vendors hawking their wares. He completed a full circuit of the piazza and, having failed to catch so much as a glimpse of her, he retraced his steps, stopping this time when he reached Stout Bess, once again presiding over her ropes of onions hanging from their pole.

"Back again, are you?" she asked, giving him a knowing look.

Since he'd deliberately cultivated the idea that his interest in Jenny was romantic, there seemed to be no point in disabusing her of the notion. "Yes. I'm looking for Jenny. Have you seen her?"

"No." She frowned thoughtfully. "And I'll admit, I'm a bit worried about her."

"Oh?"

"It's not like her to be shirking." She nodded in the direction of the large clock adorning the pediment of St. Paul's church. "Regular as clockwork she is, most days."

"I don't suppose she might be ill," Pickett suggested quite truthfully, for in fact he supposed no such thing. As for exactly what he *did* suspect accounted for Jenny's absence, however, he feared very much that she was avoiding him. "Did you notice any signs yesterday that she might be sickening?"

Bess scratched the most prominent of her several chins. "I don't think it's illness, exactly," she said thoughtfully, "unless she's sick of being plagued to death with questions from some fellow who won't take 'no' for an answer. Lud, you're just like your father!"

"I am nothing like my father!" insisted Pickett, bristling.

Bess gave a shout of laughter so loud that it drew curious looks, having been heard even over the bustle and noise of the busy market.

"Oh, there is a certain superficial resemblance," he admitted grudgingly. "I suppose I can't deny that, since I see it in the mirror every morning, but beyond that—"

"Always had an eye for the ladies, did your father," she recalled, heaving a sentimental sigh. "It would've been just like something he'd do, your following poor Jenny home yesterday. Did you catch her, by the bye?"

He sighed. "No. She caught on to me somehow, and

146

managed to give me the slip."

"Better for you that she did," said Bess, nodding sagely. "She'll have been sure to tell Roger by this time, and right jealous he be. If he should catch up to you one dark night, it'll be very much the worse for you, you mark my words."

"I'm not trying to seduce her," Pickett insisted. "In fact, it's Roger I'm trying to find, but no one will tell me anything!"

Bess shrugged. "Well, and who can blame 'em? Everyone knows what Roger would do to the cull who set a— a Bow Street Runner"—she lowered her voice, as if afraid to speak the words aloud—"onto him, now, don't they?"

"He can't do anything if he's busy dancing the Newgate jig," Pickett pointed out. "If he's that fearsome, I should think someone—anyone!—would be willing to rat him out just to be rid of him."

"Aye, but his place might be filled with someone even worse." As Pickett heaved a sigh of frustration, she appeared to have a change of heart. "All right, I'll tell you this much, for your father's sake: Jenny and Roger and a fellow named Jud live in a house east of Seven Dials. Now, don't ask me no more, for that's all you'll get from me." In proof of this statement, she pressed her lips tightly together with her thumb and forefinger.

Pickett removed his occurrence book from the pocket of his coat and made a note of this newest name. "And it's just the three of them living in the house? There isn't a fourth? A child, perhaps?"

It soon became obvious that Bess misunderstood the question, but this was not necessarily a bad thing, as she apparently considered women's concerns a safe enough subject. "Jenny don't have any brats, neither by Roger nor anyone else, so far as I know, so if ever she was in the pudding club, she contrived to get rid of it."

"That's not—that is, I don't mean an infant in leading-strings, but an older child. An apprentice of sorts, you might say."

"No, not that I've ever heard tell of," Bess said, curiosity having overridden her determination to keep her lips sealed. "See here, Johnny, what's all this about?"

"I'm not going to tell you that," Pickett said. She made a contemptuous noise in the back of her throat that would have done his magistrate proud, and Pickett, suppressing a grin at the thought, added hastily, "I'm not trying to be disobliging. But if it should be as you say, and Roger should get wind of it, you can tell him quite truthfully that you know nothing about it."

With that Bess had to be content, a state of mind aided considerably by the shilling Pickett dropped into her plump hand.

Seeing that nothing was to be gained by loitering about the market hoping Jenny might eventually put in an appearance, Pickett retraced the route he'd followed the previous day to the star-shaped junction of streets known as Seven Dials. It was here, as he recalled, that he'd been thrown off the scent by the boys who had taken Jenny's wheelbarrow into the maze of streets west of the Dials—in exactly the opposite direction, if Bess were to be believed, from the house Jenny shared with Roger and a second man named Jud.

Alas, the streets to the east of the notorious intersection were just as confusing as those to the west, and his passage was further complicated by the fact that during the daylight hours the narrow streets swarmed with children, half of whom were charged with blocking his passage so that the other half might pick his pockets. He was aided here by the fact that he had once been among their number, and so was wise to their tricks; thus he was still in possession of his coin purse when he turned into a short, dark alley off Vinegar Lane, just north of the workhouse. There were no fewer children here than there had been on any of the other streets down which he had walked, but here the youths seemed oblivious to his existence, so fixed was their attention on something on the ground at one end of the alley.

"All right, where's the fair?" he demanded impatiently, striding into the group with the intention of rescuing whatever unfortunate stray dog or cat they had cornered. "Go home, all of you, and—"

He broke off abruptly. The group had turned at the sound of his voice, leaving a gap through which he could see past them to the object of their interest. No dog or cat cowered there.

Instead, Jenny lay on her back, her dead eyes staring up at him in silent accusation.

13

In Which Julia Prepares to Welcome Her Brother-in-Law

After seeing Pickett off to Bow Street, Julia returned to their shared bedchamber and prepared herself for a day spent shopping. In truth, this was a pleasure in which she had not indulged for some time; given that most of their income derived from the widow's jointure left her by her first husband, it seemed tactless in the extreme to make too great a show of spending it, no matter how many times her present husband assured her that she might.

Still, the prospect of their small family doubling in size from its present two members to four in less than three months could not but bring with it certain expenditures, and while it was true that the anticipated birth of their child gave them sufficient time in which to assemble all the necessary paraphernalia, the same could not be said of the arrival of her young brother-in-law. Any day now, John might return from Bow Street with a ten-year-old boy in tow, and she would *not* oblige the child to bed down on a pallet on the floor; to be caught thus unprepared would, she feared, betray her own lack of eagerness for the boy's arrival, and she would not for worlds have John guess her reluctance to see their domestic idyll interrupted by an outsider.

And so, armed with several issues of *Ackermann's Repository* and accompanied by Andrew (who, as footman, would have the honor of carrying any purchases she might make), she donned her pelisse and bonnet and set out on her quest. In deference to her husband's sensibilities, she stopped first at a cabinetmaker's showroom in Leicester Square, a somewhat less fashionable district commanding prices not quite so high as one might expect to find in the corresponding shops of Old Bond or Oxford Street.

"Good morning, good morning!" exclaimed the young man behind the counter, rubbing his hands in anticipation at the sight of the well-dressed client entering his establishment with a liveried footman at her heels. "What may I show you today?"

"Good morning," Julia answered. "I am in need of furniture for a child."

"Certainly! Er, a crib, perhaps?" he suggested tactfully, observing the bulge that her pelisse could no longer conceal.

She shook her head. "Eventually, but not today. In fact, my husband's young brother is about to make his home with us. I need something sturdy enough to withstand the predations of a ten-year-old boy. And since I don't know exactly when he will be joining us, I fear I haven't the time to wait while something is custom made. Do you have anything already made up that might be delivered on short notice?"

The young man, who upon her entrance had entertained visions of elaborately scrolled and gilded cabinets or Egyptian-inspired tables and commodes in the style made fashionable by Mr. Hope, abandoned these rosy dreams with a sigh of regret and ushered her to the back of the showroom, to which an unassuming four-poster had been relegated, leaving the more elaborate pieces pride of place in the windows fronting the square.

"As you can see, it is not a very ornamental piece," he said regretfully, "but it is constructed of solid oak, capable of defying even the most boisterous young gentleman."

Privately, Julia had more confidence in the four-poster than she had in the "young gentleman," but that being the case, she judged it best to err on the side of caution. She agreed to purchase not only the bed, but also a chest of drawers and a clothes-press of similar stout but utilitarian design, then gratified the young man by opening one issue of *Ackermann's Repository* and asking if it was possible to have an infant's crib made to the design pictured in the periodical.

"Of course," cried the shopkeeper, seeing that his fondest hopes might yet be realized. "That is, I shall ask my father— he and my elder brother do most of the actual woodwork, you see, while I tend the shop—but I'm sure he will agree. If you will forgive my asking, how long"—he broke off, blushing— "that is, when do you expect to need it?"

"December," she said. "I shall need the four-poster much sooner, however."

"It will be delivered before nightfall," he promised.

From the cabinetmaker, Julia went to the shop of her own dressmaker, where she inquired after a wardrobe suitable for a boy of ten.

"I'm afraid I haven't his measurements," she told *Madame* apologetically. "In fact, I have not yet made his acquaintance. He is my husband's young brother, you see, and he will be coming to live with us very shortly."

"*Vraiment*, would it not be better then to wait? Surely his own clothes will suffice until then, *oui?*"

"I fear he has been living up to now in very, er, straitened circumstances," Julia explained, displaying a hitherto unsuspected talent for understatement. "I don't know the condition of his current wardrobe, but I confess, I am not optimistic. I daresay I shall be returning to order more clothing for him very shortly, but I should like to have something ready for him upon his arrival. Tell me, do you have anything already made up that might serve the purpose?"

"Ah! I have it, the very thing. You shall take it to this child, and if it does not fit, I shall have one of my own apprentices make whatever alterations may be necessary, *oui?* But come and see!"

Julia followed, feeling much encouraged—until she beheld the garments *Madame* displayed and realized that that ambitious needlewoman had the fixed intention of outfitting a child of the slums in a skeleton suit of light blue velvet worn over a shirt with a wide collar of fine white cambric edged with lace. The buttons (of which there were many) were made of mother-of-pearl, and served not only to fasten the close-fitting jacket, but to attach it to the ankle-length trousers. The question of how any boy thus clothed might answer nature's call was answered by the front fall; the flap of this, too, made use of mother-of-pearl buttons. If she were to present her young brother-in-law with such a costume, Julia reflected, he would hate her for the rest of his life. And she wouldn't blame him.

"Is very pretty, *oui?*" prompted the dressmaker, seeing her client struck speechless by the beauty of this garment.

"Er, very pretty," agreed Julia without enthusiasm.

"I shall have someone wrap it up, shall I?"

"Not just yet," Julia put in hastily, before Madame could issue such a command to one of her apprentices. "I'm afraid the child's upbringing has—has not been all that it should have been. I am persuaded he would only ruin so fine a costume. I think perhaps something a bit less, um, frilly?"

Madame gave a disdainful sniff that conveyed her opinion of children who failed to recognize the genius at work behind their apparel. Although, now she thought of it, she seemed to recall seeing something in the popular broadsheet *Aunt Mildred's Parlour* (such a pity that it was no longer being printed, for it had been so useful in keeping her abreast of the goings-on in the lives of her aristocratic clients!) that had hinted very broadly at this particular client's second marriage—quite the *mésalliance*, if *Tante* Mildred were to be believed. And in Madame's experience, she usually was. Furthermore, Lady Fieldhurst's—*non, Madame* Pickett's— speculations as to her young brother-in-law's behavior seemed to support it. Madame sighed. It would be a pity to be obliged to drop a client who set off her creations to such advantage. One could only hope *Madame* Pickett's fears would prove to be groundless. In the meantime, however…

"I know just the thing," she announced, with considerably less enthusiasm than her first pronouncement.

This time "the thing" proved to be a blue coat cut very much like the elder Pickett's, only lacking the tails, as it was cut straight across the back, and a pair of ankle-length trousers of brown nankeen. To this costume Julia readily agreed, and soon these, along with a white cotton shirt, stockings, and smallclothes, were wrapped in brown paper, tied with string, and surrendered to Andrew to carry. Shoes, Julia supposed, must wait until she could take the child to be measured.

There remained the schoolroom to furnish, as well as the toy soldiers her husband had particularly requested. Fortunately, the last letter she'd had from her sister had made mention of a bookstore that catered exclusively to children, offering (in addition to its extensive library of juvenile literature) a wide assortment of playthings of an educational or improving nature. While Claudia, living in Somersetshire, was obliged to order items for her own daughter's nursery and have them sent from London, Julia had the advantage of being able to visit this establishment and make her selections in person.

And so, after leaving the dressmaker's shop, Julia made her way to the business Claudia patronized and soon found herself lost in a fantasy world of dolls, toys, games, and books. These last, however appealing, presented a new dilemma: She had no idea what sort of education, if any, the boy had received. Could he read at all? If so, how well? To present an already literate boy of ten with an alphabet primer suitable for a child half his age would be insulting; on the other hand, to offer him reading material beyond his capabilities would only lead to frustration. She asked Andrew for his opinion, but the footman, when applied to, confessed somewhat sheepishly that he had never been much for book-learning. It appeared, then, that she must rely upon her own judgment. But where in the world was one to start?

Where in the world, she reflected. *The world...*

The world, in fact, was just the place to begin. The globe, rather. One need not be literate, after all, to learn to identify England on a map, and this simple discovery might well lead to a desire to know more: where France was, for instance, along with England's other enemies and allies. Then, too, there was the celestial globe that showed the positions of the stars.

Julia happily selected a pair of globes, the terrestrial and celestial, each mounted within a wooden frame that allowed the sphere to be turned on its axis. However, once this task was accomplished, she was obliged to return to the original dilemma: how much education, if any, did the boy already possess? She began selecting books from the shelves at random, leafing through them, and putting them back, hoping against hope that she might stumble upon the answer within the pages.

"Pardon me," a voice interrupted this fruitless activity, "but you appear to be having some difficulty. May I be of assistance? I'm a schoolmaster, you see," he added, as if he feared she might suspect him of making inappropriate advances, "and so am accustomed to selecting literature that might appeal to a variety of interests and skill levels."

Julia turned and beheld a tall, almost gaunt man of at least seventy, with wispy white hair, a slight stoop, and pale blue eyes framed by wire-rimmed spectacles. His clothing was years out of fashion, but had been well-cut when it was new, by a tailor who had known how. She had no doubt he had spoken the truth when he'd claimed to be a schoolmaster; in fact, if she had set out to draw a portrait to represent the breed, he was exactly the man her imagination would have supplied.

"That is very kind of you," she said warmly, "but I shouldn't want to put you to any trouble—"

"It's no trouble at all, I assure you. How old is the child, if I may ask?"

Julia, deciding it would be not only ungracious, but foolish in the extreme to look such a gift horse in the mouth, answered, "The child is ten. But as for his interests or skill level, I'm afraid I haven't the faintest idea. He is my husband's half-brother, you see, and he will be coming to live with us very shortly. I should like to be prepared for his arrival, but—" she broke off with a helpless little gesture indicating the embarrassment of riches on the bookshelves.

"Hmm." He considered her dilemma with puckered brow before saying, "If I may make a suggestion, I shouldn't worry too much about his reading ability, at least not at first. It might be better to choose books he might enjoy, even if you or your husband must read them aloud to him. If you find he reads ahead of you, or asks about certain words, it will give you some idea of what books he might be able to read for himself."

"At which point," Julia said with a sigh, "I shall be obliged to return and select still more."

"Very true," said the schoolmaster, his mild blue eyes twinkling behind his spectacles. "But in almost forty years devoted to the development of young minds, I flatter myself that I have formed some idea of the perennial favorites of my own students. Shall I write a few titles down for you?"

"Yes, please!" Julia consented with real gratitude.

He groped in the pocket of his coat, but to no avail. "Oh dear, I seem to have come off without my little note-book. If you would not object to furnishing me with your name and direction, ma'am, I should be pleased to write out a list and send it to you by post." Sensing some hesitancy on Julia's part, he added quickly, "And after I post the letter, I shall put the card on the fire, so you need have no fear of my someday turning up on your doorstep uninvited."

Julia gave a self-conscious little laugh. "Very well, you have convinced me, Mr.—?"

"Butterworth," he said with a courtly little bow. "Mr. Hiram Butterworth, yours to command."

It occurred to Julia, fumbling in her reticule for her card, that her husband might not be best pleased at her giving this information to a complete stranger, and certainly not after the harrowing events of the summer just passed. Still, her instincts assured her that this man was exactly who he claimed to be, and that he would do exactly as he said he would. And so she did not hesitate to hand Mr. Butterworth the card with her name and direction engraved on it.

He took it and glanced down at it, then looked at it again, more keenly, before subjecting her to an oddly penetrating stare.

"Mrs. Pickett?" he asked sharply. "Mrs. John Pickett?"

"Er, yes," Julia agreed somewhat cautiously.

"And your husband—is he with Bow Street, by any chance?"

"Why, yes," she said again, taken aback by his sudden interest. "Why do you ask?"

"Because I know him. In fact," he added with a rather satisfied smile, "it was I who taught him to read."

"Did you indeed?" Julia exclaimed delightedly.

"Oh, yes. Not that I had to do much," he added. "He seemed to soak it up like a sponge. I've thought of him often over the years. Tell me, how does he go on?"

"Very well, thank you. He has an enthusiastic patron in his magistrate."

"I'm pleased to hear it." He glanced at the man behind the counter, waiting patiently for them to make their selections and pay for their purchases. "I fear we are keeping this good man from his work, Mrs. Pickett. I believe there is a tea room only a couple of doors down; do say you will join me there, where we may dissect your husband's character to our hearts' content."

The temptation was too great to resist. It was not that her husband was secretive about his criminal past; in fact, he had insisted upon making a clean breast of the thing before allowing her to agree to their marriage, unaware that she'd already had the whole story from Mr. Colquhoun. Still, there was a great deal about his early years that she did not know, and this man seemed more than willing to enlighten her.

And so, after paying for her purchases and telling Andrew that after he had seen to it that the two globes were tied securely to the boot of the carriage, he might amuse himself at the public house across the street for the next hour, she and the schoolmaster traversed the short distance to the tea room. He seated her at a table against the wall about midway between the front and back of the shop; Julia suspected he had deliberately chosen a place far enough from the large windows to shield her from prying eyes, yet not so secluded as to suggest anything of a clandestine nature.

The hour that followed was educational, to say the least. Some of Mr. Butterworth's recollections regarding her husband had her choking back whoops of laughter, while others moved her very nearly to tears. It soon transpired that Mr. Butterworth had taught not only John, but his half-brother as well.

"Sharp as a tack," he assured her, "but he lacks Johnny's—Mr. Pickett's, I suppose I should say—focus. Your challenge there will be in finding a tutor who will not allow him to become bored."

"But he can read?"

"Oh, yes. Although whether he chooses to do so may prove to be quite another matter."

"Mr. Butterworth," Julia said, obeying a sudden impulse, "I don't suppose you would be interested in coming to us as his tutor? We cannot pay you lavishly, I fear, but I believe your wages would compare favorably to those of the master of a charity school."

"God bless you, Mrs. Pickett," he said, smiling somewhat regretfully at her. "It's very kind of you to offer, but I fear I must decline."

"But—surely you will wish to retire soon," Julia began.

He shook his head. "I have enough put back to support me in a comfortable, albeit not luxurious, retirement when the time comes. But I cannot justify living in comfortable idleness so long as there is one child who may be rescued from poverty by means of education. Besides," he added on a lighter note, "lads of Christopher Pickett's temperament require the services of a younger man—one who can keep pace with him physically as well as intellectually."

From this stance he refused to be moved, and likewise would not allow her to settle the reckoning for their tea and biscuits.

"It has been many years since I moved in fashionable circles, Mrs. Pickett, but I hope I am not so ungallant as to allow a lady to pay for my tea!" he protested indignantly, but his air of offended propriety was belied by the twinkle in his eyes.

"On the contrary," she retorted in like manner, "if half the things you have told me about John are true, it appears I ought to pay you for a great deal more than that!"

"Now, there you are mistaken, ma'am. As it happens, he repaid me himself, not so very long ago."

"Oh?"

"Yes, indeed. Twenty-five shillings, as I recall."

Twenty-five shillings, she thought. His entire week's

wages.

While she pondered this revelation, Mr. Butterworth added, "Whatever he may have been in his youth, ma'am, your husband is a man of honor."

"Yes, he is," she agreed, misty-eyed. "To a fault, at times."

And he would be returning to Curzon Street soon, she realized, noting with some surprise the lateness of the hour. If he were to arrive there before her, he would no doubt wonder at her absence; she had told him she intended to do some shopping, but she'd not expected to make a day of it.

Alas, she'd said Andrew might have an hour free before his services would be required, and it still lacked twenty minutes to the appointed time. Since she could not leave yet in any case—after all, she could hardly invade a pub and call for him—she returned to the shop where she had met the schoolmaster. During their tea, Mr. Butterworth had mentioned one or two books which had been particular favorites of "Johnny's," and she decided to purchase them while the titles were still fresh on her mind. John might be pleased to revisit them, even if they should prove to hold no appeal for his brother. While she was about it, she might as well pick up a few things for the nursery; both Claudia and Emily Dunnington had warned her that during the last weeks of pregnancy, swollen feet and an aching back would very likely make shopping more of a punishment than a pleasure.

Collapsing wearily onto the seat of the heavily-laden carriage some time later, Julia regarded the mountain of packages wrapped in brown paper and arranged neatly in a stack at her feet, then thought of the larger ones tied onto the boot and was rather taken aback to realize exactly how much money she had spent. Just that morning John had said she didn't have to ask his permission, and she feared she was about to put his indulgence to the test.

When she arrived at the Curzon Street residence full of apologies and explanations, only to be informed by the butler that Mr. Pickett had not yet returned from Bow Street, she hardly knew whether to be sorry or glad.

"But," Rogers added quickly, "the furniture you ordered has been delivered and taken up to the largest of the second-floor bedrooms. Thomas, Andrew, and I await your instructions as to its arrangement."

"What? Oh, yes!" Julia exclaimed, brightening as she untied her bonnet and tugged off her gloves. No doubt his tardiness meant he had located his brother, and would soon be bringing him home—which meant she had better make sure the room was in readiness for the boy's arrival. She did not take the time to change clothes, but snatched an apron from a cupboard and tied it over her fashionable walking dress, then started up the stairs.

Julia spent the next half-hour issuing instructions to the male staff as they positioned the bed with its headboard against the wall ("No, not that wall; the one adjacent to the wall with the window. Now, move it about six inches to the left...") and the clothes-press against the wall opposite. Once the heavy pieces were in place, she dismissed the servants, and she herself performed the task of making up the bed with the best spare linens; not for the world would she have either of the Picketts, man or boy, suspect that she regarded the newcomer's arrival with anything less than delight. Finally, she folded the boy's new clothes into the clothes-press, then changed her mind, took them out again, and spread them out on the bed.

Having made the bedroom ready, she debated as to whether to begin work in the schoolroom, unwrapping the books and other accoutrements to learning and arranging them on the bookshelves. But no, she had no desire to make her young brother-in-law's acquaintance while clad in an apron and with the hem of her skirts two inches deep in dust. The schoolroom, she decided, could wait until morning, after the housekeeper had had sufficient time to see that it was dusted and scrubbed clean.

"No sign of Mr. Pickett yet, Rogers?" she called down to the butler as she descended the stairs. In fact, she knew the answer quite well, for as the window in the boy's room overlooked the front of the house, she would have heard any footsteps on the portico directly below, especially those footsteps to which her ear had become attuned over the past six months.

"No, ma'am, I'm afraid not," Rogers said. He sounded almost apologetic, as if he were somehow responsible for Pickett's absence.

"Never mind," she said with a sigh. "He will no doubt arrive soon enough. In the meantime, I should like to have a fire lit in the drawing room, and you may inform Cook to hold back dinner."

"Very good, madam."

Rogers departed to communicate her instructions to the cook, and Andrew arrived a very short time later to light the fire. Her wishes having been carried out, Julia curled up at one end of the sofa and opened a book, prepared to amuse herself by reading while she awaited her husband's return.

She could not have said at what point she began to grow uneasy. She was only aware, at first, of a certain restlessness of spirits that made it difficult to concentrate on her book no matter how thrilling the gothic tale contained within its pages. The feeling gradually increased as, below stairs, the roast beef that was to have been their dinner dried out, and the gravy intended to accompany it slowly congealed in the pan.

And still he did not come.

14

In Which Maxwell Interferes Once Again

Pickett pushed through the knot of children and knelt before the body, then took one of Jenny's limp hands in his. Her skin was cool. *No big surprise there*, he reasoned. It was the middle of September, and the weather was growing cooler, especially at night. Still, he suspected she had been dead for some time, probably killed the night before and her body dumped here under cover of darkness.

The cause of the poor girl's death was not far to seek, for a thin red line traced a circle around her throat where something—a thin cord or string, perhaps even a wire—had bitten into the flesh, cutting off the flow of air to her lungs. Her last, desperate struggle for life was suggested in the scratch marks above and below this line, where she had clawed at the garotte in a futile attempt to tear it loose.

He frowned thoughtfully at the sight of another mark, not so easily explained. This one was not red, but the bluish hue of a deep bruise. Although wider than whatever it was that had strangled her, it was perfectly aligned with the red line, as if something—a locket, perhaps, or a keepsake of some kind— had been threaded onto the cord. Suddenly he remembered quite clearly the first day he had spoken to her in Covent Garden, and had glimpsed a string that showed from the neckline of her dress. Something she'd worn about her neck, then, something that had been pulled so tight that it had strangled her to death. With a mental apology to the dead girl, he ran his hand beneath her bodice, but found nothing. Whatever she had worn, it was gone now. What had it been? Some lover's token from Roger? Not on a plain string, surely; a chain or even a ribbon would have been far more likely. Something more mundane, then. A coin, with a hole punched through so it could be threaded onto a string as a deterrent to theft or loss? Or a key, perhaps.

Yes, thought Pickett with growing conviction. A key, so that she could lock the door of her residence behind her when she left for Covent Garden in the morning and let herself back in when she returned in the evening. And it had been removed after the murder, lest it should lead him (or perhaps Maxwell) to the bolt-hole of the man who was, Pickett strongly suspected, both lover and killer of the dead girl. He could almost picture Roger, or else his henchman, Jud, throwing her lifeless body over his shoulder with no more thought than Pickett himself had once given to the sacks of coal he'd carried in much the same manner.

Or had Jenny's body been brought here in the very same wheelbarrow she'd used to convey her cabbages to Covent

Garden? The hope that he might discover some telltale footprints or wheel tracks died half-formed. It was true that any cobblestones that might once have covered the ground here had long since gone, leaving nothing but packed earth in their place. But any patterns that might have been left in the dirt the night before had surely been obliterated by the swarm of children who'd got here ahead of him.

The children...

"Who found her?" he asked, glancing back to address the gaggle of juvenile onlookers.

To his surprise, the crowd was much smaller now than it had been when he'd come across them only moments ago; clearly, several had slipped away at the approach of Authority, even so unassuming Authority as himself. At his question, those who remained turned as one to regard a strapping youth about thirteen or fourteen years old.

"I did," the youth confessed with obvious reluctance, adding quickly, "But she were already like that when I first seen her."

"What time was it?" Receiving no answer beyond a dozen blank looks, he rephrased the question. "How long ago was it?"

Still no answer. It was hardly surprising, really; time meant very little to children, and still less when every day was much like the one before, and the one that would follow.

"Did any of you touch the body? Move it in any way?"

The question was not as macabre as it sounded, for setting aside the opportunity for thievery, there were those, especially among the uneducated classes, who believed the touch of a corpse could cure all manner of ailments. Still, there was no answer beyond a ragged girl who seemingly spoke for them all when she shook her head to indicate the negative.

"Did anyone take any of her personal effects? A coin purse, perhaps, or a trinket of some sort?" Lest any young thief be afraid to make a confession, he aligned himself on their side by adding sympathetically, "After all, it's not as if she'll be needing them anymore, is it?"

"I wouldn't 'alf mind 'aving 'er shoes," one of the older girls admitted, gazing somewhat wistfully at the dead girl's scuffed but sturdy half-boots. "But she's Roger's dolly-mop, and if 'e was to see me wearin' 'em, 'e wouldn't think twice about cutt'n' 'em off me, feet 'n'all."

Several of the heretofore silent children spoke up in emphatic agreement with this claim. Pickett nodded in understanding, then turned to fold the lifeless arms across her chest and rose to address the children once more. "I need one of you to go and fetch the coroner."

They stared silently at him for a long moment before the eldest youth spoke up. "Dunno where to find 'im, do we?"

"All right, then, go to Bow Street and tell the first man you see to send for the coroner."

"*Bow Street?*" the boy reacted as if Pickett had suggested he drop in to hell and give his regards to Old Nick. "They'll think I done it, sure as check!"

"No, they won't," Pickett said, his impatience tempered somewhat by recognition that he would have reacted in exactly the same way a dozen years earlier. "If anyone attempts to clap you in irons, you have only to let him know that John Pickett sent you."

"'oo's 'e?"

"He's me!" Pickett retorted ungrammatically, perhaps justifiably incensed. "The magistrate at Bow Street is a—a personal friend of mine," he added, hoping Mr. Colquhoun would not think it presumptuous on his part to claim such a relationship.

"Keep yer hair on," grumbled the youth. "I'll go, already."

"No, let him," Pickett said, nodding toward a somewhat younger boy who had been observing the proceedings in silence from the edge of the little group. "I'll need you to help me carry her to the nearest pub—I suppose that'll be the Anchor and Crown," he added to the youngster designated as messenger. "You can have the coroner meet me there."

The child gave a nod and took to his heels. Pickett, watching him go before turning back to issue instructions for the transportation of the body to the Anchor and Crown, only hoped the boy would not wash his hands of the whole ugly business as soon as he had turned the corner out of sight.

* * *

He need not have worried. Whether through fear of reprisal should he fail to carry out this command, or simple curiosity that any such claim as friendship with a magistrate— let alone one attached to Bow Street—might contain any grain of truth, the boy set out at a run and did not slacken his pace until he had burst through the door of the Bow Street Public Office.

"Need the—the crowner," he panted, stumbling on the

unfamiliar word. "There's a dead girl—it's Jenny—her wot sells cabbages."

"Here now, what's this?" asked Mr. Colquhoun, abandoning his bench so that he might question the newcomer more closely.

"A girl is dead," the boy reiterated, a bit more clearly this time as his breathing returned to normal. "It's Jenny, her wot sells cabbages in Covent Garden. I'm to tell you to fetch the crowner and have him meet the fellow at the Anchor and Crown."

"What 'fellow'?" asked the magistrate, scowling down somewhat fiercely at the boy.

"He says he's a friend of yours," the visitor insisted, although not without a healthy dose of skepticism that anyone should claim friendship with the terrifying personage now looming over him. "Calls hisself John—John—" He struggled, albeit without success, to recall the last name.

"Was the name Pickett, by any chance?" asked a new arrival, a man who walked with a slight limp, and yet conveyed the impression of a military man, for all that. "John Pickett?"

"Aye, that was it!" exclaimed the boy, his brow clearing at having his dilemma so easily resolved.

"And you say he's at the Anchor and Crown?" inquired the first man, the one with the thick white eyebrows drawn together over the bridge of his nose.

"Aye. Not that Jenny was there when she was done in," he added hastily. "It's just that this John fellow told Digby that 'e was to 'elp 'im carry 'er there. So as to get 'er off the street,

SHERI COBB SOUTH

you might say."

If it were possible, the scowl grew even fiercer. "I see."

"If you'll have a message sent to the coroner," the soldier fellow said to the scary man, "I'll join Mr. Pickett at the Anchor and Crown."

The magistrate nodded, and the lad was obliged to follow the soldier from the office without, he thought regretfully, ever knowing for sure whether that John fellow had told the truth when he'd said the magistrate was his friend. And that the man with the beetle brows was the magistrate, he had no doubt; surely no lesser mortal could make a fellow quake in his shoes only by looking at him.

Worse still, he didn't even have a chance to ask the soldier if the extraordinary claim was true, for aside from being hard-pressed to keep pace with the fellow's long stride in spite of the limp, he was further hindered by the fact that the man kept asking him questions—some of which he could answer, like where Jenny's body had been found, and others, like just how this John Pickett had happened to be upon the scene, he could not.

Upon reaching the Anchor and Crown, they were met with the information that the poor girl's body had been taken to the storage room in the rear of the establishment, this chamber having the dual advantages of being both cooler and some little distance removed from the prying eyes of curiosity-seekers. Apparently their host did not number himself among this group, for after waving them behind the bar, inviting them to "step this way," and ushering them through the door that led into the back room, he lingered longer than necessary in the hopes of hearing some of the more lurid details of the murder.

Alas, he heard nothing more than a rather dull conversation between the two men.

"Mr. Pickett," the Bow Street man commented, nodding to the young man who had brought the poor dead girl in, "fancy meeting you here."

Mr. Pickett made no response to this, but merely asked, "Has the coroner been sent for?"

Another nod. "He'll be on his way by now. Or, if not by now, then soon enough." And then, after a pause, "I suppose you found the body?"

"Actually, they did," Mr. Pickett said, indicating the two boys.

"How fortunate that you happened to be in the vicinity."

The publican's gaze sharpened. For just a moment it seemed as if there were some hidden meaning behind this observation—in which case the conversation was not nearly so dull as it appeared.

But no.

"Yes, wasn't it?" the younger of the two men, the one named Pickett, agreed blandly. "I was just on my way to pay a call on my stepmother when I came upon these two and some of their friends."

"I seem to remember having been told that she lives somewhere hereabouts. But you mustn't let this sad business keep you from your visit. I'll meet with the coroner, shall I? Hullo, what have we here?" the man from Bow Street asked, bending down for a closer look at the body stretched out on a table hastily cleared off for the purpose. "Strangulation, it appears."

"I don't mind staying—" Pickett began, but was overruled.

"No need at all. In fact, the young woman is indirectly involved in a case I'm working. I'm obliged to you for the offer, but there's no need for it."

"The coroner may require my evidence," Pickett protested.

"I'll be sure to give him your name, if you wish, but it's not as if you were the one to find the body, is it?"

"Well, no, but—"

"Then there's no reason why this"—Maxwell indicated not only the body lying on the table, but the two youths and the curious publican as well—"should oblige you to change your plans. The boys and I can tell the coroner anything he may need to know. Can't we, lads?"

The boys were quick to agree, and in the end, there was nothing for Pickett to do but go. And perhaps, he reasoned, it was just as well; given the telltale marks on Jenny's neck, the coroner's jury would certainly bring in a verdict of willful murder, with or without his testimony. Perhaps it was best that he leave Maxwell to deal with the formalities while he set about the more urgent task of finding where Jenny's lover (and very likely her killer as well) had gone to ground.

With this end in view, he set out first for his stepmother's house. He had promised her another half a crown if her information regarding Jenny had been accurate, and it had; he had to give her credit for that. In fact, Pickett couldn't be entirely certain that he, or Maxwell, or perhaps the two of them together, hadn't been in some measure responsible for her death. But whatever the cause, it had not been his hand, nor had it been Maxwell's, that had tightened the string about her neck until she lay dead.

No, it was Roger's; Pickett was almost certain of it. It was merely the latest (although surely the most heinous) of the crimes the man must be required to answer for. How many more would there be, Pickett wondered, before he was finally brought to book? Perhaps of more immediate concern, at least to him, was the question of how long his half-brother could hope to survive under such a master. Pickett found himself in the curious position of hoping Roger and his cohorts were planning some new robbery for which the boy's services would be required. For if Roger hadn't hesitated to murder the young woman who had shared his bed, he wouldn't think twice about dispatching a child who had outgrown his usefulness.

And so it was that he entered Moll's house a short time later with an air of grim determination and said, without preamble, "Put down the bottle and talk. I need you to tell me where I can find Roger Thorne."

Far from obeying this command, Moll clutched the bottle to her bosom as if afraid he might attempt to take it by force. "What d'you mean, barging into the house without so much as a by-your-leave? I said I don't know, didn't I?"

"Oh, so you *do* know the name of the man who bought your son, do you?"

She gave him a singularly ugly look, but said merely,

"There aren't many in St. Giles who *don't* know Roger—aye, and fear him, too, which is why you'll get nothing more out of me! Besides," she added resentfully, "you said as how you'd give me another half a crown if I'd told you the truth about Jenny, but I haven't seen it, have I?"

Taking his cue, Pickett withdrew a coin purse from the inside pocket of his coat and extracted a silver coin, which he dropped into the palm of Moll's waiting hand. She did not close her hand around it, but regarded the bulging coin purse with an avaricious gleam in her eye.

The object of her interest was not lost on Pickett. "You said yourself that he wouldn't part with the boy for nothing," he reminded her. "I had to come prepared—and I'm not letting you bleed me dry before I so much as set eyes on him!"

In fact, the little stash of coins was not the only preparation he'd made. Keeping the coin purse company in his pocket was the small pewter figure of a soldier. Had it been only a few hours since he'd tucked it into his pocket before joining Julia at the breakfast table? It seemed like a lifetime ago. And for Jenny, at least, it had been.

"Although," he said thoughtfully, "if you were to tell me where I could find Roger, I might be willing to cough up a bit more."

"I said I don't know, didn't I? I told you to ask Jenny."

"I did."

"And?"

He shook his head. "I couldn't persuade her to talk."

This seemed to please Moll immensely. "Ha! I don't doubt it, for it's like I said: you're not the man your father was, not by a long chalk!"

And thank God for that, Pickett thought. Aloud, he merely said, "Apparently not."

"You'll just have to ask her again. Maybe you can wear her down."

"I suppose I could try," Pickett said doubtfully. "But if she wouldn't talk before, she surely won't now. Jenny is dead."

"*What?*" asked Moll, shocked into a state approaching sobriety. "When—how—"

"Strangled. Sometime last night, I should think."

She groped behind her for the chair she'd vacated upon his entrance and collapsed onto it. "Jenny, dead," she breathed. "D'ye think he done it?"

"I'd be willing to bet on it." He gave her a moment to ponder this revelation, then added, "So if you have any idea where I can find him, you must tell me, before he kills— someone else."

He didn't call his brother by name, but she apparently had no difficulty recognizing exactly what "someone else" he had in mind. Shaking her head vehemently (to the further detriment of her already disheveled yellow curls), she leaped to her feet so abruptly that she almost lost her balance.

"Oh, no you don't, John Pickett! Don't you go blaming me for anything that bastard might do to my boy, not when I was just trying to see him esh-established"—she stumbled slightly over the word—"in a trade, same as any mother would! I told you I didn't know where he lives, and it was God's own truth—though I'll not deny I'm that glad of it, for

177

it's not what you'd call healthful to be too curious about Roger's comings and goings. As you'll find to your sorrow, if you keep poking your long nose where it don't belong!"

From this stance she refused to be budged, and Pickett was obliged to abandon what was clearly a lost cause. To give Moll her due, it appeared she was telling the truth when she said she didn't know where Roger might be found, but even if she wasn't, he would have got nothing from that source; she was obviously too terrified of retaliation on Roger's part to say anything that might be regarded as a betrayal. And Pickett had to admit that her fears were not without cause: only look at what had happened to poor Jenny.

Still, it left him with a new dilemma. With the strangulation of Jenny—and Maxwell's appropriation of that case in addition to the robberies—it had become all the more urgent for him to find his brother before the boy's life was forfeit, either to the murderous rage of his master or the more reasoned workings of the Law. But with Jenny dead and Moll either ignorant or uncooperative—and very likely both—he didn't know where else to turn. Stout Bess seemed friendly enough, but she was leery of his connection with Bow Street, and Mr. Colquhoun didn't seem to think it likely that the crippled soldier on the portico of St. Paul's would offer him any assistance, not when his first loyalty was to Maxwell, a former brother-in-arms.

Pickett's steps slowed as he remembered that he did, in fact, have one more connection in the area. He had hoped, especially since his marriage, not to be obliged to make use of this particular source again before leaving Bow Street forever;

it seemed uncomfortably like a betrayal of his wife to do so. But in the absence of any more viable plan of action, he heaved a sigh and turned his steps in the direction of Seven Dials, and a certain house where resided one Lucy Higgins.

15

*In Which John Pickett Visits a Brothel,
and Gets More Than He Bargained For*

The junction known as Seven Dials consisted of seven streets, each radiating outward from a central axis adorned with a column topped with the clock faces that had given the intersection its name. Pickett had once heard, or perhaps Mr. Colquhoun had told him, that the area had been developed a little more than a century earlier with the expectation that it would become the most fashionable residential address in London. Pickett only hoped its developer had not lived long enough to see what his vision had eventually become. For as long as he could remember, the Dials, as it was known colloquially, had housed the poorest of London's poor, who existed cheek by jowl with the criminal element that always seemed to spring up wherever the struggle for survival was at its most brutal. Even the central column had long since disappeared, as if it no longer wanted to be associated with the area to which it had given its name.

The house where Lucy lived and conducted business was not situated in one of the seven streets connected directly to the central axis, but in Lombard Court, a dark, cramped passage bisecting Tower Street. Although it was only mid-afternoon, the shadows of the tall buildings falling across the narrow lane cast it into gloom. As his eyes adjusted to the premature twilight, Pickett identified Lucy's building by the fact that two of its occupants lounged on the front stoop, smoking clay pipes and no doubt enjoying their last bit of leisure before clients began to arrive with the nightfall. Both of them looked up at his approach.

"Well, here's a pretty lad," said one, regarding him with a lascivious smile from which several teeth were missing. "I'll flip you for him, Peg."

"Right-o, Sarey," agreed Peg, and plunged a hand into her bodice, apparently in search of a coin. "I call heads."

"No!" Pickett interrupted before matters could progress further. "I'm not—That is—I'm here to see Miss Higgins."

Peg gave a snort of derision. " 'Miss Higgins,' is it? Hoity-toity!"

"*Lu-ceeee!*" the gap-toothed woman called Sarey bellowed, tilting her head back to direct this summons toward one of the upper-story windows. "Pretty fellow here's asking for you. Better grab him quick, before Peg makes you fight her for him!"

A voice called down from the second floor, and although the voice itself was familiar, the words it uttered were indistinct.

"G'on in," Sarey interpreted, jerking her head in the

direction of the door before taking another pull on her pipe. "Upstairs, second door on the left."

Pickett thanked her, then entered the house and started up the stairs. He had called on Lucy before on more than one occasion, when he'd needed some assistance from her in the course of an investigation, but these consultations had always taken place in the relatively innocuous environs of the ground floor, in a shared space which functioned, he supposed, as a drawing room of sorts. The floors above, he knew, would be where the women practiced their profession, and the knowledge that he drew nearer to this uncharted territory with every step he took was unsettling in the extreme.

He reached the top of the stairs and turned to the left. The first door was closed—and occupied, if the grunts and moans emitting from beyond the unvarnished wooden panel were anything to judge by. The next door was slightly ajar, however, and as he drew nearer, he saw Lucy standing in the opening, draped against the doorframe in a sultry posture. At the sight of her caller, she so far forgot herself as to abandon her pose.

"*John Pickett?* Look at you—you've had your hair cut"—she raked her fingers through it, as if seeking confirmation—"Lud, you even smell different," she added, her nose twitching fastidiously.

"You needn't sound as if I used to stink!" he objected, very much on his dignity.

"No, you didn't stink, but nor did you smell like— like—" She sniffed at him again, struggling to pin down the unfamiliar odor.

"Like what?"

"Like money."

"Do I?" Pickett asked, taken aback by this claim. A moment's reflection was enough to inform him that it was probably true. He was sure that Mrs. Catchpole, his landlady and charwoman, had done her best during the five years he had lived beneath her roof, but the strong lye soap she made in the tiny, weed-choked patch of garden behind her shop could not compare to the fine scented bars that Julia purchased from Mr. Pears's shop in Soho. His linens, which Mrs. Catchpole had laundered for him every Friday, now benefitted from the attentions of a laundrymaid dedicated to their care, while the familiar old brown serge tailcoat was brushed every evening by Thomas, his valet, who also smoothed away any wrinkles by pressing it with a flatiron. Yes, he supposed Lucy did find him changed, in ways that he had not even been aware of.

"But I haven't seen you this age! Where've you been keeping yourself all this time?" Lucy's question, and the conversation that would inevitably follow his answer, brought his attention back to the matter at hand.

"Er, Mayfair, mostly," said Pickett, with what he hoped was a careless shrug. "When I'm not at Bow Street, that is."

"Mayfair, is it?" echoed Lucy, regarding him closely. "Which means you're still wearing the willow for that viscountess, I'll be bound. How long does it take to get an annulment, anyway?"

"We, um, we decided against it."

Lucy's jaw all but hit the floor, and her black eyes grew

round in astonishment. "You *didn't* get an annulment? You mean you're *married* to her? For real, married?"

He nodded. "For real, married." He did his best to restrain the smile that threatened to break free at these simple words—flaunting his new status would do nothing to help his cause—but he could no more hide his happiness than he could cease breathing.

Her response to this revelation was not what he had feared. In fact, it was worse.

"Married to a viscountess, you say. And yet, here you are at last!" Her voice was smugly triumphant. "So the wanting was better than the getting, was it?"

She grabbed his cravat and pulled him into the room,

"Lucy, no—you don't understand"—he seized her by the shoulders and tried to hold her at arm's length, even as she tugged at his cravat until the knot gave—"that's not—I only wanted to—*will you stop that?*" This last as she showed every indication of setting to work on the fall of his breeches.

"What?" Startled by his vehemence, she halted and looked up at him, both of her hands filled with bunched-up cambric; he had interrupted her in the process of pulling his shirt loose from his breeches.

In the charged silence, the noises from the adjacent room carried easily through the thin walls. Pickett had known, of course, what men and women *did*, but until six months earlier, this knowledge had been theoretical rather than practical. Now, however, he could picture all too clearly what was taking place in the next room—the same thing, in fact, that Lucy intended for him on the rumpled bed pushed up against the opposite wall. The heat rose to his face, and he knew he was blushing.

"What?" she demanded again, impatient at having been interrupted in her work.

"Lucy, that's not why I'm here—you know it isn't!"

She released his shirt and set her hands on her hips, arms akimbo. "Then why'd you come upstairs?"

"Because you called down and told me to!" he reminded her.

"Since when have you ever done what *I* said?" she grumbled under her breath.

"I need some information. No one else is willing to talk, so I thought you might help. It concerns a young woman named Jenny who sells cabbages in the market at Covent Garden—"

Lucy gave a derisive snort. "Oh, I know all about her."

"You do?" He had long been aware that news traveled fast in the crowded buildings and narrow lanes of the rookery, but surely word of Jenny's murder could not have spread so rapidly as this. "How—?"

"And let me tell you, John Pickett, if you're going to play that viscountess of yours false with anybody, it ought to be me!" she insisted, jabbing her finger into his chest. "I've been waiting the longest."

"I'm not going to play her false with you, or Jenny, or anyone else! Besides, if it was Jenny I wanted, I'd be out of luck, wouldn't I?"

Lucy looked oddly bewildered for someone who had just claimed to know all about the young woman she seemed to consider a romantic rival. "What—why—?"

Pickett gave an exasperated sigh. "Because her lover just killed her, didn't he?"

Her reaction astounded him. She turned deathly pale, and collapsed onto the edge of the dirty mattress as if her legs were suddenly incapable of supporting her. "Jenny's—dead?"

"I—I'm sorry," Pickett said. "I thought—you said you knew—I shouldn't have told you like that. I'm sorry."

"I only meant I knew who you was talking about," she insisted, her voice as hushed as if they were speaking in a church instead of a brothel. "When did it happen?"

"Sometime last night. Her body was found this morning. She'd been strangled."

"And—and he did it?"

"I have no proof—at least, not yet—but I'd be willing to bet on it. I'd been talking to her—asking questions. I've been trying to find him. He must have got wind of it, and—" He shook his head, seeing again Jenny's wide, sightless eyes.

"What do you want him for?" Lucy asked, still speaking in that unnaturally subdued voice.

"I've only recently discovered that I have a younger brother—half-brother, actually—"

"A brother?" Lucy echoed, brightening somewhat. "How old is he?"

"Too young for you," Pickett informed her bluntly. "Roger supposedly took him on as an apprentice, but he's actually using him as a snakesman. I'm trying to get him away from there before he ends up accompanying Roger to Newgate. If you have any idea where I can find him—Roger, that is, not my brother—I wish—I wish you would—"

He broke off in some consternation, for Lucy appeared to be having some sort of fit. She jumped to her feet, jerking her head and rolling her eyes in the direction of the room from which the all too graphic sounds emitted.

"Lucy? Are you all right? Should I—?" He broke off as comprehension dawned. "Do you mean to tell me"—he lowered his voice just as she had done—"he's in the next room?"

She nodded her head emphatically. "Aye, he's with Liza," she said in a hushed whisper. "But they've been at it for a good while now, and I'm thinking it won't be long before he'll be on his way."

"Thank you, Lucy," Pickett said, turning toward the door. "I'm obliged to you."

"Oh, no you don't." She moved swiftly to put herself between him and the door. "You'll not be coming around here, wanting me to squeak beef on the most dangerous man in the Dials, putting my life in danger and me not a penny the richer for it."

"Fair enough," Pickett sighed, reaching again for his coin purse. He was not such a fool as to wander about this part of London with a fat coin purse, and at the rate he was doling out his modest store of coins, he would have nothing left with which to tempt Roger. He dug out a silver shilling, then took her hand, turned it palm up, and closed her fingers around the coin. "Thank you, Lucy."

She stepped away from the door somewhat reluctantly. "You take care of yourself, John Pickett."

There was a curious note of finality to the words. Pickett nodded in acknowledgement, not quite certain whether she was concerned as to his safety—she appeared to be fully conscious of the danger he courted by attempting to beard the lion in his den—or if she knew without being told that, having married above his station, he would soon be leaving Bow Street, and thus their own association would be at an end.

But he could not think of that now. It had been an unlooked-for piece of luck, his calling on Lucy at the exact moment when his quarry was engaged in sampling the wares next door, and he could not afford to let it go to waste. He had to exit the house with all due speed and establish himself in some position from which he could watch for Roger's departure and follow him to his bolt-hole.

He said his goodbyes to Lucy and then quickly but quietly made his way down the stairs.

So intent was he upon his own purposes that he quite failed to notice that the noises that had so disconcerted him had now ceased.

* * *

A few minutes later, Pickett was leaning against a building at the corner of Lombard Court and Tower Street, trying to look as if he were only one more vagrant begging for the wherewithal to buy a bottle of cheap gin. He wished he might at least set his clothing to rights—his cravat was untied and his shirt partially untucked so that it hung below his waistcoat, the top two buttons of which were undone—but he acknowledged that his disheveled state might well make his appearance a bit less conspicuous. He supposed he ought to be grateful to Lucy for giving him such a disguise, but in fact her very flattering attentions only made him very uncomfortable.

Some distance down Lombard Court, Peg and Sarey regarded him curiously, but neither of the women made any attempt to call out to him, which was a relief in more ways than one: when he'd first exited the house after leaving Lucy, their crudely expressed speculations as to his points had made his ears burn. He dared not move out of their line of vision, however, for fear of losing his man should he fail to see Roger making his exit. It suddenly occurred to him that he had no very clear idea of what the fellow looked like, beyond Maxwell's vague description. A pretty fool he would look, if he were to follow the wrong man!

Suddenly Peg and Sarey turned away from him to look up at the house, and Pickett realized the door must have opened. *Roger*, he thought, his gaze sharpening. But no, it was a female who stepped out onto the portico, no doubt another housemate who toiled in the same profess—

The soft tread of a footstep close behind him made him turn, and suddenly he was struck so hard that his head cracked against the brick wall. Indeed, the brief intimation of danger that had caused him to turn his head was the only thing that prevented him from slamming into the wall face first.

"I hear you've been looking for me," murmured a rough voice close to his ear. "Your lucky day, then, innit? You found me."

16

In Which Another Family Reunion Takes Place

R oger Thorne, I presume," Pickett said in as cool a tone as it is possible for one to take while pinioned to the wall with one cheek pressed against the soot-stained brick. The trickle of blood from one nostril suggested that while his nose might have been spared the worst of the impact, it had not gone entirely unscathed. "I mean you no harm. I only want to talk to you."

Roger gave a skeptical snort. "Aye, prig-nappers are always after me for the pleasure of my conversation."

It was not a promising opening, but the pressure of Roger's weight eased, and Pickett was no longer pinned against the rough brick. He turned to face his attacker, and Roger's fist slammed into his belly, a blow so unexpected that it doubled him over and left him gasping for breath.

I'm going to die here, Pickett thought. *He's going to beat me to death, and no one will lift a finger to stop it.* On the contrary, any spectators would be far more likely to form a circle around them from which they could observe the combatants unimpeded, placing wagers and cheering on their favorite. Pickett knew instinctively that he would not like their choice of champion.

As if in confirmation of this statement, Sarey bellowed in the direction of the second-floor window, "Lookee here, Lucy, that pretty lad of yours is about to get his face rearranged!"

"Give him another one, Rog'!" shrieked the new arrival, confirming Pickett's suspicion that here was the woman whose favors Roger had been sampling only moments earlier. If that were indeed the case, then the man would have expended considerable energy already. If he could only stay alive long enough, perhaps the constable would come along. At the moment, he would even welcome Maxwell's arrival.

All he had to do was stay alive. His brother's life depended on it.

Taking as deep a breath as he was able, he pressed his hands to the wall at his back and pushed off, straightening upright so that the crown of his head drove into Roger's chin, snapping his head back so hard that Pickett could hear the man's teeth clack together.

Alas, it had been a very long time since Pickett had been obliged to defend himself with his fists. He contrived to land the odd punch or two, and took a great deal of satisfaction in the grunts that these elicited from his opponent, but the end was never in doubt. With a sigh of something akin to relief, Pickett—bleeding copiously from his nose, and with his right eye rapidly swelling shut—sank, insensible, to the pavement.

* * *

"There's something I need you to pick up," Roger informed Jud bluntly, entering the house and swiftly bolting the door shut behind him. "I left it at the end of Lombard Court, where it joins Tower Street."

Jud grimaced. "Lud, Roger, you've never offed another one!"

Roger scowled fiercely at him, then shot a quick glance at the boy, who had stuck his finger between the bars of the bird's cage and was trying to coax the creature to perch on it. "He's still alive. Leastways, he was when I left him."

The significance of that glance was not wasted on Jud. Lowering his voice to a near-whisper, he asked, "Is it true, then, what the brat says?"

"Has to be. He's as like the boy as be-damned." He glowered at the back of the boy's head, still bent over the bird cage. "The little bastard failed to mention that the fellow's a Bow Street Runner."

"*What?*"

"You heard me. He came to the bawdy house in Lombard Court, asking one of the girls about me. I was in the next room. Heard every word."

Jud let out a long, low whistle, which the bird echoed.

"I jumped him from behind," Roger continued, "but I can't be sure he didn't get a good look at me. That's why I need you to fetch him. So he can't go carrying tales to Bow Street."

"You, er, you want me to finish him off?" Jud inquired

delicately.

Roger shook his head impatiently. "No, don't. I thought of that, but it might be better to keep him here, just to make sure the brat behaves himself. After this last job, well, we'll have no need of either one of 'em. Best take your blanket to throw over him, just in case you should happen to run into the watchman."

As his blanket had already been pressed into service once for a very similar purpose, Jud was perhaps understandably nettled. "Why does it have to be my blanket? Why can't it be yours this time?"

"Are you saying you don't like the way I run things, Jud?"

Roger spoke softly enough, but there was something in his voice that, while subtle, contained enough of a threat as to make the boy look up from the bird perched precariously on the tip of his finger. It was doubtless some stiffening on the child's part that caused the creature to dart away in a flurry of flapping wings, but the sudden movement seemed to suggest that it, too, lived in fear of provoking Roger's displeasure.

"N-no, Rog', of course not," his henchman was quick to demur. "It's just that I thought—that is, I wondered if—but I reckon I was wrong."

Roger nodded in approval. "Just so. Now, go, before somebody else comes along and does the job for you."

Jud did not have to be told twice. He fetched Jenny's wheelbarrow from its usual corner and left the house without further protest.

* * *

Jud returned a short time later, still pushing the wheelbarrow, which was now piled high with what appeared to be secondhand clothes.

"*There* you are!" Roger moved swiftly to shut and lock the door behind him. "Anybody see you?"

Jud shook his head. "Naught but the usual."

Roger glanced down at the wheelbarrow's load. "Still alive?"

"Aye. Leastways, he was when I found him." Jud hesitated for a moment before adding, "Er, what was you wanting me to do with him?"

"I don't know how much longer we can count on him being out. Before he comes 'round, I'm gonna need you to help me tie him up. First, though"—he turned toward the door to the back room and raised his voice—"Come here, boy! Your Uncle Jud has a present for you!"

"He's not my uncle!" retorted the boy, appearing in the doorway nonetheless.

Roger chose to ignore this retort. "You know how you're always going on about that brother of yours?"

He inched cautiously forward, his brown eyes, too large for the pale, thin face, growing suddenly wary. "What of it?"

"Come pay your respects to your brother John," Roger said, and Jud, obeying some unspoken signal, tipped the wheelbarrow forward to disgorge its burden onto the floor.

It was no pile of castoff clothing, but a man—that much, at least, was readily identifiable, although little else could be determined from his face, so battered and bruised it was. The nose was caked with dried blood, and a thin line of blood still trickled from one nostril, its crimson trail impeded somewhat by the fact that one side of the mouth was swollen. More swollen still was his right eye, so much so that he could very likely not open it at all.

It wasn't supposed to be like this, he thought desperately. His brother John was supposed to be big and brave and strong. This was only a quite ordinary fellow, no more capable of standing up to Roger than he was himself.

"Is he...dead?"

The words had been scarcely more than a whisper, but as if in answer, the figure on the floor emitted a soft moan.

"He's coming 'round," Roger said briskly. "Better step lively. Jud, you take his feet and I'll take his shoulders. Boy, go into your room and set that straight chair in the middle of the floor. I'll take no chances on him laying his hands on anything that he might use as a weapon. Go! Now!" he said again, impatiently, when his cohorts were slow in carrying out his commands.

The rickety straight chair usually stood against the wall opposite the door, right next to the boarded-up window that should have looked out onto the tiny patch of waste ground in back of the house. In accordance with Roger's orders, Kit dragged it away from the wall, around the foot of the straw-filled pallet where he slept, and into the center of the room. Apparently Roger intended for him to share his sleeping quarters with the new arrival. Kit wasn't quite sure how he felt about that. It might be nice, not being completely alone anymore, especially now that Jenny was...gone. And yet there the fellow would be, bruised and broken, a constant reminder of how his own desperate hopes had been dashed.

At that moment, Roger entered the room, backing through the doorway with Jud close behind and the unconscious man slung between the two of them like a hammock. They plopped their prisoner down onto the chair, then Roger ordered Jud to hold the fellow in place while he fetched a rope. For one horrifying minute, Kit feared they intended to string the poor man up from an overhead beam—two such beams were clearly visible, thanks to decades of crumbling plaster—and kick the chair out from under him. Alone or not, he had no desire to have a corpse for company, be he brother or no. But Roger returned with several short lengths of rope and soon had his prisoner trussed firmly to the chair on which he sat, his wrists bound tightly to the uprights of the chairback, and his ankles to its front legs.

"There!" Roger pronounced with a final tug to the knot securing Pickett's left ankle. "That should hold him."

"What—what are you going to do with him?" asked Kit, finding his voice at last.

Roger rose slowly to a standing position, looking down at the boy from his superior height. "Depends on you. You want him left alive, you'd better toe the line. No more back talk, y'hear me?"

Kit's head bobbed up and down in hasty reassurance. Then, seeing no further disclosures were forthcoming, he was emboldened to ask, "And if I do? Toe the line, I mean. What then?"

"I guess we'll have to see about that, won't we? Fellow said he wants to talk to me; tomorrow he'll have his chance.

Right now I'm for bed. You'd best turn in, too, Jud." Upon reaching the doorway, Roger turned back to issue one final order. "He wakes up and tries to make any trouble, you let me know, you hear?"

Kit nodded in agreement, but knew all the while that he was lying. If the prisoner did wake up, he intended to ask him a few questions.

With any luck, maybe he would discover that this battered and bloody excuse for a man was no relation of his, after all.

* * *

Kit was awakened abruptly in the middle of the night, although he could not identify exactly what it was that had awakened him. He couldn't see anything, but this fact alone wasn't very helpful; no moonlight penetrated the boarded-up window even when the moon was at the full—which it wasn't now, as he had cause to know. Suddenly he heard a faint groan, and realized that this must have been what had awakened him: sounds of stirring from the man he still could not believe was his heroic brother.

"John?" he called softly into the darkness.

"I'm...sorry." The answer came somewhat breathlessly, as if it hurt him to speak. "Did I waken you?"

"Yes, but I don't mind. Is—is your name John, then?"

"It is...John Pickett, at your service," he answered, and it seemed to Kit, incredibly, that there was a hint of humor in the words. "I would bow, but I can't seem to make my arms or legs move."

Yes, certainly a hint of humor, but Kit recognized the

trace of panic underlying the words; he'd felt it, too, the fear that must be concealed lest he give Roger another weapon to use against him.

"That's because Roger and Jud have you trussed up like a Christmas goose." Not that Kit had ever actually seen a Christmas goose, but he'd heard the expression.

"Oh. I see. That's a relief."

In the darkness, Kit's brow puckered. "It's a relief, being tied up so's you can't move?"

"It's better than being paralyzed, anyway."

"Oh." Kit was silent for a long moment, then the question he could no longer hold back came out in a rush. "Johnareyoumybrother?"

"I think so." The voice came cautiously out of the darkness, and Kit wished he could see him, bruises and all. "Is that all right?"

"What do you mean, is it all right? You either are my brother, or you aren't."

"Actually, I'm your half-brother. We have the same father, but different mothers."

"Oh, I knew that."

Now it was Pickett's turn to be confused. "You knew about me? How?"

"My mum. She got drunk once—"

"Only once?" Pickett said, and instantly regretted it. This was, after all, the boy's mother he was talking about.

Kit, however, appeared to take no offense. "She likes the Blue Ruin, all right, but there was only one time she got to talking about you. She started off like usual, about how my da—your da too, I expect—got sent off halfway 'round the world leaving her with nothing but two great hulking lads to feed, and both of 'em—us—good for nothing but eating our heads off. I'd never heard of another one, so I asked her who was the other one, and she said there was an older one named John, but he was gone now."

"I see," Pickett said thoughtfully. "What else did she tell you?"

"Nothing! I asked her again next day when she was sobered up a bit, but she just clapped her mummer shut and wouldn't tell me anything. I thought maybe you was dead, and so she didn't like talking about you, but then Dick Robbins—he's what you might call my stepda—he said it was no such thing, only she was just jealous and didn't like to think of Gentleman Jack—my da—I suppose he must be yours, too—having a brat by no other woman."

"Kit—it is Kit, is it not?—Kit, if you could—look, can they hear us up there?" Pickett jerked his head in the direction of the floor above their heads, knowing quite well that Kit could not see this gesture.

The boy, however, had no difficulty in interpreting this somewhat cryptic query. "I don't think they can, so long as we're quiet. I think Jud's in the room directly above, and Roger's in the one beside it, the one that faces onto the street."

"Good." Pitching his voice low so as not to be overheard, Pickett asked, "If you could—escape—from Roger, would you want to go back to Moll—to your mum?"

Kit gave a bitter little laugh. "What, so she could send me back to him, or sell me to somebody even worse?"

And that, Pickett thought, was the saddest thing about the children of the rookery. It wasn't the poverty or the hunger—at least, it wasn't *only* the poverty and hunger—it was the fact that one could be so cynical at only ten years old, so utterly devoid of hope, as if life would never offer them anything better than it did right now. And in most cases, they were very likely right.

"Kit, I would like very much for you to come and live with me," he said as gently as possible through lips so swollen that they struggled to form the words. "If I can get you out of here, would you be willing to do that?"

It was everything he'd hoped for from the time he'd first learned of his brother's existence, everything he'd dreamed of from the time Roger had taken him from his home, and that with his mother's full cooperation. And it came, not from the heroic figure of his imagination who would have made very short work of both Roger and Jud (very likely at the same time, blindfolded, and with both hands tied behind his back), but from one who was just as much at the mercy of Roger as he was himself.

Kit, to his shame, felt hot tears gathering behind his eyelids. *Don't let anyone see you cry. Don't give them a weapon to use against you.* "You couldn't even save yourself from Roger," he said scornfully. "What makes you think you could save me?"

And so saying, he rolled over on his pallet in the hopes that the crackling of the straw beneath him would drown out the sobs he could not quite suppress.

17

In Which Julia Takes Charge

Reluctantly emerging from slumber in the middle of a most delightful dream, Julia rolled over and stretched her hand out toward the side of the bed where her husband slept. Her fingers met not warm flesh, but cool sheets. She opened her eyes, all traces of sleep suddenly banished. It was true that he had not come home by the time she'd sought her bed on the previous night, but she had been quite certain he had climbed into bed at some point; that was, in fact, the least interesting of the things she remembered him doing. But it appeared she had dreamed the whole thing, or else he'd awakened early and got up. And not only had he got up early, she realized with growing conviction; he must have been up for some time, for the sheets no longer retained the heat from his body.

The discovery, following as it did the interrupted dream, left her feeling restless and wanting. Then she noticed his pillow, and frustration turned to something much more ominous. The feather-stuffed pillow was perfectly smooth, with no indentation where his head would have lain. Nor, when she examined it more closely, could she detect any trace of the indefinable scent of him which, after six months of marriage, would have enabled her to correctly identify him out of a dozen men in a dark room.

He had not come to bed last night.

Had he come home at all?

Throwing back the covers, she rolled out of bed and thrust her feet into her slippers, then shrugged on her dressing gown and started for the stairs. If he had any ideas about sleeping on the sofa rather than risk waking her, she would very soon put paid to any such notions. But upon reaching the drawing room, she found it empty. A sound of clinking cutlery emanated from the dining room, and she hurried after it, hoping to find him at the breakfast table. But no, it was only Rogers, laying the table for the morning meal.

"Good morning, madam," he said, looking up as she entered the room.

"Good morning," she replied. "Rogers, have you seen Mr. Pickett this morning?"

"No, ma'am, I'm afraid not." After a brief but awkward pause, he added, "In fact, it was my understanding that he had not yet come home. Thomas went up very early to fetch his boots to be polished, but they had not been left in the corridor for him as is the young master's usual practice."

"I see," Julia said thoughtfully, but her brain was awhirl. Surely he would have sent word if he had intended to be absent overnight—wouldn't he? Unless, of course, he was unable to… "Pray go and fetch Andrew. Tell him I want him to deliver a message to Mr. Colquhoun at the Bow Street Public Office."

"Yes, ma'am," Rogers said, and turned away to carry out these instructions.

"No, wait! I shan't need Andrew, for I am going myself!"

Some time later, a carriage drew up before the Bow Street Public Office, and the footman leaped down to open the door and assist her to alight; Andrew had, in fact, been needed after all, but only to accompany milady's carriage, and only after Rogers had observed, with great diplomacy, that the Young Master might be distressed to think of her journeying alone to so insalubrious a part of Town. Rogers might speculate, but Julia was quite certain as to what the Young Master's sentiments would be on this particular subject. And so it was that she now accepted Andrew's aid in stepping down from the carriage and even restrained herself from charging ahead of him, keeping instead to a pace that would allow him to reach the door first and open it for her.

Once inside, however, it was another matter entirely. Scanning the room in search of a familiar figure, she saw only a sea of male faces, all regarding her with expressions ranging from astonishment to frank admiration. Most appeared to be members of the Foot or Horse Patrol, if the blue coats and red waistcoats they wore were anything to judge by. Of the magistrate, Mr. Colquhoun, there was no sign.

"Pardon me, ma'am." One of them approached her, a man of about forty whose dark gray tailcoat, to say nothing of his air of quiet competence, identified him as one of Bow Street's principal officers. "Is there anything I can do for you?"

"Thank you," she said, turning eagerly to address him. "I should like to have a word with Mr. Colquhoun, if you please. I—"

She broke off abruptly as another man entered the room through a second door at the back. Like so many of the others, he wore the uniform of the Foot and Horse Patrols; the film of dust coating his clothing strongly suggested the latter. It was not his clothes that interested her, however, but his face, which was remarkably handsome and crowned with a headful of stylishly cropped golden hair. It was also familiar—a fact which, at the moment, was of far greater interest to her than any degree of manly good looks.

"Mr. Carson!" she exclaimed.

His eyes met hers, and immediately he stood straighter, and his steps as he approached her held more than a hint of a swagger. She might have found the change in his demeanor amusing, had her mind been less taken up with worry and fear.

"Mrs. Pickett? What are you doing here?"

"I was just telling Mr."—she turned back to the man in gray—"I'm sorry—I don't—"

"Maxwell," he said, sketching a little bow. "Robert Maxwell, ma'am. Yours to command."

"Oh!" Her eyes widened. So this was John's "Maxwell," was it? She had best have a care for what, and how much, she divulged; then again, Mr. Maxwell might be in a better position than anyone to know what might have happened to her husband. "I'm pleased to meet you, Mr. Maxwell, although I wish I might have done so under happier circumstances. I must see Mr. Colquhoun. It's John, you see—Mr. Pickett, that is. He never came home last night."

The explanation was made to the two men equally, but it was Maxwell who frowned and said, "That explains it, then."

"Explains what?" Julia asked.

"There was an inquest this morning. I'd expected to see Mr. Pickett there."

"But he wasn't?"

Maxwell shook his head. "No."

"Who"—Julia's face turned pale, and her voice was hardly more than a whisper—"who died?"

"No one you would know, ma'am," Maxwell assured her. "A Covent Garden costermonger. A young woman who sells cabbages."

"Oh," Julia said, hardly knowing whether to be horrified or relieved. "Then—it was not—?"

She broke off abruptly, and Maxwell's frown deepened. "Not who?"

"Never mind—I don't—I hardly know what I'm saying," Julia demurred quickly. After all, she could hardly admit to this man, of all people, that for a moment she had been afraid that it was her husband's young brother who was now dead. "Tell me, is Mr. Colquhoun in? May I see him, please?"

"I'll take you to him," put in Carson, not at all pleased at being ignored when a beautiful woman was present.

"I'm very much obliged to you both," Julia said, and although her words were directed toward Maxwell, it was

Harry Carson whose arm she took.

Carson, nothing loth, quickly steered her through the crowded room to the magistrate's office and rapped upon the door.

"Who is it?" called Mr. Colquhoun from within.

"Carson, sir," Harry called. "You have a visitor."

"Yes, well, send him in."

"Not a 'him,' I'm afraid, but a 'her,' " Julia confessed, sweeping into the room as soon as Carson opened the door.

"Why, Mrs. Pickett!" exclaimed the magistrate, rising from his desk with every appearance of pleasure. "What brings you here this morning?"

"It's John—Mr. Pickett, that is," she amended hastily, recalling that while they were at Bow Street, the bond between her husband and his mentor must be a strictly professional one. "He never came home last night. In fact, I have not seen him since he left the house yesterday morning."

Mr. Colquhoun's bushy white brows drew together in a fierce scowl. "The devil, you say!"

"He wasn't at the inquest this morning either, sir," put in a deep voice from somewhere over her shoulder, and Julia realized Mr. Maxwell had followed them into the magistrate's office.

She was not best pleased with this turn of events. She would have preferred to speak to Mr. Colquhoun in private; Mr. Carson was unlikely to leave unless and until Mr. Maxwell did, and so long as Mr. Maxwell was present, she would be obliged to guard her tongue.

The truth of this assumption was confirmed when

Maxwell turned to her and asked, "Did he say anything yesterday morning about where he planned to go, what he intended to do?"

Her eyes met Mr. Colquhoun's, and something in his expression told her that he was aware of her dilemma. The realization gave her courage. "I believe he said something about paying a call on his stepmother," she said. "But I don't know where she lives."

"I do," Maxwell told the magistrate. "Queen Street, number seven. I'll be glad to escort Mrs. Pickett. It's hardly a place for a lady to go alone."

"Thank you, Maxwell, but I need you here. I want a full report on this morning's inquest. Mrs. Pickett"—he turned to Julia—"you may ask any of the men out front to accompany you. Tell him he has my permission."

"What about me?" objected Carson, never slow where the companionship of a beautiful woman was at stake. "I'll go with you," he said, addressing Julia.

"You mustn't keep your horse standing," Mr. Colquhoun said in a voice that brooked no argument. "Mrs. Pickett, if you will call again and tell me what you have discovered, I would be much obliged."

"Yes, of course," she agreed warmly, then added, "Thank you, sir," with so speaking a look that he was left in no doubt as to exactly what he was being thanked for.

Having conveyed this silent message, she departed the magistrate's office. Had the three men observed her exit, they might have found it curious that she made no effort to enlist the escort of any of the Bow Street men in the outer, public room, but walked straight through, exchanged a word with her coachman, and allowed Andrew the footman to hand her into the carriage.

* * *

In truth, Julia's determination suffered a severe setback when the carriage drew up before number seven, Queen Street. She had, of course, heard her husband speak many times of the streets in which he had grown up—and for which he retained no sentimental fondness—but beholding these conditions with her own eyes, she realized he had spared her many of the more alarming details.

The brick houses lining both sides of the narrow street must have been handsome at one time, but that time had long since come and gone. Now there were places in the walls where the bricks had fallen out, and many of the windows were boarded up, suggesting that the glass panes were broken. A few of the houses were in such imminent danger of collapse that long wooden beams had been wedged between their upper floors and the upper floors of the houses directly opposite, so that the more they sagged toward their twins across the street, the more securely they remained upright, supporting themselves and each other through shared misery.

The inhabitants of the street were equally unpre-possessing. A mangy dog of indeterminate breed, its ribs clearly visible beneath the skin and its tail tucked between its legs, poked through a pile of refuse in search of something to eat. Some little distance up the street, a man in ragged clothes leaned against the wall smoking a clay pipe; Julia was struck with the fanciful notion that he, like the beams jammed between the opposing houses, was all that held the wall up, and if he were to walk away, the house would come crashing down behind him. Nearer at hand, three men appeared to have been engaged in pitching pennies, or some similar game, but they had apparently lost interest in this entertainment and were now staring with unconcealed amazement as her carriage approached. On the front stoop, and looking down on the players, sat a slatternly woman alternately taking long pulls from a bottle and calling encouragement to the men. At least, Julia thought it was encouragement; the words she spoke were obviously the English tongue, but Julia could make no sense of them. If the ribald laughter which greeted this speech was anything to judge by, it was probably just as well.

The carriage lurched to a stop, and a moment later Andrew flung open the door. The stench assailed her. And yet this hellish place had, miraculously, produced John Pickett. What might have become of him, she wondered, had not Mr. Colquhoun intervened? For that matter, what had become of him now?

"Are you sure this is the right place, ma'am?" Andrew asked dubiously, glancing down to avoid stepping in a puddle of something probably better left unidentified.

"I'm afraid so," she said, grimacing. She took the footman's proffered hand, grateful for his assistance in helping her avoid the puddle, then glanced up at the coachman. "You may walk the horses, but don't go so far that you could not hear me if I called. Andrew, you may climb up on the box with him. It will be more difficult for anyone to accost you that way."

"Yes, ma'am. But first I'll knock on the door for you, shall I?"

"Thank you, but I think not." She had given quite a lot of thought as to how to approach this meeting, and decided that to meet Moll on terms of relative equality would likely yield the best results.

"Yes, ma'am." Andrew sketched a bow, then turned and clambered up onto the box where the coachman sat. The carriage rolled slowly up the street.

And then she was alone. She took a deep breath, then stepped up to the door and knocked, trying not to notice the curious stares aimed in her direction by everyone from the diseased dog to the slattern with the bottle. Receiving no response, she knocked again.

"All right, all right, keep yer hair on. I'm coming."

The voice did not come from within the house, but from somewhere outside, and only a very short distance away. To Julia's dismay, the woman sitting on the stoop rose to her feet, still clutching her bottle in one hand while brushing with the other hand any dust from the back of a skirt that was long past any help this gesture might have offered.

"Who are you, and what d'ye want?"

"Mrs.—Miss—" Too late, Julia realized she had never heard the woman's surname, still less her marital status. "Moll?"

"What if I am?"

As the woman drew nearer, Julia could see that she had once been pretty, perhaps even beautiful. The fine bone structure of her face was still there, although one had to look closely for it beneath the bloated, reddened skin. In spite of all that her husband had told her about this woman, Julia could not help feeling a surge of pity for her.

"How do you do?" she asked, offering her gloved hand. "Mrs. John Pickett."

Moll did not take the hand, but planted her own hands firmly on her hips. "Now, that I ain't, and never was, damn his eyes!"

"Dear me, no," Julia protested quickly, fearing she had botched the thing before she'd even set foot in the door. "I'm afraid I wasn't very clear. *I'm* Mrs. John Pickett." Lest Moll require further elucidation, she added, "I believe I may be your daughter-in-law."

Moll's eyes gleamed with avarice as she took in every detail of her visitor's appearance, from the high-poked bonnet framing her face to the fashionable pelisse of bronze-colored lutestring and the swell of her abdomen beneath it.

"So you've married my dear Johnny, have you? Well, let's not stand here jawing for all the world to hear! Come in, come in! Have a seat, won't you, and I'll put on the kettle for tea."

Julia, entering the house with some misgiving, silently acknowledged that she could not refuse to sit on the stained and threadbare armchair Moll offered without giving offense, but silently resolved that nothing could induce her to ingest anything that had been prepared in this house. It was not the poverty that repelled her. One could, after all, be poor and still maintain basic standards of hygiene; in fact, she could remember certain indigent women in the village where she had lived as a child who had considered it a point of pride to do so. No, it was the slovenliness, apparent in the cobwebs in the corners, the heap of empty bottles littering the floor, and the thick layer of dust that coated every surface, that forced her to repress a shudder as she seated herself on the chair.

"No, no, that won't be at all necessary," Julia assured her with perhaps more haste than tact. "I would not wish to put you to any trouble. In fact, it was about John that I wanted to see you."

"Oh?" Moll had already picked up the kettle and blown the dust from it, but at Julia's words she set it down with a clatter, plopped down on a chair, and picked up the bottle that, Julia suspected, was never very far away. "What about him?"

"When did you last see him?"

Moll heaved a sigh. "John and me ain't on what you'd call visiting terms. And after I'd raised him and loved him like a mother! What his poor father would say, if he knew how shabbily I've been treated—"

"John has been gone since yesterday," Julia interrupted, cutting off what threatened to be a very lengthy recital. "I am trying to discover what has happened to him."

To her alarm, Moll seemed to find this wonderfully funny. She threw back her head and laughed so loudly that Julia had no doubt it could be heard in the street.

"Oh, I can tell you what happened to him!" Moll said, choking back her laughter as she gestured toward Julia's middle. "He's gone and done a bunk, and left you with a pudding in the oven, same as his father did to me!"

"I am quite certain that he has not," Julia informed her

roundly. "But before he left the house yesterday morning, he told me that he intended to call on you. I should like to know if he did, and if you have any idea of what he might have done or where he might have gone after he left you."

Moll regarded her with a calculating look. "A lot's happened since yesterday morning," she said. "I might be persuaded to remember, though—for a price."

Julia gave a half-hearted chuckle, thinking it might be to her advantage to indulge the woman's little joke, however unamusing she found it. But Moll's expectant look never wavered, and Julia realized she was quite serious.

"Mrs.—Moll—I'm afraid you don't understand," she said, more than a little taken aback by this discovery. "I think John may have fallen into some danger. It is imperative that I discover where he is, and what has happened to him."

Moll extended one chapped hand, palm up. "Then I guess you'll be wanting to pay up, won't you?"

Julia stared at her in blank astonishment. "Surely you cannot be thinking of money when at this very moment your own flesh and blood—"

"Easy not to think of money when you've plenty of it," retorted Moll, snatching her hand back since Julia appeared disinclined to put anything into it. "As for him being my flesh and blood, well, that's just what he's not, and I'll thank you to remember it! She that bore him's been dead these twenty years and more, and I haven't forbade having her name spoke in my presence all this time for you to go dragging her up now, d'you understand?"

Twenty years and more, thought Julia. In spite of the

urgency of the situation, she could not help taking just a moment to think of that small motherless boy, forbidden to speak his dead mother's name, nor permitted to hear anyone else speak it, either, his memories of her growing dimmer with every year that passed until, finally, the man would have no recollections of her at all. *I'll take very good care of him*, she silently promised her deceased mother-in-law, *if only I can find him.*

Aloud, she said, "John may not be your own flesh and blood, but there is another boy, is there not, who is yours? A boy named Christopher?"

Moll's eyes narrowed in suspicion. "Aye, what of it?"

"John has been trying very hard to find him. He believes your son may be in danger."

But surely Moll must have known this already, mustn't she? Even if John had never reached her house the previous morning, he had sought her out once before on the subject, for it had been from Moll that he'd first learned of Jenny. Unless, of course, he had on that earlier occasion couched his words carefully so as not to frighten her, and had succeeded so well in this endeavor that the seriousness of the boy's situation had escaped her entirely.

"I'll tell you just what I told him," Moll said. "I bound the boy over as an apprentice, so's he could learn a trade. I'd've done as much for John, too, same as any mother would, but Jack—him what's the boys' father, you know, or maybe you don't—Jack wouldn't hear of it, though his brat had already turned seven, and there was a sweep wanting him as a climbing boy—offered us good money for him, too!" she added resentfully, as if the loss of this income still rankled even after eighteen years. She spat in the general direction of the dented brass spittoon at her feet, and didn't seem to notice that she'd missed.

Julia felt more than a little ill, but it wasn't the blob of spittle glistening on the bare wooden floorboards that made her press her hands to her belly. No, it was the thought of John—*her* John—forced up chimneys day in and day out from the tender age of seven, until his growth was stunted and his bones grew twisted. Most climbing boys, she knew, were orphans, for few parents were so desperate for money that they would force their children into such a life. Even if Moll could summon no tender feelings for John himself, what sort of woman could do such a thing to the child of a man she loved?

"And you say you've told John of the boy's apprenticeship," Julia said, as much to distract her own thoughts as to steer Moll back onto the subject for which she had sought her out. "Was that yesterday, or on his earlier visit?"

"Something for nothing, my fine lady?" Moll asked, holding out her hand again.

Hating herself for it, but recognizing that it was the only way she would get any cooperation from the woman, Julia took a silver shilling from her reticule and dropped it into the palm of Moll's hand.

"He did stop by here yesterday," Moll said, stuffing her ill-gotten gain into her bodice. "Told me Jenny was dead, and that it was probably Roger what done it. Wanted to know if I knew where he might find him."

"And did you?" Julia prompted her eagerly, hardly knowing what to hope for. Certainly it would be just like her husband to confront the man fresh from the murder of his lover, knowing quite well that such a brute would have no compunction about killing him next.

"No. But even if I had, I'm not such a fool that I'd be ratting him out, it not being what I call healthy—and so I told John!"

Julia tried to press her for more details, but Moll's ignorance as to the man's whereabouts seemed to be genuine, and her finely honed self-interest would certainly have deterred her from attempting to discover more. At last, Julia was forced to concede that she was unlikely to learn anything more from this source, and rose to take her leave.

"You never know but what I might remember something more," Moll said as she accompanied her visitor to the door. "For a price."

Julia stopped and turned to confront her. "You'll not have so much as a farthing more from me, no matter what you claim to 'remember.' It went very much against the grain with me to give you as much as I did, so I suggest you enjoy it while you may."

Moll's expression turned ugly. "Hoity-toity! You might think different when all your fine neighbors see your poor mum-in-law begging on your doorstep, and you and your husband too high-and-mighty to spare even a ha'penny for one who stood in the place of a mother to him."

Julia's eyes locked on Moll's, and she ground out through clenched teeth, "Make no mistake about this, Mrs.—

er—Moll. Between the pair of us, John and I have friends in very high places, from the magistrate at Bow Street to the Earl of Dunnington and his countess. If you make any further attempt, even the slightest, to extort money from me or mine, you will discover just how highly John is regarded at Bow Street and elsewhere."

Moll instinctively retreated a step. "I'm sure I never meant—"

"Oh, I think you meant exactly what you said. If you have any doubt that *I* also meant what *I* said, you have only to try me. Good day."

And so saying, she left the house without a backward glance.

18

In Which John Pickett Faces His Captor

In another house in London not so very far distant, a pounding on the other side of the door made Pickett jerk upright in his bonds. Had he really been asleep? It seemed hard to believe he had actually slept in his present condition, but although he ached in places he didn't even know he had, his brain lacked the dull, disoriented feeling that came, as he had cause to know, with a return to consciousness after a prolonged period of insensibility.

"That'll be Jud," Kit said with a sigh of resignation, throwing back his thin blanket as the pounding on the door was renewed. "He won't half like it if I'm late for breakfast."

Breakfast, Pickett thought, noticing for the first time the thin slivers of light filtering into the room between the boards covering the window. *Which means it's morning, and I've been here all night.*

What must Julia be thinking by now, after waiting all

night for him to come home?

It only means someone will be looking for you, he told himself. *Julia will make sure of it.*

He would have smiled a little at the notion of his gently-born wife descending upon Bow Street with news of his disappearance, but the effort made his face hurt. Besides, he could not think of Julia now. He was painfully aware of having lost face with his young half-brother the previous night, and had only a very short time in which to retrieve his position before Roger could put him at some further disadvantage.

"Kit," he said, "before you go to breakfast, I—I have something for you. It's in the inside pocket of my coat. I'm afraid you'll have to get it; I can't—" He gave a little shrug, which made the ropes tighten painfully about his wrists.

Kit regarded him warily for a long moment, then scrambled to his feet and approached the chair where Pickett sat bound.

"This side," Pickett said, dipping his head toward the right front of his tailcoat.

Kit reached into the pocket, and Pickett had the satisfaction of recognizing the exact moment at which the boy realized what he was holding.

"It—it—" Kit stared down at the toy soldier in his hand as if he had just been given the crown jewels. "Where did you get it?"

"The magistrate at Bow Street gave it to me, so that I could return it to you. It was discovered outside Coutts after the robbery and taken in as evidence."

Kit looked up sharply. "Bow Street? It's true, then, about—about you being a Bow Street Runner?"

"Yes."

Pickett didn't have to ask how he knew; he had no doubt his unloving stepmother would have divulged the information quickly enough in order to stay on good terms with a man who would be a powerful and dangerous enemy. Well, he was not without powerful and dangerous connections of his own, as Roger would soon discover.

He cast a furtive glance at the door, then spoke quickly and quietly. "Listen, Kit. The Bow Street Runner who is investigating the Coutts robbery is new, but he's determined, and he's making progress. He got a good look at you and told the magistrate that you looked just like me. I realize that hardly seems like a compliment at the moment, but it might just save your life. Bow Street is hard on Roger's heels. They may not get him today, or even tomorrow, but sooner or later, he's for Newgate. And I'm going to get you well away from here before you end up going to the gallows with him."

"That so?" Kit's expression grew skeptical as he took in every detail of Pickett's injuries, as well as the bonds that prevented him from so much as putting a hand into his own pocket. "And just how d'you think you're gonna do that?"

"Well, I obviously can't lick him in a fight," Pickett observed, and Kit thought, incredibly, that he was smiling, although his swollen face made it hard to be sure, "so I suppose I'll have to outwit him, won't I?" Although, he added mentally, it was a pity he hadn't begun by recalling that the house where Lucy plied her trade would very likely have a back door giving access to Little St. Andrew Street. Instead, he'd left his flank unprotected, and that, no doubt, was how Roger had been able to take him unawares.

This rather unproductive train of thought was interrupted by Jud, who flung the door open and advanced into the room. "You want anything to eat, you'd better get your arse out here," he informed the boy, then turned to Pickett. "As for you, Roger says he wants a word with you."

Tied to the chair as he was, walking into the next room was clearly beyond Pickett's powers. Before he could point this out, however, Jud seized the back of his chair and tipped it onto its back legs, then dragged it into the outer room. Pickett let out a long breath. For one terrifying moment, he'd thought Jud intended to let the chair fall all the way to the floor, and there wouldn't have been a thing he could do to stop it. Still, he found himself sitting as tightly wound as a watch-spring, tilting his head slightly forward to prevent it from striking the floor just in case Jud should decide to let go. Jud gave a grunt that seemed to indicate amusement, as if he knew exactly what Pickett was thinking. Then he turned the chair in a tight half-circle so that it faced the middle of the room and set it back on its front legs with a *thunk*.

And for the first time, Pickett got a good look at his attacker.

I've seen you before, he thought, studying the figure as closely as he could through the one eye that wasn't swollen almost completely shut. *And quite recently, too. But where? Where have I been lately that we might have crossed paths?*

He hadn't the luxury of pondering the question for long,

for Roger was speaking to him.

"Now, there's a face only a mother could love."

He sounded, Pickett thought indignantly, as if he were quite pleased that his handiwork had yielded such excellent results.

Aloud, he said, "I wonder whose fault that might be?"

"Got a mouth on him, this one does. Want me to shut him up, Rog'?" Jud said, and although Pickett could not see him, since Jud still stood behind the chair, he could hear the cracking of the big man's knuckles and knew he was prepared to make good on the threat.

But Roger shook his head and put up a restraining hand. "No—he said he wants to talk to me."

Pickett was aware of something deep inside him uncoiling as the tension in his body lessened. Upon regaining consciousness sometime during the wee hours of the night, one of the first things he'd done—one of the few things he *could* do, trussed up as he was—was to run his tongue over his teeth. He'd been relieved to discover them all still there, and still tight in his gums; he would hate to lose them now, this late in the game.

"So, go ahead." Roger dragged a second chair out from beneath the table, turned it around, and straddled it, leaning his forearms against the top of the chairback. "Talk."

Pickett had prepared in advance what he'd intended to say if and when he ever found Roger, but so much had happened in the past twenty-four hours that he struggled to call it to mind. Then, too, there was the fact that his mouth did not appear to be working properly, as half of it seemed disinclined to move. He had no intention of giving Roger the satisfaction of knowing this, however, and so he took particular care not to slur his words any more than he could help as he said, "I've come on behalf of the boy's mother. She's changed her mind, and wants him back. She is prepared to reimburse you the two pounds you paid for him, plus another twelve shillings for your trouble."

Roger gave a derisive snort that might, if one were inclined to be charitable, have been considered a laugh. "You'll have to try another one. Moll never in her life had twelve shillings all at one time. Anything that comes in goes for Blue Ruin before it hits the bottom of her pocket."

"Oh, so you've noticed that, have you?" asked Pickett, readily conceding the point. "But she was so torn up over the loss of her boy, and her with no way of recovering him, that I told her I'd stand the nonsense, and she could repay me later, as she had funds to do so—not that I expect I'll ever see a brass farthing," he added in a voice that invited Roger to share a joke at Moll's expense.

But Roger just shook his head, regarding Pickett with something akin to pity. "That won't wash. I saw Moll just two days ago, and I promise you, getting her hands on the brat was the last thing on her mind! You want the little bastard because it suits your own purposes, though I'll be hanged if I know what they are."

Oh, I hope so, Pickett thought. *But you're not taking him with you, not if I have anything to say to the matter.*

"Well, maybe I'll let you have him, and maybe I won't, but I can tell you this: it'll cost you a hell of a lot more than two quid twelve." Roger leaned forward, his pale eyes boring into Pickett's one-and-a-half functioning brown ones. "Ten pounds sterling. Not one farthing less."

"*Ten pounds?*" Pickett didn't have to feign shock. He knew exactly how much he'd put into his coin purse the previous morning, and it hadn't come close to ten pounds even before he'd been obliged to dole out payments to first Lucy and then Moll. He glanced toward Kit, who had finished his breakfast and was now crouched on the floor next to a small bird in a cage, crumbling bits of bread through the bars and talking softly to the bird as it hopped about snatching up the bread in its beak. Pickett wished he might lower his voice, but to show any consideration for the boy's feelings would only give the lie to the claim he had to make. "Why the devil should I give you ten pounds for the brat? I never laid eyes on him until yesterday!"

The thin shoulders stiffened, and Pickett knew he had heard—and felt—every word. *I didn't mean it*, he thought, trying desperately to convey the silent message with his eyes, or what could be seen of them. But even had his face been less swollen and bruised, the brothers were not sufficiently well-acquainted for such unspoken communication. Kit rose to his feet with a pathetic sort of dignity.

"He says the Bow Street Runner who's looking for us is new," he announced, clearly ranging himself on Roger's side. He uncurled the fist in which he'd been clutching the toy soldier. "And he said the magistrate gave him this to take back to me, but I don't believe him. Besides, I don't want it anymore."

Without another word, he returned to his bedchamber, pausing only long enough to be certain Pickett could see him hurling the soldier into the fireplace before slamming the door shut.

Pickett would have gladly given ten pounds, and a great deal more besides, if only he could have called him back. But even if he were free to rise from his chair and go after the boy, he could not; Roger was making a counter-offer, and he must pay attention so he could counter it with a lesser offer of his own. And so he did, unaware that only six years earlier, his magistrate had entered into a very similar transaction over his own fate.

At last he and Roger agreed upon terms, with Pickett, at least, feeling quite pleased with himself. Knowing to the last farthing how little remained in his coin purse, he had been obliged to take a hard line, professing such complete indifference to the boy's fate that Roger eventually agreed to a price low enough to enable Pickett to pay the ransom and still have a little bit—a *very* little bit—left over. He only wished Mr. Whitmore of the Bank of England had been present to witness this neat bit of ciphering, all performed in his head without benefit of either pencil or paper.

His pride suffered a severe blow a moment later, however, when he remembered that he could not access his own coat pocket. "Er, I'm afraid I can't—that is, you'll have to—" He only hoped Roger didn't help himself to the entire purse.

Roger did not offer to untie him, but instead stood up and swung his leg free of the chair he'd occupied, then strolled up to Pickett, grasped the front edge of his coat, and jerked at it so savagely that for a moment Pickett feared he intended to pull the chair over, allowing the captive to land on his face. He was spared this indignity, although the truth was not much better. Roger plunged his hand into the inside pocket and drew out, not a coin purse, but a small notebook and pencil.

"I don't like being made a game of," Roger snarled, tossing Pickett's occurrence book onto the floor.

For the first time, Pickett was glad that it was Maxwell, and not he, whose occurrence book would contain all the notes on the investigation of the Coutts robbery. But if the coin purse wasn't in his pocket, then where—? *Kit*, he thought desperately. Kit, who was angry and hurt, and so would do nothing to help him now, even if the boy had somehow contrived to take the coin purse at the same time he'd retrieved the toy soldier, and even now had it secreted away somewhere under his mattress.

"No game, I swear," Pickett said hastily, before Roger could make good on any of the threats he ground out through clenched teeth. "It was there, just yesterday—"

Yesterday, he recalled with a sinking feeling in the pit of his stomach. Kit couldn't have taken it, for it was already long gone. He had no idea how long he'd lain unconscious on the pavement before someone—he rather thought it had been Jud—had come for him with the wheelbarrow. Still, he was familiar enough with the Dials to know that anyone spying a man lying insensible—not an unusual sight by any means, given the availability of cheap gin in the area—would not hesitate to relieve him of any valuables he was stupid enough to carry upon his person. He was lucky the thief hadn't bashed his head in with a bottle and stripped him naked while he—or she—was about it.

"He didn't have nothing on him when I picked him up yesterday," Jud put in. "If he did have any money, somebody had it off him before I got there."

Roger looked a bit disappointed at being deprived of the chance to further rearrange Pickett's face, but said only, "How now, then? With no rhino and no means of getting any, if you want that brother of yours, I guess you'll have to come up with some other plan."

Some other plan. Pickett wasn't sure why the phrase should make alarm bells go off in his head. *Some other plan...* Not that any of his plans seem to amount to much lately; he'd told himself he would tender his resignation at Bow Street as soon as he could come up with some other plan, and look what had happened there, with Mr. Whitmore at the Bank of England treating him like a felon...the Bank of England, where he'd tried to make a dignified exit and only got himself lost instead...the Bank of England, where he'd almost knocked a man off his feet, a lean man with a shabby coat and pale, cold eyes...

"Good God," Pickett breathed, staring at Roger as the full import of that chance encounter became clear. "You're going to rob the Bank of England."

19

In Which the Brothers Pickett Plot Their Escape

W ho said anything about the Bank of England?" demanded Roger, instantly on the defensive.

"No one," Pickett assured him hastily. "But I saw you there one day—ran into you, in fact, as you were coming in. Scouting out the lay of the land, I daresay."

"All right, so you have me," Roger admitted, spreading his hands in a gesture of surrender. "We're gonna rob the bank, and the brat is gonna help us, and we don't mean to let some damned Nosey Parker from Bow Street blow the gaff this late in the game. So if you want to stay alive, you'll dub your mummer."

In fact, Pickett was surprised they'd allowed him to live this long. He wondered if, by murdering Jenny, Roger had surprised himself, perhaps even frightened himself a little. Surely there was no other reason that might account for the fact that he was still alive. He wondered if this unexpected lenience might extend to untying his hands so that he might eat breakfast, but thought it best not to push his luck. To his surprise, it was Roger who raised the subject.

"Untie one of the fellow's hands, but *only* one, and give him something to eat," he commanded Jud, then added, for Pickett's benefit, "I'd thought to let the brat do it, but I expect right now he'd just as soon let you starve."

And that appeared to be all he had to say on the matter. Jud dragged Pickett's chair over to the table, then plunked down in front of him a slice of bread smeared with something that Pickett, eyeing it with disfavor, supposed must pass for butter, along with a somewhat withered apple. Apparently he was not to be allowed the use of one of the mismatched pewter plates visible in an ancient Welsh dresser; presumably, he might try to use it as a weapon.

Expressing some disappointment that he was to be denied the enjoyment he might have derived by watching the captive try to pick up his food using only his mouth, Jud set to work on the rope pinning Pickett's right hand to the arm of the chair. Pickett offered no response to a remark that was clearly intended to goad him into some reckless action that would give Jud some justification for landing a blow or two. No, he would keep to himself the observation that if he were only to be allowed one hand, he would have much preferred that it be his left; the information might possibly give him some element of surprise over his captors, and with so few weapons in his arsenal, he could not afford to pass up any advantage, no matter how insignificant.

In the meantime, there was breakfast. Although he'd had

no dinner the previous night, Pickett had not realized until food was set before him just how hungry he was. Heavy footsteps from somewhere behind him indicated that both Roger and Jud were going upstairs, leaving him to eat in relative privacy. And eat he did, setting to with a will in spite of the unappetizing fare set before him and trying not to think of mounds of fluffy yellow buttered eggs and rashers of bacon, washed down with strong, hot coffee.

He was not quite finished with the apple when the thud of footsteps on the stairs heralded the return of his captors, and a moment later Jud appeared with rope in hand, ready to bind his wrist once more to the arm of the chair. But something had changed. Whereas before Jud had been clad in his shirtsleeves, he now wore a moth-eaten wool coat from which a button was missing.

"I'm going out," Roger announced. Pickett could just see the man out of the corner of his eye, and noticed he, too, was dressed for the street in the same shabby coat he'd worn that day at the bank. Addressing his henchman over Pickett's head, he added, "Be sure to lock them back up before you leave the house."

Jud, nothing loth, grabbed the back of Pickett's chair and dragged it back into the room at the rear of the house. Just before he turned the chair to face the wall, Pickett had a glimpse of the boy sitting rigidly erect on his pallet, his back turned very pointedly toward the door and, presumably, his elder brother. Then the door was closed and locked, leaving them in a twilight darkness relieved only by the slender bands of light, somewhat brighter now as the sun rose higher, penetrating the boards that covered the windows.

They sat there in silence while Pickett kept his ears pricked for the sounds of their captors' departure. Once he was certain they were alone in the house, he ventured a question.

"Do they always keep you locked up like this?"

Craning his neck, he could just see over his shoulder the boy's shrug. "Sometimes they do, sometimes they don't."

"Oh."

The long silence that followed was suddenly broken by the sound of something scrabbling across the floor. Pickett was just about to ask, somewhat warily, if Kit was troubled by rats when he caught the spark of a flint, and a moment later, a candle flared sputteringly to life. Pickett wondered why the boy had not lit it sooner; then again, his own face, in its present condition, was probably better unseen. He only hoped Julia would not share these sentiments; he thought it very likely that she would take exception at Roger's efforts toward rearranging it, for he had reason to believe she'd rather liked it the way it was.

But he could not think of Julia now. He had no idea how long Roger and Jud would be gone, and he had certain things to communicate to the boy—yes, and certain things to learn from him, as well—before they returned. At the moment, however, it was clear that Kit was engrossed in thoughts of his own. Pickett had assumed the boy's facing the opposite wall was intended to express his contempt for his elder brother by quite literally turning his back on him, even lighting the candle so that Pickett could not fail to be aware of this gesture,

231

as well as its meaning. Gradually, he came to realize that Kit was not merely ignoring him, but was gazing at the fireplace where the toy soldier still lay in the ashes. Although he couldn't see the boy's face, regret and longing could be read in every line of the stiff shoulders—along with the pride that prevented him from retrieving the prized possession he had so recklessly thrown away.

"I was just thinking," Pickett said, breaking the long silence, "if you don't want the soldier after all, would you mind fetching it out of the fireplace and putting it back in my pocket? I'm sure the magistrate would prefer to have it back than to discover that a valuable piece of evidence has been burned to cinders."

Having been provided with such an excuse, Kit did not have to be told twice. He crawled over to the fireplace and snatched the plaything out of the ashes, then began polishing it clean with the corner of his blanket. "I'll fetch it, but it'll be for me, not no magistrate," he said belligerently, then added, "Besides, it can't be burnt up. Chimney's been blocked up for years. Roger says so."

Pickett accepted this snub meekly, noting with some satisfaction that his young brother was, at least, looking him in the eye, albeit not without hostility. At this point, even so small a victory was encouraging.

"Kit," he began a bit tentatively, "I'm sorry for what I said out there—sorry you had to hear it. I didn't mean it, you know. I just couldn't let Roger see that it mattered—that *you* mattered. I couldn't give him so powerful a weapon."

While he was making his apology, Kit had shown every

sign of rejecting it out of hand, but at his mention of a weapon, something seemed to flare in the boy's eyes. No, not exactly hope, Pickett thought. Not so much hope as recognition. Pickett realized that Kit knew, no doubt through bitter experience, never to let anyone see that he cared about anything or anyone, lest it, or they, be taken from him. And here, perhaps, was a way he might gain his brother's confidence.

"I expect that up to now you haven't had much reason to trust anyone," he said gently. He couldn't tell whether or not the boy was listening anymore, for Kit's gaze was now fixed firmly on the soldier in his grimy hands. Still, he hadn't offered any kind of a retort, so Pickett was emboldened to continue. "But I can promise you that there are people who care about you, people you can depend on. And I hope that, in time, you'll come to think of me as one of them."

Another long silence met this speech, and Pickett braced himself for another cutting remark as to his ability to save himself, much less his brother. And so the question, when it came, took him completely by surprise.

"Where do you live?"

"I—I beg your pardon?"

"You said you wanted me to come and live with you," the boy reminded him. "So, where do you live?"

"Oh, I see. I live in a house in Mayfair." Seeing his brother regarding him with an expression of incredulity, Pickett felt compelled to offer something more, an odd combination of explanation, confession, and apology. "The house—well, it actually belongs to my wife, but—"

"It's a real place, then?"

"What, the house?" asked Pickett, all at sea.

"Mayfair. I've heard of it, but I thought it was just make-believe."

"No, it's quite real," Pickett said with a hint of a smile. "After we get out of here, I hope you'll let me show it to you, even if you don't choose to live there."

There was another silence while Kit considered this offer. When he spoke again, his words were stilted and awkward, as if forced from his unwilling throat.

"I—I'm sorry I told Roger. What you said about Bow Street, I mean."

"There's probably no harm done," Pickett assured him with, perhaps, less than perfect truth. "In fact, it might even help, if it makes Roger take Maxwell too lightly." *And won't Maxwell just love my making a gift of his name to one of the thieves he saw fleeing Coutts,* Pickett thought. Still, if he hoped to win the boy's trust, then it couldn't hurt to demonstrate a little trust in him first.

In any case, he was rewarded with a diffident smile. Pickett decided to press his luck.

"But I'm going to need your help if I'm to get you away from here before Maxwell finds Roger's hidey-hole and comes to arrest the lot of you. Tell me, do you know where we are?"

Kit's timid smile vanished, replaced with a look of utter bewilderment. "We're locked in the back room of Roger's house."

"Well, yes, I suppose I deserved that one," Pickett

admitted. "I meant where is the house? What street is it in? Do you know?"

Kit's brow puckered in deep concentration for a long moment. "N-no," he said at last. "I never heard Roger or Jud say."

Pickett tried a different approach. "If you were to leave the house, would you know how to get to, say, Covent Garden?"

" 'Course I would!" Kit sounded a bit indignant at having his navigational skills called into question. "Jud used to let me visit Jenny at the market. Sometimes she would give me a penny and let me buy a muffin." His air of bravado faded, and suddenly he was no longer a cheeky street urchin, but a very frightened little boy. "He killed her, you know. I saw him. And that night, Jud put her in her wheelbarrow and took her away, and then when he came back the next day with you in the barrow, I thought—I thought—" He broke off with a sniff and wiped his nose on the sleeve of his shirt.

"I know." Pickett spoke as gently as he dared. It would not do to encourage any display of weakness, lest the boy yield to a bout of tears which he would certainly hate himself for later, and as a result feel compelled to hold his would-be sympathizer at a distance. "But I'm here, and intact—well, relatively intact—and I need you to tell me all you know about Roger and Jud. Where have they gone?"

"Jud's gone to buy food, now that Jenny's—gone. I don't know about Roger. He don't answer to nobody."

"We may not have much time, then. Can you untie these ropes, do you think?"

It was an agonizingly slow process, and Pickett was certain that their captors might return at any minute, but at last both of his hands were free. He would have liked a minute or two to work the circulation back into his arms, but he dared not take any longer than necessary. He set to work on one of his ankles while Kit took the other.

He didn't waste time trying the door, since he'd heard the turn of the key in the lock before Jud left the house, and had nothing on his person with which to force it. Then, too, even if he succeeded in opening it, he would still have to deal with the front door, and the very real danger of walking straight into Roger, or Jud, or both, returning from wherever it was they'd gone. In fact, he had thought of another possibility, but only as a last resort, if all other options had failed. And so he crossed the room to the boarded-up window and ran his hands over it until he located the seams through which shone those thin shafts of light, indicating (or so he hoped) a weakness that might be exploited.

"There's been a fire here," he remarked to Kit, gesturing toward the blackened lower corner of one board.

"That was me," Kit said, not without a hint of pride. "I thought maybe I could escape by burning the boards off. But Jud smelled the smoke, and when he told Roger what I'd done, he didn't half give me a thrashing!"

Pickett regarded his brother with something akin to horror. "I can't say I blame him. You might have burned the house down!" Recalling Kit's activities only a few minutes earlier, he added, "I'm surprised they let you have a candle at all."

"They don't. I stole it," boasted Kit with simple pride.

"You terrify me." Pickett made a show of mopping his brow on the sleeve of his coat, which drew a reluctant grin from his young brother. "Still, between your attempt at arson and the ravages of time, the board or the window frame, or both, may have been weakened to the point that, with any luck, we can force them loose."

Alas, it soon became evident that their luck was out. Pickett drove his shoulder into the boards until it ached, and once even tried to kick the boards out—an operation that ended with him sprawled on the floor, to Kit's loudly expressed amusement—but in spite of their dilapidated appearance, both the window frame and the boards fitted inside it were surprisingly stubborn.

"We could try the chimney," Kit said doubtfully.

"I thought you said it was blocked," Pickett reminded him.

"It was Roger that said it was blocked, but maybe he just made it up, him not wanting to waste coals on a fire."

Pickett shook his head. "Even if it isn't blocked, I'm not sending you up the chimney like you were some climbing-boy."

"I can at least *try!*" insisted Kit.

"No, you can't. God knows it's a dangerous enough operation even for the boys who know how." Seeing his young brother was inclined to argue, he added on a lighter note, "Besides, where would we be if you were to get stuck halfway to the roof? Roger would be bound to suspect something if he came home and found the chimney howling like a banshee. I'll bet even Jud could figure that one out, and between you and me and the lamppost, he doesn't appear to have much in his brain-box."

"I wouldn't howl," Kit insisted, grinning nevertheless. "I wouldn't get stuck, either."

"Maybe not, but I'm not going to take the chance."

"Then how *do* we get out?"

Pickett sighed. "I'm afraid we don't, at least not today."

"But—"

"I have an idea," Pickett assured him, "but I need time to think it through."

"What is it?" The boy's wide eyes shone, glittering with the reflected light of the candle flame. "Tell me!"

"I can't, at least not yet."

"But *when?*"

"I promise, when it's time you'll know, and you'll walk out of here as free as a bird." It probably wasn't the best choice of words, given the caged goldfinch in the next room, but Kit didn't seem to notice.

"What about you?"

"I'll walk out, too," Pickett said, and for just an instant there was something in the tone of his voice, or perhaps it was something about the expression on his battered face, that gave Kit an uneasy feeling in the pit of his stomach. Then just as suddenly it was gone, and his brother was asking for his help. "In the meantime, there's something I need you to do for me."

"You mean I get to help?" Kit exclaimed delightedly, as if the rescue he had so desperately longed for were nothing more than a prank to be played on a schoolyard bully.

"Of course! We're in this together, aren't we? Do you remember the little notebook I had in my pocket?"

"The one with the pencil attached to it?"

"That's it. Roger threw it on the floor out there," Pickett reminded him, gesturing toward the locked door to the front room. "The next time they let you out there, I want you to get it, if you can manage the thing without being seen, and bring it in here. Don't put it back in my pocket—that's the first place Roger would look, if he were to think of it. Hide it under the corner of your mattress. And if he asks, you don't know anything about it."

"Right! Anything else?"

"I think you'd better tie me back up," Pickett said with obvious regret. "We don't know how long it might be before Roger or Jud returns, and it won't do to let them know that I can slip my bonds whenever I've a mind to. I can tie my own ankles, but I'll need you to do my wrists."

Having lashed his ankles to the legs of the chair, Pickett surrendered his hands to Kit, who had to be chided for tying the ropes so loosely that Roger could have seen at a glance that they'd been tampered with.

"I feel *mean*," the boy confessed, tightening the knot as his brother had ordered.

"You need not, for by the time I'm done with you, you may wish Roger had thought to gag me, as well," Pickett said with a flippancy he did not feel. "Tell me, do you know when he plans to make his attempt on the bank?"

Kit's face puckered in concentration. "I know he told Jud they would wait 'til the new moon." He cast an inquisitive look up at Pickett from where he still knelt beside his brother's chair. "Is that the same thing as a full moon?"

"No. In fact, it's just the opposite. It means you can't see the moon at all."

"Oh. I guess that makes sense. They would want it to be dark, wouldn't they?"

"You would think so," Pickett agreed thoughtfully, "but the moon didn't stop them from robbing Coutts, did it?"

Kit nodded sagely. "That was because Roger needed money. I heard him tell Jenny, but he didn't say what he needed it for. Maybe she already knew." His face grew solemn. "It's too bad about Jenny, isn't it? I bet she would've told me, if I'd asked her."

Pickett offered no comment, and Kit soon grew restless. Without bothering to stand up, he crawled over to his pallet and snatched up the toy soldier. A few seconds later, he was on his knees before the boarded-up window, marching the soldier back and forth across the sill like a sentry watching for Roger's return. *This* John, he felt certain, would have got them out by now. At the very least, he would have contrived to kick the boards from the window without ending up in a heap on the floor. He stifled a giggle at the memory.

"What's so funny?" Pickett asked from his chair on the opposite side of the room.

"Nothing," Kit said, unconvincingly.

"Liar," Pickett said without heat.

And that was the curious thing, Kit thought. His real brother was nothing at all like his imaginary one.

And yet, he thought he just might like this one better.

20

In Which John Pickett Makes a Very Interesting Proposal

Pickett, meanwhile, had been given a great deal of food for thought, and was finding it not at all to his liking. If Roger was waiting only for the new moon before making his attempt on the Bank of England, then the night fixed for the robbery could not be far away, he reasoned, recalling the thin sliver of moon hanging low in the western sky as he walked home from Bow Street the previous night. But no, he thought, sitting up straighter in his bonds. He'd never returned to Curzon Street at all last night; he'd spent the night here, in this very room, bound hand and foot to his chair. And if the waning crescent moon had been scarcely visible two nights ago, what must it be like now? Was it possible that the thing was set for tonight? Or tomorrow night, at the very latest?

Either way, he hadn't the luxury of slowly wearing Roger down, especially not if the fellow made a regular practice of absenting himself for long stretches of time. No, it would have to be the method of last resort. He supposed it was a good thing he hadn't had a long time in which to consider the matter, to try and talk himself out of doing what he knew now must be done. This way, too, Julia would be spared an endless succession of nights in which to wonder and worry over where he was and what had become of him. He, too, would have little time to mourn the breaking of a vow kept for more than a decade...

"Kit," he said abruptly, his voice unnaturally loud in the quiet room, "come here, will you? I—There's something I need to talk to you about."

Kit, nothing loth, left the toy soldier to his guarding of the window sill and crawled across his pallet to plop down on the floor at Pickett's captive feet. "What?"

"You say you know how to find your way from here to the piazza at Covent Garden," he began, choosing his words with care.

"The *what?*" Kit asked, scowling as he considered the unfamiliar word.

"The piazza," Pickett repeated, then added by way of explanation, "where the market is."

"Oh, *that!* Why didn't you say so?"

"Do you know how to get from there to the Bow Street Public Office?"

Kit stared at him. "Why would I want to go *there?*"

"Never mind that now; do you know the way?"

"I do, but only so's I can avoid it."

Pickett, his mind troubled by weightier matters, decided to let this pass. "I'm going to tell you how to get from there to

Curzon Street. That's where I live."

"In Mayfair," said Kit, still trying to grasp the fact that it was a real place.

"In Mayfair," Pickett agreed, nodding. "I'll draw you a map, once I have my notebook, but there won't always be streetlamps to read it by, so it's better that you know the route from memory."

Kit regarded him with a look of utter bewilderment. "Why can't I just follow you?"

"We, er, we might become separated in the dark. Now, listen carefully, so you can repeat it back to me. From Bow Street, go back to the piazza, then take Southampton Street until you reach the Strand…"

* * *

It was not long afterward that they heard the sound of the outer door creaking on unoiled hinges, and footsteps in the room just outside their own.

"It's Jud," whispered Kit.

"How can you tell?" Pickett asked, lowering his voice to match the boy's.

Kit shrugged. "His footsteps are heavier, aren't they? Him being heavier than Roger, and all."

"Observant lad," Pickett remarked approvingly, and was disconcerted when Kit responded to this mild praise by looking up at him with something alarmingly akin to hero-worship in his eyes. "By the bye," he added hastily, "it might be better if we let Roger and Jud think we're not on terms. Don't be hurt if I say dismissive things about you to Roger, like I did earlier. In return, you may talk to me as disrespectfully as you please."

"Just like real brothers!" exclaimed Kit, grinning broadly.

"Just like real brothers," echoed Pickett.

They reached this agreement not a moment too soon, for the door suddenly swung open. Jud stood there regarding Pickett menacingly. Kit had turned his back on the prisoner, and was deeply engrossed in carrying out military maneuvers on the window sill. At Jud's entrance, however, Kit leaped to his feet and darted past him into the outer room.

"What did you get us to eat?" he shrieked, sounding, at least to Pickett's ears, like any ordinary ten-year-old boy; if he'd learned anything from two weeks spent in Scotland with the three Bertram brothers, it was that the juvenile male of the species was perpetually hungry. As if in proof of this assessment, Kit called, in quite a different tone, "There's not very much food here!"

"We're not going to be here much longer," Jud retorted, turning away from Pickett to deliver a scold, "so you'll eat what you're given, and like it!"

Not much food here, Pickett thought. *We're not going to be here much longer.* It appeared he was correct in thinking the robbery would take place very soon. Which meant he had better waste no time in persuading Roger to relinquish his claim to his little snakesman.

He received further confirmation of his theory only a few minutes later, when the leader of the thieves returned, apparently quite pleased with himself.

"All taken care of," he announced, and Pickett, the only

one of the four not in the front room, wished he was at least facing the door, so that he could discover what he might by Roger's gestures and facial expressions. "By this time tomorrow, we'll be on a ship bound for Amsterdam."

Unlike his leader, Jud *was* in Pickett's range of vision, and at this proclamation, he cast a nervous glance in his captive's direction. "Are you sure you ought to—?" He broke off, but rolled his eyes in toward Pickett.

"Why not? It's not like he can do anything to stop us, can he?" He took a few steps further into the room so that he could grin at Pickett, seemingly still tied fast to the chair to which he'd been bound the night before. "Y'hear that, Bow Street? We're sailing for Amsterdam at dawn, and we're gonna have a nice little present from the Bank of England to take with us."

Pickett took a deep breath. It was now or never. He turned his head to meet Roger's gaze, doing his best to look no more than mildly interested. "Are you? Brave man!"

"Brave, am I?" Roger's smug expression wavered slightly. "How so?"

"Only that I wouldn't want to risk *my* neck on the skills of a brat scarcely breeched."

"Hey!" put in Kit, every bit as indignant as Pickett could have hoped for.

"This brat knows what he's doing," Roger said, and although his confidence appeared to be unshaken, Pickett dared to hope he was trying to convince himself as well as his prisoner.

Pickett shrugged. "At Coutts, maybe. But you've seen the Bank of England; the place is a fortress! I doubt there's a space small enough for a mouse to get through, much less a lumping great lad eating his head off."

Never had Pickett thought he would be actually grateful for Moll's unflattering description of himself; furthermore, the fact that Kit had discovered an apple amongst Jud's purchases and was just sinking his teeth into it when all eyes turned in his direction added considerable verisimilitude to Pickett's claim.

"Maybe we won't need to get a mouse in," Roger replied, giving Pickett a very ugly look. "Maybe we'll just pick the lock and walk through the door, bold as brass."

"Maybe so," Pickett conceded, apparently all admiration for this alternative plan. "By the bye, did you know some of the senior bank officers live right there on the premises, and their families with them? I didn't, until I took a wrong turn and got lost. Found myself in the private section of the building, sure as check. I'm afraid I gave one poor lady quite a turn, walking into her drawing room without so much as a by-your-leave," he added, embellishing his experiences wandering about the bank without so much as a blush.

"I said this one had a mouth on him," put in Jud, clenching his fist and rhythmically smacking it against the palm of his other hand. "Do you want me to shut it for him, Rog'?"

"No, let him talk," Roger said, dismissing this suggestion with an impatient gesture before turning back to Pickett. "You say people live there? How many?"

"Nearly fifty, or so I've heard," said Pickett. In fact, he was deriving considerable satisfaction from the knowledge that he had presented Roger with a conundrum he had not anticipated—a feeling that proved to be premature.

"He's lying!" Jud growled and, without waiting for permission from Roger, strode up to Pickett's chair and struck him across the mouth.

"That's enough, Jud," Roger chided his overeager henchman.

"*Now* he says so," Pickett muttered. He ran his tongue over his lips, and tasted blood. While he might have wished for a gentler distraction, there was no denying that Jud's attack had served a very useful purpose: Out of the tail of his eye, Pickett had seen Kit's hand dart out and snag the notebook. In the next instant it had disappeared, presumably up the sleeve of the boy's shirt. Although his young half-brother's hands were still childishly soft, his fingers were long and nimble—perfectly suited, in fact, to the task Pickett had assigned him. *Lord, what our father might have achieved with you,* Pickett thought. If he accomplished nothing else, perhaps he could at least prevent Kit from being obliged to make a career of the skill; its practitioners tended to be short-lived.

"I was going to say," he informed Roger with an air of wounded innocence, "perhaps you're right in taking the babe along. It would be easier for him to hide if the wife of one of the bank officers should discover you. Then, too, if he were caught, he could always cry. She would very likely feel sorry for him, and—"

"I'm not a 'babe,' and I don't cry!" put in Kit indignantly, although he had paled perceptibly at Jud's rough treatment of his brother.

"Still," said Pickett, ignoring the interruption, "I don't envy you. I'd hate to think the only thing standing between me and Newgate was a cub still wet behind the ears."

"I don't remember hearin' anybody ask you," Roger said with a sneer. "And Jud don't like it when folks speak out of turn, so unless you've got a better idea—"

"Actually," Pickett said, "I think I do."

Jud emitted a low growl.

Roger said skeptically, "Oh, do you? And what might that be?"

"I could rob the bank for you."

21

Which Finds John Pickett Playing a Double Game

W hat the hell d'you mean by that?" demanded Roger, moving closer to tower over his captive.

"Exactly what I say. I'll break into the bank for you."

"Aye, but not before you've got every man jack at Bow Street waiting there to welcome us!"

Pickett dipped his head to indicate the ropes that held him fast to the chair. "If I can do that in my current state, I'm not just a Bow Street Runner; I'm a bloody magician."

"I don't think you're making the offer out of the goodness of your heart," observed Roger. "So, what's in it for you? What is it you want in return?"

"I want you to release the boy."

Roger gave a snort of derision. "Not much of a bargainer, are you? His mum would hand him right back to me, and then where would you be?"

"I didn't say return him to his mum. I said release him.

Set him free, turn him out—let him go wherever he pleases."

"He wouldn't last the night," Roger predicted grimly, seating himself in a chair facing his prisoner.

Pickett shrugged. "Maybe, maybe not. But that's not your lookout, is it? You'll still get into the bank, and that's all you wanted the brat for in the first place; what do you care what happens to him?" Roger was silent, apparently considering the matter, so Pickett plunged ahead. "This job could set you up, you and Jud, for the rest of your lives. Who do you trust to do the thing right: a boy still in short coats, or a man whose father was none other than Gentleman Jack Pickett himself?"

"That won't wash," protested Jud, speaking up for the first time since Pickett had made his offer. "The brat's Gentleman Jack's spawn, too."

"Ha!" scoffed Pickett. "He never clapped eyes on the man! I, on the other hand, learned the business, as you might say, at my father's knee."

Roger folded his arms across his chest. "And yet you left the diving-lay to go to Bow Street, where you've been building yourself a nice little nest egg by squeaking beef on others of the brotherhood."

"No worse than Jonathan Wild did," protested Pickett, invoking the name of the notorious thief-taker of a century earlier. "He worked both sides of the law; why shouldn't I?"

"He also ended his career swinging from a rope at Tyburn," Roger pointed out, quite truthfully.

"Because he didn't know how to play the long game," agreed Pickett, nodding sagely.

"And I suppose you do?"

Pickett could not fail to notice the sarcasm in Roger's tone, but he chose to take the question at face value. "I haven't done too badly," he admitted modestly. "I haven't stolen anything in more than ten years, when I pinched an apple from a costermonger in Covent Garden."

"Why not?" asked Jud, curiosity overcoming skepticism.

Another careless shrug. "No need to! It served the purpose, what with it getting me arrested and hauled before the magistrate—"

"D'you mean," Jud demanded incredulously, "that you *wanted* to be taken in?"

"Of course I did!" Pickett replied scornfully, as if annoyed at being asked so stupid a question. "How else was I going to get the attention of the magistrate who'd had my father transported?"

"And after you got his attention?" Jud sounded almost eager. "What then?"

"What do you think? Lonely lad, father sent away at his instigation—he felt responsible for me. Got the notion that if only I was given a chance, I could grow up to be a fine, upstanding individual. So he arranged for me to be apprenticed to a wealthy coal merchant."

Jud frowned. "That don't sound like much of an improvement to me."

"Only because you've never seen the coal merchant's daughter," Pickett replied. "Eventually, though, her father wised up. Tore up my contract of apprenticeship, and forbade me from ever seeing the wench again. So I went back to the magistrate and told him my sad story: how the girl was mad for me to marry her, and when I refused, she threatened to tell the old man that I'd given her a slip on the shoulder. Lord, if I had, it would have been the easiest seduction ever attempted," he added, with a trace of bitterness that was quite sincere.

"And so the magistrate brought you to Bow Street," concluded Jud.

"As you say," agreed Pickett, inclining his head, "and I've been there ever since. But although I'd pocketed my share of rewards for arrests and convictions, I was ready for something bigger. So only last year, when one of the wealthiest nobs in the country got himself stabbed to death, I inserted myself into the middle of the investigation. I convinced the widow that she was likely to hang for her husband's murder, and I was the only one who could prove her innocence. After the trial, I married her. She was very grateful to me, you see." He glanced from Jud back to Roger, who had been listening to this account in silence. "Like I said—the long game." *And what Julia would say if she knew I was telling such bangers, I can't even begin to imagine,* he thought.

Jud pondered this story for a long moment. "But if you was going to marry money in the end, why didn't you take the coal merchant's daughter?"

The question caught Pickett off his guard, but only for a moment. "Because I wasn't the first apprentice to set his sights on the girl. Her father had tied her dowry up in such a way that her husband wouldn't be able to touch it, or at least, not enough of it to make it worth his while to take the jade to wife. And glad I was to discover it in time, too," he added, although gladness had not, in fact, been uppermost amongst his emotions at his parting from the fair Sophy.

"I'm sure this has all been very interesting," put in Roger in a tone that conveyed quite the opposite, "but it still doesn't explain why you want the boy."

Pickett contrived to look sheepish. "It has to do with my wife," he confessed. "In fact, her widow's jointure turned out to be just as tied up as ever Sophy's dowry was. As I said, Ju—the lady who now bears my name is very, shall we say, grateful. But her gratitude doesn't always take the form I might wish."

"Makes you beg for it, does she?" asked Roger, not without satisfaction.

"Every last farthing," grumbled Pickett, ignoring the earthier connotations of this question. "A man doesn't want to have to account for every penny he spends. She's especially inclined to cut up stiff over my clothes. But if she turns herself out as a lady, why shouldn't I look the part of a gentleman? I ask you: Is that fair?"

Jud, by this time quite entranced with their unwilling guest's cunning, was heard to say that it was not. Pickett paid no heed.

"That's where the brat comes in. It's plain as a pikestaff that he's my brother—half-brother, anyway—so she can't object if the poor lad comes to live with us, now, can she? And if a bit of her pin money goes missing from time to time, well, she's got so much of it, she's not likely to notice the difference."

Roger and Jud exchanged long, silent looks. At last, Roger said, "Here's the deal: You'll get us into the bank, but I'm the one in charge, and you'll follow my orders, you understand? After the job's done, we'll let the brat go."

"Right, then," Pickett said briskly. "What have you got so far?"

"We leave the house when the clock strikes two. The ship sails for Amsterdam on the ebb tide. Tide turns just after half past five, according to the fellow who sold us passage."

"Not much time, then," observed Pickett, mentally subtracting the time it would take to walk to the bank from, he thought, somewhere in the general area of St. Giles, as well as the time Roger and Jud would require to reach the wharf after the robbery.

"Time enough for a man who knows what he's doing," was Roger's reply. "And the less time spent loitering about the wharf after the deed's done, the better our chances of getting clean away. What will you need? Jud here can go out and buy any supplies while we plan our attack."

Pickett would have liked an opportunity to do a bit of reconnoitering, just as Roger had done on the day they'd crossed paths at the Bank, but he knew his chances of being granted any opportunity to make his bid for freedom were somewhere between slim and none. No, he would have to rely on his own recollections, combined with the bits and pieces he'd picked up from those older and more experienced Runners who'd had dealings with the Bank before. The irony was that Roger need not have worried that Pickett would attempt an escape; he would not have left his brother behind, in any case.

"I'll need a length of good, stout rope, and a dark lantern, and, say, two or three sacks of heavy canvas," Pickett told Jud, feeling no small satisfaction in being able to order his erstwhile tormentor about as if the man were his own personal lackey. "A ball of twine might prove useful as well, and something long and pointed. That should do the trick."

"That's it?" Roger asked. "You're sure?"

Pickett answered in the affirmative, and Roger dug inside the open collar of his shirt and pulled out a small coin purse worn about his neck on a leather thong. He tugged it open and counted out several coins—remnants, presumably, of the Coutts robbery.

"Don't be all day about it," he told Jud, pouring the coins into his henchman's open hand. "We've lots to do, and we'll need to make an early night of it."

After the door had closed behind Jud, Roger turned back to Pickett. "Not exactly what I would have expected you to ask for, but I reckon you know your own business best."

Pickett offered no explanations, instead merely asking, "Tell me, are you by any chance afraid of heights?"

"What the devil is that supposed to mean? The printing office is on the ground—"

"The *printing office?*" Pickett echoed in a very fair imitation of incredulous revulsion. "Do you mean to tell me we're risking our necks for nothing but *paper money?*"

"You can't deny it's a hell of a lot lighter and easier to carry than coins!" retorted Roger, bristling.

"Lighter, yes." Pickett readily conceded the point. "And utterly useless, once you reach Amsterdam."

"I can convert them to guilders once I make port," Roger insisted.

"Of course you can," agreed Pickett. "Provided you can do the thing and then disappear before the Dutch banks hear reports of a rather spectacular bank robbery in London."

"We'd have the same trouble with coins—aye, and it'd take a damn sight more of them to make it worth the risk!"

"Who said anything about coins?"

"Look here," demanded Roger, "if you don't like paper money, and you're not interested in coins, then just what are you getting at?"

Pickett answered the question with a couple of his own. "Have you ever noticed how much wider the Lothbury entrance is than the ones on Threadneedle or Princes Street? Have you ever wondered why that is?" While Roger pondered these seeming *non sequiturs*, Pickett continued, "It's wide enough to drive a wagon through, in fact. And if you drove a carriage through that entrance, you'd find yourself in a court-yard. On the opposite side of that courtyard is a covered passage, and at the end of that passage"—a slight pause for effect—"is the Bullion Yard."

Roger's eyes widened, gleaming with avarice. "*Gold.*" He breathed the word almost reverently.

"And welcome in any country you care to name."

Roger was silent for a long moment, considering the dangers inherent in making off with a fortune in gold bars. "They'd be a heavy load to carry," he said at last.

"Nothing Jud couldn't handle." Pickett touched his tongue to the corner of his mouth. "I can vouch for his strength."

Apparently satisfied, Roger rose and started for the stairs, no doubt eager to make his own preparations for the night's adventure. He stopped with his foot on the fourth tread, and turned back to his co-conspirator.

"Just in case you have any ideas about bubbling me, let me remind you that I'll have a knife on me, and won't be afraid to use it."

And having delivered himself of this warning—or was it a threat?—he climbed the remaining stairs without waiting for a reply.

* * *

Jud returned later that afternoon, and after his purchases were spread out on the table for Pickett's approval, Roger ordered everyone to their respective beds (everyone but Pickett, anyway), to get what sleep they could before setting out for the Bank at two o'clock.

After the cessation of thumps and creaks from above their heads indicated that Roger and Jud were asleep, Kit asked, "Was I all right?"

"You were brilliant," Pickett assured him. "In fact, you were so brilliant that there's something else I need you to do. You'll have to untie me first, though."

Kit was more than willing to do so, and while he fumbled with the knots by the uncertain light of the single candle, Pickett had him recite once more the route that would take him from Covent Garden to Bow Street and thence to Curzon

257

Street. Once he was satisfied that Kit could find his way alone, Pickett moved on to the next step in his plan.

"I need you to deliver a couple of letters for me. I'm going to write them now, and you can tuck them inside your shoes so Roger and Jud won't see them. Will you do that?"

Kit answered emphatically in the affirmative, and so Pickett drew up his chair to the window sill and retrieved his notebook from its hiding place beneath Kit's mattress. He positioned the candle so that his own body blocked the light, allowing Kit to sleep undisturbed, and began to write.

The first letter was fairly easy. It was brief, almost terse, and if it could not undo the act of betrayal he was about to commit, Pickett took what comfort he might in the knowledge that he had mitigated, as much as possible, the results of that act.

The second letter was another matter entirely. How did one, how *could* one, communicate in a few short lines the depth of a love for which a lifetime would have been insufficient to give expression? And, in addition to this declaration, to convey an apology, a request, and, finally, a farewell? It was impossible. Pickett drew a line through the inadequate words and began again.

He worked on this missive for fully an hour, forbidden from starting afresh on a clean page by the possibility that Roger or Jud might discover the rejected attempts and realize that he had plans of his own above and beyond simple bank robbery. At last, having affixed his name to this model of the epistolary art, he folded it, then folded it again, and finally, moving as quietly as possible so as not to awaken his brother, tucked it inside the boy's shoe.

"John?" a sleepy voice spoke out of the darkness.

"Did I wake you?" Pickett asked, returning his chair to the center of the room. "I'm sorry."

"I was already awake."

"Is anything troubling you?"

"John, what's going to happen to King George?"

"King George?" echoed Pickett, thinking his brother had chosen a very odd time to be worrying about the monarch's periodic bouts of madness.

"Jenny's bird," Kit said. "She said his red head and gold wings looked like he was wearing a crown of rubies and a golden robe. So she called him King George."

"Oh. I see."

"Roger and Jud won't be taking him on the ship with them, will they?"

"I shouldn't think so."

"D'you think Roger would let me keep him?"

"Perhaps," said Pickett, quite determined not to waste what little bargaining capital he possessed in negotiating the ownership of a goldfinch. Unless, of course, the goldfinch was not really what worried his brother…

"I wish I could come with you," Kit said. "I—I don't want to be left here all by myself."

"You won't be, I promise," Pickett assured him. "Roger doesn't know it yet, but there's going to be a last-minute change of plans. You're leaving at the same time we are, not after the job is done."

"Roger won't like it."

SHERI COBB SOUTH

"Very likely not. But he'll agree to it, all the same. He wants that gold, and he needs me in order to get it. I didn't give away all my trade secrets, you know."

"Then maybe we could come and get King George tomorrow, after Roger and Jud are gone," said Kit, brightening somewhat.

It had come, then, the moment Pickett had been dreading ever since he'd made his deal with the devil. "Kit," he began, seating himself on the chair, "come here, will you? There's something I need to talk to you about."

Kit climbed out from under his threadbare blanket and approached Pickett's chair. "What is it?"

"Kit," Pickett said again, putting his hand on the boy's shoulder as he struggled for words, "you need to understand— you need to be prepared—" He broke off, took a deep breath, and tried again. "You know, don't you, that I won't be allowed to survive?"

22

In Which the Brothers Pickett Part Ways

K it stared at Pickett, eyes wide and gleaming with what
might (although it was hard to tell in the uncertain light)
have been unshed tears.

"They can't let me just walk away," Pickett explained. "I
know too much."

"You could promise not to tell anybody," Kit said
urgently.

"You want me to lie? That letter, the one I asked you to
take to Bow Street—it has all the details of the robbery."

Yes, those were definitely tears in the boy's eyes.
"But"—his voice cracked on the word—"but you said I was
going to come and live at your house in Mayfair!"

"And so you are," Pickett assured him. "It's just that,
well, I won't be there." *At least, not in a form you can see,* he
thought. *But if the dead are allowed to watch over the people
they love, then some part of me will always be wherever Julia*

261

is. And speaking of Julia... "My wife will be there, though. Oh, I know you heard what I told Roger, but it's not really that way at all. Her name is Julia. She's very pretty and very kind, and I love her very much. I expect you will, too, once you've come to know her. And then, in a couple of months, there'll be a baby to play with. You'll like being an uncle, won't you?"

Kit shook his head vehemently. "Not without you," he insisted, by this time sobbing in earnest. "I know I said I didn't want you to be my brother, because you weren't brave and strong, but I didn't mean it! You're the b-bravest and b-best p-person I know!"

Pickett made no attempt to refute this charge, unworthy of it though he knew himself to be, but gathered the boy onto his lap and murmured comforting words into the disheveled brown curls so like his own. Some time later—he scarcely knew whether it had been minutes or hours—the boy's sobs had dwindled to an occasional hiccup, and his slender bulk felt like a dead weight; Kit had fallen asleep, his tousled head pressed into the curve of his elder brother's neck. Thinking the boy would be far more comfortable in his own bed, Pickett slid his arm beneath Kit's knees and braced himself to stand up with his burden, but the boy mumbled a faint protest and burrowed in more closely still. Abandoning this tactic, Pickett closed his eyes and pressed his cheek into the nest of curls.

And so they slept, the brothers Pickett, until the appointed hour.

* * *

"Pssst! Kit!" Pickett whispered close against the boy's ear. "Wake up! They're moving around upstairs. I don't want

Roger to come down and find me untied."

Kit stirred and muttered something incomprehensible.

"Kit!" Pickett gave his brother a little shake. "I need you to wake up. You've got to tie me to the chair." *The things you never thought you'd hear yourself say...* "Wake up, Kit!"

Kit's eyes opened and he blinked several times, his sleepy gaze taking in his empty pallet as well as his brother, upon whose lap he had apparently passed the night. He slid off Pickett's knees and onto his own two feet, and stood looking fixedly down at them.

"I thought—I hoped maybe it was just a dream."

"No, I'm afraid not," Pickett said, bending to lash his left ankle to the leg of the chair. "We've got a busy few hours ahead of us, so we'd best get moving. Do you remember what to do?"

"I think so," Kit said without enthusiasm, "but—but I don't think I *can!* I'm not brave like you are!"

Pickett had already set to work on his right ankle, but at Kit's anguished tone, he sat upright. He'd thought the lad would be embarrassed by any reminder of the weakness he'd shown a few hours earlier, but apparently he was wrong.

"Not brave?" he echoed incredulously. "You? I've only been here a little over twenty-four hours; you've been at Roger's mercy for weeks, forced to climb through windows and down chimney flues—"

"That's not the same as being brave!" Kit insisted. "I only did it because I was afraid of what he would do to me if I didn't."

Pickett set his hands on the boy's shoulders and looked

263

him squarely in the eye. "Listen, Kit. Bravery isn't the same thing as not being afraid. Being brave just means you're determined to do what has to be done, even if you don't want to. And I don't just *think* you can do that; I *know* you can! And do you know how I know?"

"How?" Kit asked, returning Pickett's gaze with an expression on his face that was half hope and half doubt.

"Because you're a Pickett," his elder brother said firmly. "And we Picketts do whatever we must. It's how we survive growing up in the rookery. Do you understand?"

Kit's head lifted, and his attempt at a firm jaw might have been funny if it hadn't been so pitiable. *Who would have thought*, Pickett wondered, *that I could grow so attached to any spawn of Moll's?*

Aloud, he said, "I've got my ankles, but I need you to tie my hands. And hurry; I think I hear them coming down the stairs."

This suspicion was proved correct a few seconds later, when the door rattled and then swung open to reveal Jud, bearing down upon Pickett with a knife.

"All right, then, let's go."

Pickett held his breath as Jud slashed through the ropes that he and Kit had only just succeeded in tying. He suspected the knots would not have borne close inspection, so it was probably just as well that Jud chose this way of freeing him, little though he liked the blade in such close contact to his skin. Unbound at last, he stood and stretched his arms and legs in a gesture entirely unfeigned; although he had not been tied fast the entire time, as Jud supposed, he had supported Kit's weight for most of the night, which amounted to very nearly the same thing.

Having released the captive, Jud returned to the outer room, leaving the brothers alone.

Pickett stooped and picked up the toy soldier that lay on Kit's unused pallet. "Don't forget this fellow."

"John."

"Hmm?"

"That's his name," Kit said, clutching his prize. "I named him John. After you, I guess you could say. I mean, I used to pretend he was you. Before I met the real you."

"I'm—honored," Pickett said, and meant it. Feeling some further response was called for, he added, "I'm glad I got to meet you, Kit. Even if only for a little while."

Kit gave him a rather timid little smile, but whatever he might have said was interrupted by Roger. "Aren't you ready yet? Time's wasting."

As if in proof of this statement, the bells of a distant church tolled twice. St. Giles-in-the-Fields, Pickett thought, or perhaps St. Paul's—the church in Covent Garden, not the cathedral. Any native Londoner worth his salt—a group of which Pickett was certainly a member—could identify any one of the City's churches by the sound of its bells, and thus ascertain his location within a few streets. At the moment, however, Pickett could not bring his mind to focus on the conundrum. He told himself that it hardly mattered; wherever he was, he would not remain there for long.

"Coming," he said, and left the room with Kit at his heels.

"What's this?" Roger scowled down at the boy. "Go back to bed, boy! Like I told you before, you're not needed for this job."

If Roger had previously been unaware of the shift in Kit's allegiance, his suspicions were now fully roused by the fact that his little snakesman, far from returning to his pallet on the floor, cast uncertain eyes up at his brother.

"There's been a change of plans," Pickett informed the leader of the cabal. "The boy is going now."

Without waiting for a response, he strode over to the table, picked up the thick coil of rope that Jud had bought the day before, and slipped it up his arm and onto his shoulder, as if the matter of Kit's future were quite settled.

"Well?" he prompted, seeing Roger glaring at him with a very ugly look in his pale eyes. "Hadn't we best be off? As you said, time's wasting."

Roger was not accustomed to having his will crossed, and did not take at all kindly to the experience. "Not with him, we aren't," he ground out through clenched teeth.

"No, there is not the least need for him to accompany us," said Pickett, readily conceding the point. "I only meant that he's leaving your service as of now, and not after the job is done."

"Roger, our plans—" Jud began, only to be cut short.

"Hold your tongue!" Roger snapped. Turning back to Pickett, he said, "D'you think I'm going to leave the little bastard free to blab to every tag, rag, and bobtail between here and the river?"

"I shouldn't think you would have to worry," Pickett

said. "A boy his age, incoherent with fear and exhaustion—even if he should try to tell, I doubt many people could make sense of his story at all, and still less would believe it."

"You want I should draw his cork again, Rog'?" Jud cracked his knuckles and balled his fists in anticipation.

"Do that, and I might be too badly injured to break into the bank at all," said Pickett, unfazed.

Jud gave a low chuckle. "Think you've got us at a stand, don't you? You'll be singing a different tune when I start breaking the brat's fingers, one by one."

"You harm one hair on his head," Pickett said, his voice low and menacing, "and the deal's off. You can sing for your gold, for you'll get no help from me." He turned to Roger. "Well? What's it going to be? You haven't got all night, not if you intend to sail at dawn."

"Damn you," Roger breathed. Sweat beaded on his brow in spite of the chill of the unheated room, and Pickett knew he was struggling mightily against the urge to give Jud the permission he so obviously craved, weighing against it the knowledge that he had to keep Pickett alive if he was to claim the treasure that was almost within his grasp. "Just remember, I've got a knife, and I'm not afraid to use it. One false move out of you, and I'll cut you to ribbons. Aye, and I'll do it with a smile on my face, just give me half a chance and see if I won't."

And with this threat, he turned, picked up the lantern, and quitted the house, leaving the others to follow.

Even after leaving the house, Pickett could not find his bearings at once. The narrow courtyard revealed by the lantern

SHERI COBB SOUTH

might have been any one of dozens, perhaps hundreds, of similar courtyards off similar backstreets throughout London.

"Be off with you, boy," Roger told Kit, grabbing him by the shoulder and giving him a shove. "And don't bother turning up here looking to be fed, for me and Jud won't be coming back."

But Kit, it appeared, was made of sterner stuff. "I—I want the bird," he said. "Jenny's bird. I won't leave it here all by itself to starve, with nobody to feed it."

Roger muttered several choice suggestions under his breath as to what Kit might do with the bird, but ordered Jud, "Go in and get the damned bird. I'll not have the little bastard spoil everything at the last minute with his caterwauling."

Jud darted into the house and returned a moment later with the cage, a cloth thrown over it to guarantee the silence of its feathered occupant. Kit, all too familiar with the tactics favored by the two men, peered under the cloth to make sure he hadn't wrung the bird's neck out of pure spite. Apparently satisfied with what he saw, he took the cage from Jud, glanced up at Pickett, and, receiving a nod, set off down the alley. He had hardly gone twenty paces when he stopped, turned, and ran back, the birdcage swinging wildly as he flung his arms around his brother.

"It's all right," Pickett said soothingly. "You'll be fine. Just—if Julia asks where I am, just tell her I was unavoidably detained."

"Un—?" echoed Kit, stumbling over the unfamiliar words.

Pickett shook his head. "Never mind. Just give her my

268

love."

Kit nodded, then turned and retraced his steps. He didn't falter this time, but paused at the end the alley and gave Pickett one long, last look before rounding the corner into the street (Pickett still wasn't sure which street it was) and disappearing from view.

It seemed to Pickett that there was something of finality in that look, something quite aside from the fact that he would never see his brother again. No, it was the knowledge that no one would ever look at him that way again, with respect and admiration, perhaps even love, in their eyes. He had not much liked the man he'd pretended to be in order to win Roger's cooperation, but within the next hour or two, he would become that man in fact: one who worked both sides of the law, and who wasn't above playing one side against the other in order to achieve his own ends. And it was as that man that he would die tonight, hated by those he had betrayed and despised by his former colleagues, to whom he had betrayed them.

He raised a hand in farewell, although he was not quite certain to whom he was bidding goodbye: the brother he had just found, or the man he had once been.

23

In Which Julia Makes Her Brother-in-Law's Acquaintance

K it let out a sigh of relief as he turned the corner into Bow Street from Long Acre. Or perhaps he was merely out of breath; he had run the last part of the route, after having suffered a fright when a man—drunk, or mad, or perhaps both—had lurched out of the shadows and made as if to snatch at him. In his eagerness to escape, he had stepped on the tail of a feral cat who had taken violent exception to this treatment, spitting at him with teeth bared and claws unsheathed. So startled was he by this secondary attack that he'd dropped the birdcage, and then was obliged to rescue King George from a cat who had lost all interest in Kit when a poultry dinner had suddenly presented itself.

But at last he'd reached Bow Street. He could see Covent Garden Theatre looming ahead on the right, gleaming pale in the darkness, and beyond that, just out of view around the curve that gave the street its name, was the Bow Street Public

Office. He slowed his pace, and by the time he entered its portals, his breathing had returned to something very nearly normal.

Several men were present even at so late an hour, most of them gathered around a large map that had been pinned to the wall. All of them turned at the sound of his entrance. There was silence for a moment that seemed to Kit like an eternity, then one of the men spoke.

"Mighty late for a sprout like you to be wandering about." The words, spoken in a kindly tone by a man with grizzled hair and muttonchop whiskers, did not appear to be threatening, nor did he seem to represent any danger when he added, "And if your name ain't Pickett, you may call me a Dutchman."

Aside from his brother's name, only one word of this speech made any sense to Kit, and so he asked in some bewilderment, "Are—are you going to Amsterdam, too?"

A burst of laughter was the only answer he received.

"Amsterdam?" the man echoed. "Well, now, that's a long way for a lad to be going so late at night. You'll get your feet wet, too," he added with a wink.

"I have a letter," Kit said, tugging at one corner of the paper that stuck out of his shoe. "I'm supposed to give it to—"

Kit had not noticed another door, hidden as it was behind the magistrate's bench, but at that moment it opened, and another man entered the room, his bearing erect although he walked with a slight limp.

"Mr. Dixon, has anyone thought to check the—" He

broke off abruptly at the sight of Kit. "*You!* I hadn't thought you would be so obliging as to turn up on our doorstep, but now that you're here, I'm placing you under arrest for the—"

Kit didn't wait to hear more. He uttered a strangled cry, then dropped the letter and took to his heels, while King George added his own piercing cries to the general confusion. Maxwell made as if to give chase, but the magistrate's voice halted him before he reached the door.

"Let it go, Mr. Maxwell."

"But, sir"—he gestured toward the rectangle of blackness beyond the door, which the boy had not bothered to close—"that was—"

"Aye, I know," Mr. Colquhoun agreed as he joined the others gathered around the map.

"If we could bring the boy in, we might persuade him to talk. He could lead us to the others."

"He might," conceded the magistrate. "Or we could have a look at that paper he dropped, and see what we might learn from it."

Mr. Dixon, who had been roasting the boy about walking to Amsterdam, now stooped and retrieved the paper, then handed it to Mr. Colquhoun. The magistrate unfolded it and scanned it from beneath beetling white brows.

TO WHOM IT MAY CONCERN: (it read)
THE BANK OF ENGLAND WILL BE ROBBED TONIGHT SHORTLY AFTER 2 A.M. BY THE SAME MEN WHO BROKE INTO COUTTS. THEY ARE ARMED. SHOOT TO KILL.

Nothing could be discerned from the handwriting, which consisted of neat block capital letters that offered no clues as to the writer's identity. Unless…

He peered more closely at the paper, wishing he hadn't left the spectacles he wore for reading on the desk in his office. Yes, there were distinct signs of smudging. Granted, the slight blurring of the letters was quite possibly the natural result of its being tucked into the lad's shoe while he walked for what was very likely a considerable distance. But it might also be the result of someone dragging the side of his hand across the words he had already written—someone, in fact, writing with his left hand. And although John Pickett was certainly not the only left-handed person in London, it could surely be no coincidence that this letter had been delivered by his half-brother.

At least he was alive, or had been until quite recently; to be sure, no trace of his body had been discovered in any of the ditches, canals, or other places where the bodies of murder victims were wont to turn up. Where, then, had he been for the last two days, and why hadn't he delivered the message in person? The magistrate heaved a weary sigh. Perhaps he should have given Maxwell leave to pursue the lad, after all, so they could've had the tale straight from the horse's mouth, so to speak. He covered his own mouth and yawned widely. He had not left the Bow Street Public Office since he'd learned of his protégé's disappearance from that young man's distraught wife, and her anxiety had communicated itself to him. He feared the strain—to say nothing of the lack of sleep—was beginning to affect his reasoning.

"Excuse me," Maxwell's voice interrupted this train of thought, "I don't want to rush you, sir, but the letter says shortly after two, and it's almost half past. Shouldn't we— some of us, at least—be heading toward Threadneedle Street?"

"In a minute," the magistrate answered with a heavy sigh. "First, Mr. Maxwell, will you step into my office for a moment? I'm afraid I have a confession to make. I owe you an explanation, along with an apology…"

* * *

Julia, going to bed alone for the second time in as many nights, was roused from an uneasy slumber by a light scratching on the door of her bedchamber. Fully awake on the instant, she flung back the counterpane and snatched up her dressing gown.

"*John!*"

But when she threw open the door, it was not her husband, but her butler who stood there.

"I'm afraid not, madam," he said apologetically. "I'm sorry to disturb you at so late an hour, but there is a child downstairs who—well, I think you had best come down and see for yourself."

"Yes—yes, of course." She could think of only one child who might come to her house at such an hour, although why he should arrive alone was beyond her powers of imagination. "You need not wait up; I shall see to our guest."

Except, of course, that he was no guest. This could be none other than her husband's young half-brother, and he had come to stay. Arranging her face in what she hoped would appear to be a welcoming smile, she descended the stairs and entered the drawing room.

He stood in the middle of the room with his back to the door, so she had the briefest of moments to examine him unobserved. Her first impressions were not encouraging. His clothing was threadbare and dirty, and his hair a tangled mass of brown curls. In fact, he bore all the appearance of one who would be greatly improved for having been plunged into a tub of soapy water and given a good scrubbing.

Still, she tried to hide her revulsion and say in what she hoped was a friendly tone, "Mr. Christopher Pickett, I presume. Or should I call you Kit?"

He jumped, obviously startled at the sound of her voice, and turned. And Julia, who had dreaded with every fiber of her being this child's invasion of her home, looked into the wide brown eyes regarding her with an odd mixture of hope and fear, and lost her heart to him just as completely as, a year earlier, she had lost it to his elder brother.

"Oh, how very like your brother you are!" she cried warmly, holding out her hand to him. "I am your sister— John's wife, you know—and you must call me Julia. But surely you did not come all this way alone! Where is John?"

Up to this point, Kit had been staring at his newly discovered sister-in-law in rapt astonishment. His brother had said something about a baby, and although Kit had a general knowledge of where babies came from—privacy was a luxury not usually afforded to the denizens of St. Giles—the idea that this glorious creature would allow his very own brother to do *that* to her was enough to deprive him of speech.

But now, discovering in this angelic being an un-expectedly sympathetic audience, Kit blurted out, "He's gone off with Roger and Jud to rob the Bank of England."

Julia regarded him with a puzzled smile. "John has—*John* is going to rob the Bank of England? Surely you must have misunderstood—misheard, perhaps—"

Kit shook his head emphatically. "He's gone off to rob it, sure as check. And they'll kill him after he's done it—he told me so himself!" He reached down and pulled off his shoe, then extracted a creased rectangle of paper from it. "He told me to give you this."

As she took it from him, her hackles rose; she recognized the paper as having been torn from his occurrence book. She unfolded the single sheet, and as she scanned the lines written in the familiar hand, she felt strangely as if the ground beneath her feet were beginning to crumble. Like one in a trance, she moved to the sofa and sat down, still staring at the paper as she struggled to make sense of the words written there.

My dearest love,

You will no doubt have guessed by now that things have gone amiss. I was able to retrieve my brother, but only by offering my services in exchange for his. By the time you read this, I will be assisting Roger and his henchman in robbing the Bank of England. I cannot reconcile it with my conscience to take part in such a scheme without informing Bow Street of it, even though to do so means that I will be arrested along with them. In order to spare you the indignities of a trial and public execution, I have warned them that the robbers will be armed (which I have no doubt will be true, at least in Roger's case) and urged them to shoot to kill. Please try to see that the baby does not grow up thinking too badly of its father.

And please don't grieve for me. I have known more happiness in six months than many men do in a lifetime, and I go to my fate content in the knowledge that by doing so, I give my brother a chance to find some happiness of his own. God knows he's had little enough in his life up to now. I leave him to your care, knowing that he could not be in better hands. I believe you will find that he looks very much like me, and I hope that this will serve to soften your kind heart toward him, as well as keep alive the memory of one who is, was, and evermore shall be

> *yours,*
> *John Pickett*

He had informed Bow Street, or so he said, and yet she'd heard nothing from Mr. Colquhoun, who had promised to send word as soon as there was any news to be had of him.

"Tell me, Kit—" How odd, that her voice should sound so level and calm, as if the world had not just come to an end! "Did you deliver a similar letter to Bow Street? On your way here, perhaps?"

The boy nodded. "Uh-huh."

"And—and what did Mr. Colquhoun—the magistrate—what did he say?"

"I don't know," confessed Kit, shamefaced. "One of the men said he was arresting me, and I was that scared, I just threw down the letter and ran."

Mr. Colquhoun knows, Julia thought, but found little comfort in the realization. He might know about the robbery, but did he know—or would he deduce—that one of the robbers he was preparing to shoot was one of his own men, one whom he loved like a son? Should she go to warn him? But go where—to Bow Street, or his residence in Mayfair? In either case, she might not arrive there in time, for if the robbery were indeed already underway, then every available man would surely have been dispatched to the bank. Her precipitate arrival in the midst of a robbery—or worse—could only increase the danger, not only to John, but to the entire Bow Street force as well. Then, too, there was the boy to consider, as well as the child she carried.

She forced a reassuring smile. "I don't blame you for running. It must have been very frightening." Still, she could not deny that it would have been helpful if he'd lingered long enough to discover what the letter had said. For the first time, she noticed that he clutched what appeared to be a tiny bird cage, sketchily covered with a lopsided cloth. "But what's this you've brought with you?"

"It's a bird—a goldfinch. It was Jenny's." His face clouded. "But Jenny's gone, and Roger and Jud are going to Amsterdam, and I couldn't just let it be left all alone, could I?"

His tormented expression gave her to understand that it was not only the bird whose abandonment troubled him. He knew what it was to be "left all alone," first by the mother who had sold him, then by the criminal "master" who had made use of him until he'd received a better offer, and, finally, by the half-brother who had been forced to abandon him in order to set him free.

And just that simply, the decision was made. A bath would have to wait until morning, but she would see that he was given something to eat and tucked into bed for what remained of the night. It had been her husband's last (she would not let herself think "dying") wish that she take care of the boy, and she would do it to the very best of her ability.

It was the last thing she could ever do for him.

24

In Which John Pickett Reverts to His Old Ways

Still panting slightly from exertion, Pickett stood on the roof of the Bank of England, surveying the City from an angle few Londoners ever had the opportunity to experience. Roger was somewhere below, climbing up the rope with the dark lantern tied about his waist, but for now, Pickett felt as if the City was his and his alone. To the south, the sweep of the Thames could be traced, a ribbon of black broken at intervals by the bobbing of ships' lights tipping each tiny wave with gold. Less than half a mile away to the west, the bulk of St. Paul's great dome was more sensed than seen, distinguishable only by the lights it blotted out. The stars overhead shone almost unnaturally bright, and so close that it seemed as if he could reach up and touch one. He had a sudden mental image of himself stretching up his arm and plucking one from the sky, and giving it to Julia to wear in her hair.

Julia…

Julia, still farther to the west and then south, beyond the sharp bend in the river…

Julia, asleep in her bed, never dreaming that she would awaken in the morning a widow.

A *thunk* and a curse signaled Roger's arrival, and a moment later he unshuttered the lantern, dispelling the magic. Still, Pickett couldn't help feeling that view of London made what he was about to do almost worth it. Well, that and the look on Roger's face upon being told that they would not be picking the locks and entering through the Lothbury arch, but scaling the curtain wall that surrounded the bank and entering the Bullion Yard from above.

"Seems to me—would've been a hell of a lot easier—to come in through the Lothbury entrance," Roger said between gasps, breathless from his climb.

"It would have," Pickett agreed. "It would also have made us much too visible, given the number of street lamps flanking the arch. The same goes for the Threadneedle entrance. But Princes Street is narrow and darker, and most of the houses and shops on the opposite side were demolished when the bank was expanded, so—"

"Arright, arright, keep yer hair on," grumbled Roger. "I said we'd do it your way, didn't I? So what's next?"

Pickett looked out over the roof of the bank, a fantastical landscape comprising more than three acres of domes, skylights, and courtyards, these last seen only as rectangles of deeper black that spelled certain doom, should either of them be careless enough to set a foot wrong. If he were to walk ahead some little distance and to his right, he would be standing directly over the spot where he, very much on his dignity, had informed the bank's governor that he possessed no latent tendencies toward theft.

At least I was half right, he thought with a sigh. *They aren't "latent" anymore.*

He glanced uneasily to his left. Here was the weakness in making their approach from Princes Street, although the same danger would have existed had they chosen the western side of Lothbury. For it was in this northwestern corner of the bank that several of the bank's officers lived with their families—a situation complicated by the fact that Pickett, in spite of the Banbury tale he'd spun for Roger's benefit, had no idea how these residences were laid out and, thus, no idea how best to minimize the danger of discovery.

"Do you see that courtyard?" he asked Roger, pointing toward the center of the bank, and the only courtyard that was not a true rectangle. "The one whose northern edge is bowed? That's the Bullion Yard. The Bullion Office opens just off it. That's where we'll make our entrance."

He turned and loosened the rope that had taken Jud three tries to snag around one of the many decorative elements adorning the roofline, much as one might attempt the ring toss at Bartholomew Fair. Once the loop was slack, he slipped it off its anchor and wound it into a coil, prepared to take it to the Bullion Yard and use it for their descent.

"Oh, no," Roger said grimly, snatching the coil of rope from his grasp. "I'll be going first this time. I'm not giving you time to stuff your pockets full of gold while I'm still hanging from a rope."

"We'll both be 'hanging from a rope' if you don't keep your voice down! Like I said, there are people living here. And watch where you step! Don't go putting your foot through a skylight."

Roger adjusted the slits of the lantern to permit more light, then stalked off across the roof, muttering under his breath. Pickett, left alone, noticed with some misgiving that it was not quite as dark as it should have been, given the absence of the lantern. He turned to his left, and felt a knot forming in the pit of his stomach. The roof opened up on a courtyard a short distance away, near enough that Pickett could see the windows of the top floor. The curtains were parted, and in the faint candlelight he could see a small boy in a long nightdress standing in the window and watching him with wide-eyed interest. As his eyes met the child's, the boy raised one hand in a shy wave. Pickett put up his own hand and waggled his fingers, and received a bashful smile in return.

"Tommy!" cried a woman's voice. faint but clear in the quiet of the night. "What are you doing out of bed at this hour?"

The boy turned. "I'm waving at the man on the roof."

Pickett froze where he stood, unsure whether to dive for the shadows or remain motionless until the danger had passed.

" 'Man on the roof,' indeed!" scolded the woman. "You know Mummy doesn't like it when you tell tales! Now, come back to bed at once."

To Pickett's immense relief, little Tommy did as he was told. The curtains fell back into place, and Pickett closed his eyes and let out a long sigh of relief. Danger averted, at least for the nonce, he picked his way carefully across the roof in Roger's wake.

By the time he reached the big hole in the roof that indicated the Bullion Yard, Roger had the rope securely fastened for their descent, and tied the shuttered lantern once more about his waist with a short length of twine. Pickett watched as Roger inched his way down the rope, and waited until the lantern's shutters flicked open once, then twice, signaling that the rope was free for his own descent.

"Buck up, old boy," he muttered to himself as he took the rope in a firm grip. "At least this time the building's not burning down around you."

Nor, for that matter, was he carrying Julia on his back, as he had been on the night of the Drury Lane Theatre fire; his only burden now was the two canvas sacks he'd tied about his waist, just as Roger had done with the lantern.

No, it wasn't the fear of falling that tied his stomach in knots and made the palms of his hands slick with sweat. It was the waiting, the wondering how, and when, the Bow Street officers would intervene. If they intervened at all. Had Kit delivered his letter there, or had his instructions to the boy been overruled by the wariness and suspicion toward the law that seemed bred into the children of the rookery from birth?

But if Kit had delivered it—what then? Had his warning given them sufficient time to get into position? Were Bow Street officers in place even now, ready to shoot him as he and Roger made their escape with their ill-gotten gain? Granted, he'd seen no sign of anyone when they'd first arrived at the bank, but that didn't necessarily mean anything. Mr.

Colquhoun wasn't such a fool as to let any of his officers accost them too soon; there was, after all, nothing illegal about three men walking up Cheapside with nothing between them but a lantern and a couple of empty sacks. On the other hand, if they were apprehended as they exited the bank carrying bags bulging with gold ingots...

Yes, the shot would come a little later, while they were making their escape. Would he see the man who fired it? Recognize what was coming just before he felt the impact? He rather hoped not.

He glanced down at Roger waiting below, barely visible by the narrow slits of light peeking through the lantern's shutters. It was a pity, in a way, that Roger and Jud would also have a swift, merciful death without having to answer for their other crimes, including the murders of both Jenny and that poor watchman. It couldn't be helped, though, not if he was to spare Julia the ordeal of his own trial and hanging upon the scaffold at Newgate.

And then his feet were on the ground, and it was time for the next step. Three large bays were set into the eastern wall of the courtyard, each one topped with a high, arched window, and each one opening onto the Bullion Office. It was here, to these three bays, that wagons would be drawn up and loaded with gold or silver bound for the mint. Pickett had no doubt that all three would be tightly closed and locked to prevent anyone from liberating any of the precious metal before its time. A quick test of the three doors confirmed this assumption.

"So much for this brilliant plan of yours," grumbled

Roger, observing the proceedings from over his shoulder.

"Shhh!" Pickett studied the three bays in the dim light afforded by the lantern. None of the three seemed to offer any advantage over the others, so far as shadows went; on a moonless night, all were equally dark. Still, he had not forgotten his harrowing encounter with the child in the window. He tipped his head back to study the windows that overlooked the Bullion Yard from all four sides, trying to assess how the bays might appear to anyone looking down from above. It appeared that here, too, there was nothing to choose between the three, for they were almost nakedly exposed. The best he could hope for was that the windows belonged to bank offices, or the room where the new paper money was printed, or any other part of the bank likely to be unoccupied at so late an hour. In the meantime, he would be wise to get the door open quickly so that they might shut themselves up in the Bullion Office, safe from the prying eyes of any bank officer with nocturnal habits.

Pickett had instructed Jud to purchase some long, pointed tool, but the awl he'd bought from a tinker in the City was far too thick for the purpose, so in the end, Pickett had been obliged to ask Roger for one of Jenny's hairpins. He'd been more than a little uneasy at broaching what he'd thought must be a delicate subject, but Roger had been disconcertingly unemotional about this reminder of his lover's death, and at his own hands. Pickett had been simultaneously relieved and offended, for Jenny's sake, that she had been forgotten so easily. Pickett had not forgotten, however, and it was with silent thanks to the girl that he withdrew this instrument from his pocket and knelt before the big bay door.

"Give me a little light," he instructed Roger, and his accomplice adjusted the shutters of the dark lantern so that they focused a narrow beam of light onto the lock.

Seconds later, Pickett heard the faint *click* that informed him of his success. After that, it was the work of a moment to push the door open, duck inside, and close it again, sealing the pair of them in inky blackness unrelieved by starlight.

"Good work," Roger said aloud, opening the lantern's shutters completely. "I'm obliged to you."

"Shhh! Keep your voice down and close that lantern." It was probably true that there was no one near enough to hear them, but it was quite possible that the light might be seen through the three arched windows by anyone who cared to look. Either way, Pickett was taking no chances.

Roger looked annoyed, but did as he was told, closing the lantern's shutters until it emitted only enough light to allow them to look about the room. A fireplace was set into one wall, and near it stood the desk where someone—a senior clerk, perhaps, or one of the bank's officers—would keep a tally of every gold bar and silver ingot that passed in or out of the courtyard through which they had just come. A number of wooden crates were stacked against the wall opposite the bays, and here, unless Pickett missed his guess...

He approached the nearest crate, and was relieved to discover that the top had been removed; they had not brought a crowbar or any other tool with which they could have prized it open. He reached inside and withdrew a part of its contents. It was an elongated rectangle, somewhat heavy for its size,

287

and when Roger turned the lantern on it, a dull yellow gleamed in the light.

"*Gold*," Roger breathed almost reverently. He reached into the crate and drew out another gold ingot, then bit into it and regarded with satisfaction the shallow indentation made by his teeth. "If I were to send Jud back for the wheelbarrow—"

"No," Pickett said firmly. "There's no time for that, and even if there was, by the time you'd filled it up, the thing would be too heavy to push. We take only what'll fit in these two sacks."

Roger glared resentfully at him, but made no attempt to argue the matter. For the next several minutes, there was no sound but that of increasingly labored breathing as the two men filled the canvas sacks with the contents of the crate.

"Don't fill it so full it won't close," Pickett cautioned, cinching his own bag shut by the drawstring at its neck. "You don't want to lose any and, perhaps more to the point, you don't want anyone on the ship to catch a glimpse and start asking uncomfortable questions."

Once the bags were full, the men slung them onto their backs and left the Bullion Office the way they had come. Pickett would have reached for the rope, but Roger stopped him.

"No, you don't! D'you think I'm going to let you leave me down here while you take off with the gold? *I'll* be going first, if you don't mind!"

Since his tone made it very clear that he intended to scale the rope first whether Pickett minded or not, Pickett stepped back and surrendered his place to his cohort. Still, Roger's suggestion had raised a possibility Pickett had not previously considered, and he resolved not to give Roger the opportunity to carry out the plot he'd just been accused of.

The thrashing of the rope indicated the progress of Roger's ascent long after the darkness had swallowed him up, and Pickett wished it did not call quite so vividly to his mind the death throes of a man sentenced to the gallows. At last, however, its wild movements dwindled to a gentle swaying, and the light from the dark lantern flashed once, then twice; Roger, it seemed, had reached the roof. Pickett seized the end of the rope and knotted it through the loop of the sack's drawstring, then knotted it again for good measure: it would not do for the sack to fall, for the noise of its striking the paving stones would surely be loud enough to waken the soundest sleeper. Satisfied, he gave two sharp tugs to the rope as a signal to Roger, then stepped aside while his co-conspirator hauled up the rope and its burden of gold.

It returned only seconds later, giving Pickett to understand that Roger had put his knife to good use rather than waste time struggling to untie the knots. Pickett tied it to the remaining sack, once again doubling the knot to make certain it would hold. This time, however, he did not step back while Roger pulled it up, leaving him alone in the courtyard. Instead, he grabbed the rope a few feet above the sack and began to climb hand over hand. He thought he heard a hastily stifled exclamation from the man on the roof, and felt a certain satisfaction that Roger had not, in the end, had it all his own way.

Neither of them spoke of it once Pickett reached the roof, however; the next minutes were crucial for more reasons than one, and there was no time to waste on conversation. Pickett unfastened the rope, wound it into a loose coil, and looped it over his shoulder, then hefted one of the sacks while Roger grabbed the other. Once again, they made their way across the roof until they reached the arcade that marked the Princes Street entrance and here, once again, Pickett tied one end of the rope through the sack's drawstring while Roger made the other end fast to its anchor. Then Roger slowly lowered the rope until they heard, in the stillness, the faint *clink* of the ingots bumping together as it reached the ground. He waited a moment, then pulled on the rope.

He stopped abruptly. "What the devil—?"

"What's wrong?" Pickett asked, bracing himself.

"Jud hasn't untied it." He lifted the lantern and flicked the shutters open and closed, open and closed. A moment later he tried the rope again, but the same resistance met his efforts. "Hsst!" he called as loudly as he dared. "Jud!"

The voice that answered him was not Jud's. Instead, a man with a pronounced Scottish burr bellowed, "We have you surrounded! Give yourselves up!"

Roger wheeled about to confront Pickett, the lantern that lit his face from below giving him an eerie, almost demonic look. "*You bloody bastard,*" he breathed, and lunged with his knife.

290

25

In Which Mr. Colquhoun Makes His Move

M r. Colquhoun, accompanied by as many men as could be spared from their regular duties or called in at short notice, set out from the Bow Street Public Office not long after Kit had fled. As the magistrate had no desire to stumble upon the robbers en route, he eschewed the most direct route via Cheapside in favor of a more southerly course, traveling east along Fleet Street and skirting the churchyard of St. Paul's Cathedral before turning north into Walbrook. He drew up as they neared the Lord Mayor's residence, as near to the bank as they could approach and still be out of view of anyone skulking about its southern or eastern borders, and waited for the stragglers to catch up. Once all the men had gathered around him, he turned to Maxwell.

"Well, Mr. Maxwell, this is your case; what do you suggest?"

Maxwell frowned thoughtfully. "There are four

entrances, one on each side," he said at last. "We'll need at least one man at each entrance, with an extra man—two, if possible—to ferry messages between the four. We'll need to discover exactly where and how the robbers managed to gain access when the place is surrounded by a curtain wall like a medieval castle, and make sure we seal off that point of entry so that it can't be used as an escape route. Then, too, I believe there are a few bank officers living on the premises—"

"In the new northwest expansion," Mr. Colquhoun concurred, nodding. "The corner of Princes Street and Lothbury."

"I expect we'd best try to rouse at least one of them. If he can assume responsibility for the residents' safety, it would free up our own men to secure the building and apprehend the thieves."

Again, Mr. Colquhoun agreed. "Have them send a man down to unlock the doors, in case we have to come in after the robbers. I'll admit, I'd rather we didn't; the place is like a labyrinth, with entirely too many places for intruders to hide. The other bank officers should remain with the women and children, in case our friends have any ideas about taking hostages. You, Mr. Douglas"—the magistrate signaled to a member of the Night Patrol—"walk down Princes and gather up any pebbles you may stumble over along the way. Once you reach the corner, chuck them at the windows on the upper floors until you get someone's attention. But no broken glass, mind you! We don't want to interrupt the robbers before they can finish their business. Mr. Carson, go with him. Between the pair of you, surely one of you can hit your target."

"Right-o," Carson said. "But if we're going to let them get away with theft, why are we even here?"

"Did I say we were going to let them get away? I don't intend to make an arrest for breaking and entering, Mr. Carson. When we arrest them, it'll be for robbery—and murder, if I can make the charge stick. As for theft, they may find that getting their hands on a fortune is the easy part. Getting out of the bank with it is likely to prove another matter entirely."

He went on to assign the men to their positions. Since Maxwell had done most of the work on the case, it was only fitting that he should cover the main entrance on Threadneedle Street. The Lothbury entrance went to Dixon, who had been with Bow Street long enough to understand the significance of its wide arched passage, and exactly what lay at the other end.

"One more thing," Mr. Colquhoun added, after all the assignments had been made. "There are to be no shots fired, do you understand?"

"With respect, sir," Maxwell protested, "the note said—"

"Yes, Mr. Maxwell, I know what the note said. But these men must be taken alive, so they can answer for their crimes in a court of law." *And so they can be made to tell me Mr. Pickett's whereabouts,* he added mentally. *Or at least say what they've done with his body.* "If I hear a gunshot from anyone," he added, once more addressing the group as a whole, "your life had better be in mortal peril. All right, let's go."

The men dispersed to their respective posts, and Mr. Colquhoun took up a position at the corner of Threadneedle and Princes Streets from whence he could observe the proceedings at two of the four entrances. It was not long before Harry Carson came hurrying back.

"A rope," he said, panting slightly from the exertion of moving as nearly to a run as he dared without making any noise that might betray them all. "There's a rope hanging from the arcade above the Princes Street entrance, in the shadows between two streetlamps. Looks like they've got in through the roof."

"The roof," Mr. Colquhoun echoed, frowning thoughtfully. "Aye, and half a dozen courtyards open to the sky. It could be done, particularly if a man were not squeamish about heights." He set out at a fast pace down Princes Street with Carson at his heels.

"One more thing, Mr. C. We discovered a man there, too."

"Did you, now?" the magistrate asked sharply. "And what did he have to say for himself?"

Carson shook his head. "Nothing. I'm afraid I had to crown him with my truncheon before he could sound the alarm."

"Dead?"

"No, just enjoying a nice little nap. He's likely to have a bit of a head when he awakens, though."

"Very probably," agreed Mr. Colquhoun. "Well done, Mr. Carson."

"Thank you, sir," Harry said, visibly preening.

Alas for Carson, they rejoined Douglas only to find no sign of a rope, nor any other means of unlawful entrance.

"They just pulled it up," Douglas said, lowering his voice to a near-whisper as he came forward to meet them. "I thought it was best not to try and stop them. I hope that's all right," he added doubtfully, trying without much success to read the magistrate's expression in the dark.

"Exactly right, Mr. Douglas," Mr. Colquhoun assured him. "They'll have to come down one way or another, and when they do, we'll be ready for them. Did you manage to rouse any of the bank officers?"

"Not yet, sir. We saw the rope, and thought it was more urgent that we get word to you. Shall I do so now?"

"Aye, but go 'round the corner to the Lothbury side. I don't want any activity along Princes Street to rouse our quarry's suspicions."

The next half-hour seemed like an eternity. Twice Mr. Colquhoun thought he heard a noise that might signal the robbers' return, but both times nothing happened, leaving him to wonder if he had really heard anything at all. After thirty minutes of waiting in silence, he began to worry that he and his men had been discovered and, somehow, outmaneuvered.

"What the devil is taking them so long?" Carson muttered under his breath to no one in particular. "Maybe—"

"Shhh!"

A moment later the sound was repeated, and this time there could be no doubt. The magistrate and his men caught glimpses of a figure—no, two figures—moving about on the roof just above the arcaded entrance, and a moment later something began inching down the wall, something fixed to the end of a long length of rope.

"Rapunzel, Rapunzel," Carson murmured, "let down your—*oof!*" He broke off abruptly when Mr. Colquhoun trod firmly on his foot.

As it approached the ground, the pale bulge revealed itself to be a canvas sack filled with something quite heavy, if the tautness of the rope and the caution with which it was being lowered were anything to judge by. Then it touched the ground with the faint *clink* of metal against metal, and the rope went slack. The rope tightened and loosened again, and a moment later, a faint light overhead flashed once, then twice.

Mr. Colquhoun decided it was time to let their presence be known. "We have you surrounded!" he bellowed. "Give yourselves up!"

Immediately a scuffle broke out between the two men on the roof. "No honor among thieves," the magistrate grumbled.

A loud *clang* sounded as one of the combatants on the roof knocked over the lantern, and its light glinted off the blade of a knife.

"Douglas! Run around to Threadneedle and tell Maxwell to get up there!" commanded the magistrate. He turned to Carson. "How fast can you climb a rope?"

Carson, somewhat taken aback, said, "I don't know. I've never tried."

"It'll have to be the door, then. Get moving!"

Carson bounded up the three steps to the half-moon-shaped portico, but the door held fast. He turned back to Mr. Colquhoun. "It's locked."

"You've got a gun, haven't you?"

"My life isn't in mortal peril," protested Carson, pointing out the obvious.

"It will be if you don't get up there! I said I want both of them taken alive. Now, go!"

Carson drew his pistol, aimed it at the lock, and fired, then yanked the smoking door open and disappeared inside. To the sounds of the struggle on the roof were soon added those of running footsteps, punctuated occasionally by a shout or the slamming of a door.

Mr. Colquhoun, aware of his own limitations, made no effort to join the race to the rooftop, but watched (as much as the darkness allowed) the pitched battle being played out overhead. He could no longer see any light from the lantern— he supposed it must have been kicked aside, either by accident or design—but even without illumination it was obvious that one of the two robbers, most likely the one with the knife, had the upper hand. As far as he could tell, the less fortunate of the two men had been in a crouched position, or possibly kneeling, when his fellow had attacked, and was now obliged to scurry away on his hands and knees, too occupied in trying to avoid the slashing blade to waste precious time in scrambling to his feet. The magistrate could almost find it in his heart to pity the poor fellow, making what use he could of the arches of the arcade for cover as he ducked behind first one and then another, all the while trapped between the deadly blade flailing the air about him on one side and the sheer drop to the street on the other.

And suddenly there were no arches left, and nowhere else

to hide. As the man with the knife bore down upon him, a white, strained face glanced wildly behind him, as if gauging whether to jump. *Don't do it, you fool,* the magistrate silently scolded. *You'll never survive such a fall.* Of course, he was equally unlikely to survive a stabbing, but surely it shouldn't be long now until—

Suddenly the rooftop was swarming with men. Two of them grabbed the arms of the man with the knife—he rather thought they were Dixon and Maxwell—and Maxwell twisted the arm behind the rogue until he dropped his weapon, and it tumbled through the air end over end until it clattered onto the pavement. Mr. Colquhoun walked over to where the knife had fallen and picked it up; it would be added to the one held as evidence in the Coutts burglary. By the time he returned his attention to the action on the roof, a third man had hauled the remaining thief to his feet, and the rasp of metal on metal gave the magistrate to understand that the two men were being put under restraint. Then the entire company left the roof in the same way they had come, taking the two prisoners with them.

When the Bow Street men began to emerge from the bank a few minutes later, it was immediately clear that something was wrong. Their bearing was not that of a group who had successfully apprehended a pair of dangerous thieves in the very act. Instead, they shuffled out the door almost sheepishly. Many of them avoided looking the magistrate in the eye, and the others glanced at him rather shamefacedly before lowering their gaze.

And then the criminals were led out. The first man fit in every particular the description given by Maxwell of the man he'd seen fleeing from Coutts. The other...

The other man stepped off the portico and into the yellow circle of light from the streetlamp, and Mr. Colquhoun caught his breath as the reason for the men's discomfiture became clear. The thief's hands were pinioned behind him, no doubt shackled together at the wrists, and a dark trail of blood ran from a cut just below his cheekbone, probably a vestige of the recent knife attack. He was flanked by two members of the Night Patrol, each gripping one of his arms in case he should make any attempt at escape. Not that he showed any signs of doing so; in fact, he was the picture of misery and shame, the prisoner of two men who possessed not a fraction of his potential between the pair of them.

"I'm sorry, sir," said John Pickett.

* * *

Pickett sat alone on the semi-circular portico, sunk in despair. The Bow Street contingent had dispersed, Maxwell and Dixon having taken Roger and the newly revived Jud into custody. Mr. Colquhoun had commanded Pickett to "wait here," and then entered the bank in the company of one of its grateful officers.

And so he waited, with nothing to do but contemplate his disgrace. It was over. The bank robbery had succeeded beyond his wildest dreams, and Mr. Colquhoun had responded almost exactly as he had hoped. Almost. Except for the fact that he was still alive, disgraced before his colleagues and having lost forever the good opinion of the one man he respected above all others. There was nothing for him now but humiliation: imprisonment at Newgate until his trial in the Old

Bailey, after which he would endure all the shame of a public execution upon the scaffold. Even after he was dead, he would not be laid to rest in a quiet green churchyard. Instead, his body would be cut down and turned over to the Royal College of Surgeons for dissection; perhaps his skeleton would be mounted and displayed for the edification of curiosity seekers, as was the fate of the more sensational felons. He could almost see the placard in his mind's eye: *The mortal remains of John Pickett, former principal officer of Bow Street, who turned against the very Law he was charged with upholding...*

This bleak image was banished by the sound of the door opening behind him, and a moment later Mr. Colquhoun sat down beside him. For a long moment neither of them spoke, until at last the magistrate broke the silence.

"A very close-run thing. We wouldn't have known anything about it, had it not been for an anonymous letter delivered to Bow Street just after two o'clock." He turned his piercing gaze on his young protégé. " 'Shoot to kill,' John?"

Pickett slumped forward until his elbows rested on his knees, and studied his clasped hands with great intensity. "I wanted to spare Julia the shame of a trial and execution. I suppose I wanted to spare myself, too."

"Then let me set your mind at ease. The bank has no intention of preferring charges against you. Your co-conspirators, I fear, will not be so fortunate."

"*Not* preferring—?"

"In fact, I was hard-pressed to discourage them from offering you a substantial reward. I told them any such reward should rightfully go to Mr. Maxwell, who laid so much of the groundwork in the case. I trust you have no objection?"

Pickett shook his head. "No, sir. He's a good man, Maxwell. He deserves better than having me trying to throw a spanner into the works." He sat up very erect and stared straight ahead. "You will—I shall tender my resignation first thing in the morning, sir."

"What the—? Why the devil should you?" demanded the magistrate.

"Ten years ago, you made me promise—you said you would not be so lenient next time—and I've kept that promise—until today—"

And suddenly, to his abject horror, he was sobbing, his shoulders shaking, just as Kit had sobbed on the previous night, except that he was a man grown and there was no one, no one at all, who could ever put this right.

Mr. Colquhoun let out a long breath and put his arm about Pickett's heaving shoulders. "I'm very proud of the man you've become, John," he said. "I suppose I should have told you so before now, but God help me, I thought you knew."

"If that's true," Pickett said somewhat wetly, struggling to regain control of himself, "it makes my betrayal of you all the worse."

"You were in an untenable position. Have you looked in a mirror lately? Good God, one has only to look at you to see you were acting under duress."

"But that's just it—I wasn't! I *offered* to take Kit's place. In fact, I concocted the whole scheme!"

It appeared that, finally, he had made his point. Mr. Colquhoun could only stare at him and sputter. "You? The

SHERI COBB SOUTH

rope—the roof—the gold—that was all your doing?"

Pickett nodded miserably.

His mentor patted him on the back, then availed himself of Pickett's shoulder in order to hoist himself to his feet. "I think it's a very good thing I got you away from the rookery when I did. God only knows what sort of havoc you'd've been wreaking all this time if I hadn't."

26

Which Finds John Pickett Facing an Uncertain Future

Julia sat on the sofa in the drawing room hugging her arms about her for warmth. The fire had long since gone out, and she could not find it in her heart to rouse the footman to light another. Still less could she summon the energy to rekindle it herself, as she had done—more than once—while nursing her husband's injuries in his shabby little Drury Lane flat. In fact, she suspected no amount of burning coal would dispel a chill that had little to do with the weather in the pre-dawn hours of September.

Kit had finally fallen into an exhausted sleep, not in the bedchamber that had been prepared for him, but in a makeshift pallet below the foot of her own bed. More than once, she had considered leaving him in the care of the servants and hurrying to Mr. Colquhoun's residence, or even to Bow Street, but she could not quite bring herself to forsake the child left in her charge, even temporarily. It would not do for him to awaken and discover that she, too, had left him; he'd been abandoned too many times already in his short life.

And so she had resisted the urge until now, when it was four o'clock in the morning—a glance over her shoulder at the long-case clock just visible in the hall confirmed this—and it must be too late in any case. Whatever he'd intended to do must have been done by now. And yet...

And yet she did not feel like a widow. If John were truly dead, she must surely feel it, must somehow *know*, even without being told, that he was no more. Instead, she felt nothing, only a dull sense of numbness and an aching coldness that reached to her very bones, as if it were she, and not he, who had died.

She looked at the clock again. Ten minutes past the hour. How much longer must she wait, she wondered, before Mr. Colquhoun arrived to inform her of his death? That the magistrate would come, rather than assign the grim task to another, she had no doubt; he had loved him too, although he could only rarely bring himself to admit it.

She abruptly sat up straight, every muscle tensed as she strained to hear what had surely sounded, for a moment, like footsteps on the portico. The noise was repeated, rather louder this time, and then the door opened. She had no time to wonder at the visitor's letting himself in without knocking, for she recognized the voice with its Scots burr, and braced herself to receive the news she did not want to hear.

A moment later she could see Mr. Colquhoun standing in the doorway, glowering at an unkempt and unshaven young man whose swollen face was covered in bruises of every color of the rainbow, along with a light crusting of dried blood on his left cheek. She opened her mouth to speak to this unprepossessing figure, but no words would come. She could only stare mutely at him, taking in great gulps of air and pressing one hand to her bosom as if to slow the pounding of her heart.

The magistrate, however, was suffering from no such impediment. "Mrs. Pickett, I wish you would tell your fatheaded husband that there is not the slightest need for him to resign his position!"

This speech, inauspicious as it was, served to break the spell. With a choked cry, she ran to her husband, cupping his battered face in her hands and covering it with frantic kisses interrupted at intervals by disjointed utterances.

"John!—What happened to—I thought you were—you said—your letter—"

His arms came around her and held her close, and Julia caught a whiff of the same odor she'd noticed on Kit, the one that indicated the need for a bath in the very near future. Far from being repulsed by this circumstance, she clung to him all the more tightly.

"You had my letter, then?" he spoke into her hair, his breath warm on her ear. "Kit—?"

"He's upstairs asleep, the poor lamb. He didn't want to be left alone, so I made up a bed for him on the floor of our room, at least for tonight. And although I hate for him to be disturbed, I think you had best let him know you're alive. He is quite certain he killed you, or at least is responsible for your death."

"I'll go up to him at once," he said, and suited the word to the deed, albeit not before pressing his lips to her temple.

While he was gone, Mr. Colquhoun took the opportunity to enlighten Julia as to the night's activities, with the result that Pickett returned to the drawing room to find his wife sitting on the sofa and watching for his return with a rather dazed expression on her face.

"It's true, then, what Kit said?" she asked. "You really did rob the Bank of England?"

"It depends on your definition of 'rob,' " the magistrate put in before he could answer. "Strictly speaking, nothing was taken."

"Not for lack of trying," Pickett objected.

"Tomorrow's edition of the *Times*," Mr. Colquhoun continued, undaunted, "will offer for the edification of its readers a detailed account of how one of Bow Street's principal officers, at great personal risk, infiltrated a gang of thieves and stopped the theft of a fortune in gold ingots from the Bank of England."

"The readers of the *Times* might be taken in by such a pack of lies, but what about Bow Street's other principal officers? They know better."

"If any of them flatters himself that he is made privy to all my activities at the Bow Street Public Office," declared the magistrate, taking a lofty tone, "he will very soon learn his mistake."

Pickett could not agree. "They might reasonably expect to be warned that they would be obliged to put one of their colleagues in irons."

"*In irons?*" Julia's hand went to her mouth. "Oh John, no!"

Pickett fixed his gaze on the carpet at his feet, still too conscious of his own shame to meet her eyes. He would never forget the looks on their faces when they realized exactly who they were putting in shackles: Dixon's pained disappointment, Carson's wide-eyed astonishment, Maxwell's tight-lipped disapproval. Maxwell…

"Maxwell will know better, even if no one else does," he told his magistrate. "It was his case; if there had been any scheme afoot to plant an officer into the middle of the gang to smoke them out, he surely would have known about it."

Mr. Colquhoun was silent for a long moment, during which Pickett entertained hopes of carrying his point. It soon became clear, however, that he was merely taking care to frame his next argument in a way that did not denigrate one of his men before another.

"I mean no disrespect toward Mr. Maxwell, but he comes to us from a world in which orders are to be obeyed without question, and everything is either black or white. In truth, the law has many gray areas that he is not yet aware of. He'll discover it for himself soon enough, but until then, his opinions need not concern you. Just before we set out for the bank, I made a full confession to Mr. Maxwell and told him that when he'd thought you mistrusted his abilities, you had in fact been acting under, if not my orders, at least my suggestion. In the meantime, any rewards that the bank may offer will go to him—along with the reward already offered by Coutts—which ought to go a long way toward soothing any feathers that may have got ruffled over the past few days."

"I'm obliged to you, sir. It"—now it was Pickett's turn to choose his words with care—"It has not been easy, working in opposition to one of my colleagues. I'm glad Maxwell at least knows the truth about why I acted as I did, and I know you are regarded highly enough that so long as you have confidence in me, no one else would dare to question my continuing in my present position. But in all honesty, this is not—not a recent decision. I have been considering it for some time—have even begun looking about for a new situation, in fact."

Two very different pairs of blue eyes stared at him with identical expressions of shock and, yes, hurt.

"If there is some trouble I'm not aware of—" began his magistrate.

"John, why?" asked his wife at the same time. "You never said anything about leaving Bow Street before."

He took her hand and gave it a little squeeze, but addressed himself to Mr. Colquhoun. "I'm sorry, sir. I know this is a shabby way to repay you for all you've done for me—"

"Don't start that again!" chided the magistrate. "As I've told you before, any debt you owed me has long since been paid in full."

Pickett, however, had turned his attention to Julia. "I told you once, not long after we met, that one rarely made friends in my line of work. I didn't know then—I hadn't yet discovered that it was possible to make enemies. And even if I had, it wouldn't have mattered, not really. But now—anyone with a grudge against me can get his revenge by hurting the people I love. I won't put you in danger again like I did this past summer. Life as a clerk may be deadly dull, but at least you'll be safe—you, and Kit, and the baby."

"A clerk," echoed Julia, struggling to reconcile the image of a stooped man in spectacles meekly toiling over balance sheets and ledgers with the gallant young hero who had insisted on her innocence in the teeth of all opposition, who had dragged her back from the edge of a cliff to safety, who had rescued them both from a burning theatre. And for whom she had willingly given up her place in London society in order to marry. "Somehow I can't quite picture you as a clerk."

Pickett gave a bitter little laugh. "Neither could Mr. Whitmore, although I got very much on my high ropes when he implied that I wouldn't be able to keep my hand out of the till." The unswollen side of his mouth twisted. "I guess I showed him."

"I'm sure you have your reasons, John," Mr. Colquhoun said thoughtfully, "but why, exactly, a clerk? I don't mean any disparagement of clerks, mind you. A few of them—a *very* few—manage to rise in their profession, sometimes to considerable heights. But I should have thought that, after being able to see a bit of the world on Bow Street's shilling, being tied to a desk would bore you to distraction."

Pickett made no attempt to deny it. "Yes, sir, very likely. But it is at least marginally respectable work, and I won't have people saying how Lady Fieldhurst threw herself away on a coal-heaver. Not that I'm unaware of my obligation to you there, as well—" he added hastily, belatedly aware of just how ungrateful this must sound when it was his apprenticeship to a coal merchant, arranged by Mr. Colquhoun, that had eventually led to his position at Bow Street.

"Hmph!" grunted Mr. Colquhoun. "If you really felt yourself under any obligation to me, you might discharge it at once by giving up this stubborn determination to resign your position!"

"I'm sorry, sir. You may command me in anything else and be assured of my obedience, but on this I cannot, I *will* not yield. The only trouble is," Pickett concluded miserably, "I don't know how to do anything else."

"Is there no other position that might make better use of your talents?" Julia, noting with some misgiving the magistrate's lowering brow as well as the deep rumble, almost a growl, that issued from his throat, spoke up quickly before the argument could be resumed. "Some other aspect of the law, perhaps—"

Pickett shook his head. "Most legal positions require at least a working knowledge of Latin, and I don't know a *habeas corpus* from a hole in the wall."

"I didn't mean you should read for the law, exactly," Julia protested, then sighed. "What a pity Bow Street seems to be the only entity who ever has a need to investigate anything!"

"Perhaps." The magistrate turned his narrow-eyed gaze in her direction. "Then again, perhaps not. Tell me, do you remember when Lady Oversley's emeralds were stolen at Drury Lane Theatre? I seem to recall that she only sent to Bow

Street on your recommendation."

"Yes, but I only made the suggestion because I'd hoped to see John again," she confessed rather sheepishly.

"I didn't know that," said Pickett, much struck.

"As someone once told me, 'There are things you don't know about me,' Mr. Pickett," she retorted.

"The point is"—Mr. Colquhoun interrupted before the conversation could wander any further down avenues best explored in private— "that there are people, especially amongst the aristocracy, who are extremely reluctant to air their linen in public by turning their private affairs over to Bow Street."

"And then when they do," Pickett added, with a certain sense of ill-usage, "they won't tell us anything useful because they don't consider it any of our business. And they would be right, but for the fact that it was *they* who sent for *us*, not the other way 'round."

"If only there was some private citizen they could turn to instead," Mr. Colquhoun pondered aloud, "someone with the expertise of a Bow Street Runner, and yet who was at least relatively genteel—someone with an aristocratic wife, perhaps."

"You think there is sufficient demand for such a person, sir?" Pickett's tone was doubtful, but the prospect was enough to banish the bleak look from his eyes.

"Oh, yes!" cried Julia, entering into the spirit of the thing. "For you shall charge such *extortionate* fees that you will very likely become all the rage, and ladies will be inventing dilemmas only for the privilege of engaging you to solve

them. In fact," she added with mock severity, "now that I have
had time to consider the matter, I don't believe I like this idea
at all. Really, Mr. Colquhoun, what can you have been
thinking?"

"I can't think the neighbors will relish the sight of my
supposed clients calling at all hours of the day or night,"
Pickett observed.

"Oh, but you shall be very discreet," Julia said. "It's not
as if you intend to paint a sign on the door."

"I'll have to do something of the sort, or else I'll be so
'discreet' that no one will even know I'm here."

"A few lines in the *Times* ought to suffice, and perhaps
the *Morning Post* too, for good measure. Something along the
lines of 'confidential inquiries undertaken by discreet,
experienced envoy for a modest fee. Inquire in Curzon Street,
number 22.' "

"I thought you said the fee would be extortionate,"
Pickett reminded her.

"Oh, it will be," she assured him. "But they won't know
that until you have quite won them over."

"And what if, in the course of my discreet, confidential
investigation, I discover that a crime has been committed?"
Pickett's gaze shifted from his wife to his magistrate. "I'll
have no authority to act on it."

"In that case, you may apply to Bow Street, where you
may rely on the full cooperation of your former colleagues,"
promised Mr. Colquhoun. Receiving no reply, he prompted,
"Well? What do you think, lad?"

"I—I don't know," Pickett confessed. "It's all a bit

overwhelming."

"Well, it's not every night that one robs the Bank of England," the magistrate said, heaving himself to his feet. "And I daresay you want nothing more than for me to take my leave of you so you can seek your bed. I'll bid you goodnight, Mrs. Pickett. As for you, John, you don't have to make a decision tonight, you know. Give it some thought. You can always place an advertisement for a month or two, and if nothing comes of it, then you can look for that position as a clerk."

"Yes, sir," Pickett said, accompanying him as far as the door. "I daresay I shall be able to raise a hundred objections tomorrow, when my head is clearer, but at least for now I think—yes, I think it just might work."

"I have no doubt of it. In fact, the only trouble I can see—" He broke off, frowning thoughtfully.

"Yes, sir?" prompted Pickett.

The magistrate sighed. "The only trouble I can see is how damnably much I'm going to miss you."

Pickett did not quite trust himself to speak, but he stood in the open doorway for a long while, watching his mentor's retreating form until it disappeared into the darkness. It was here that Julia joined him some time later.

"John?" He had been absent from the drawing room for so long that she had assumed he must still be in conversation with Mr. Colquhoun. Instead, he stood alone, leaning against the doorframe.

"Will you think me a great coward," he asked, still staring out into the dark street, "if I say I'm afraid?"

She slipped her hand into the curve of his elbow and rested her head against his shoulder. "No one who knows you could ever call you a coward," she said warmly. "But what is it that frightens you, darling?"

He shrugged. "I don't know, exactly. An uncertain future, I suppose."

"Whatever it holds, we shall face it together," she promised. "But will you not come inside? It's very late."

Yielding to the gentle pressure of her hand in his arm, he allowed her to lead him back into the house.

"Tomorrow morning," she continued, shutting the door behind them and turning the key in the lock, "I shall ask the housekeeper for an unguent for your bruises, and I shall insist on your having a bath, but for now, I think we'd best get what sleep we can before morning. Do you know," she added in quite another tone as they started up the stairs, "it occurs to me that I have never shared a bed with a 'discreet confidential envoy.' "

"And you won't tonight, either," he said in so decisive a tone that she feared he had quite mistaken her intentions.

"Oh?"

"That pallet you made on the floor for Kit? It was empty." While she pondered the significance of this revelation, he explained, with a hint of laughter in his eyes that lightened, at least a little, the solemnity of his countenance, "He's taken your side of the bed."

Epilogue

Which Finds Young Christopher Pickett Free as a Bird

J ohn, you cannot be serious!" cried Julia, aghast.

"I'm perfectly serious," he assured her.

"You cannot mean to take a child to a—a *public hanging!*"

"A child reared in Mayfair, no," he conceded without hesitation. "But Kit didn't grow up in Mayfair. Depend upon it, he's seen more than one hanging already. They're free entertainment, you know, for those who can't afford the theatre or Vauxhall Gardens."

"That is no excuse for—"

"Sweetheart, listen." He put his hands on her shoulders and gave them a little squeeze. "He needs to know that Roger is dead and gone, that he has nothing to fear from him or Jud ever again."

She made no reply, and Pickett could tell she was wavering, no doubt recalling interrupted nights when a small boy awakened from a nightmare to find himself alone in an unfamiliar place and had to be soothed, reassured, and (more often than not) plied with warm milk and biscuits before he could be coaxed back to bed.

"I'll be with him the whole time, and if he shows the least sign of distress, I'll take him home."

She regarded him with eyes narrowed. His bruises had faded, and he once again looked like the man she had married, but for the boy's sake she was determined not to be swayed by a fluttering in her heart that no longer had anything to do with protectiveness or pity. "You promise?"

"I promise," he said, and bent to seal the bargain with a kiss.

And so it was that, on the day appointed for the execution, the throng crowded about the scaffold at Newgate included the brothers Pickett, the younger of the two puzzled and a little disappointed in his new sister's determined refusal to avail herself of the treat in store.

Roger was, as Pickett knew, both respected and feared amongst the residents of St. Giles, and so he was not surprised at the size of the mob assembled to witness the spectacle, nor at the cheer that rose up from the multitude as the felon mounted the steps to the scaffold. Jud followed a short distance behind, just as he had throughout their shared career. And while Jud looked more than a little dazed at his present predicament (Pickett suspected he had partaken very freely of the liquid consolation offered to the condemned), Roger, on the other hand, stood very erect, scanning the crowd with the same air of dignity with which a monarch might regard his subjects. Even the fashionably dressed young blades who had thought it a great lark to drive into the City and see the show, and who now observed the proceedings from the lofty vantage points of phaeton or curricle, appeared to respond to a demeanor that would have done credit to one of their own, raising quizzing-glasses or doffing high-crowned hats in acknowledgement.

Roger appeared not to notice this flattering degree of attention, for his gaze sharpened at the sight of two persons he had thought never to see again. He recognized them at once, although they had each looked very different the last time he had seen them. The elder, a tall young man several years his junior, no longer bore any trace of the beating Roger had given him outside the bawdy house in Seven Dials, while the younger, a dirty brat previously kept underfed lest he grow too tall to serve the purpose for which he had been purchased, was now a rosy-cheeked youth with glossy brown curls who looked up at him with frank curiosity.

The elder Pickett, suddenly aware of his scrutiny, put his hand on the boy's shoulder and drew him a step closer, as if daring Roger to try and take him back. Roger, deriving a certain cynical amusement from this gesture, lifted his eyebrow and gave a wry twist of his lips that might have been a smile. *What we might have achieved together,* it seemed to say, *if you'd been anybody but a bloody copper...*

Pickett caught that look, and perhaps even recognized something of the message it held, for his thoughts were running on somewhat similar lines. *Where might you be today,* he wondered, *if there had been someone like Mr. Colquhoun to take an interest in you?*

And then the hangman was there, fitting a coarse cloth

sack over Roger's head and looping the noose around his neck.

The whole thing was over in something less than half an hour, and it seemed to Pickett that Kit was unnaturally quiet on the walk back to Curzon Street.

"John?" he asked at last, once the crowds had dispersed enough that relatively private conversation was possible.

"Hmm?" *Here it comes*, Pickett thought, bracing himself not only to answer the boy's questions, but to admit to his wife that she had been right.

"I've been thinking," Kit announced very seriously.

"What about?"

"About King George."

The bird's regal name was no longer a cause for confusion, as its cage held pride of place atop the little bookcase in Kit's bedroom.

"What about him?"

"I think"—he frowned with an air of great solemnity— "I think King George would like to go free."

"Do you?" Whatever Pickett had expected, it was not that. "Won't you miss him?"

The goldfinch was, after all, Kit's only remaining link to his earlier life (well, it and the toy soldier, who had been absorbed into his new regiment—the complete set Julia had bought the boy at Pickett's request—with surprising ease), and as Pickett had cause to know, such a drastic change, even though an improvement, was nevertheless disorienting.

"Maybe," Kit admitted. "Probably, even. But you said I'll have to go to school after Christmas, and so he'd be left all alone at—at 'home.' "

He said the word tentatively, as if trying it out. Pickett could relate; it had taken some time for him, coming from the same background, to think of the Curzon Street house in those terms, too.

"And so," the boy continued, "I thought maybe he would like to be able to fly, like all the other birds."

Pickett's thoughts on the subject were mixed. The little bird's wings were quite possibly atrophied from months, perhaps years, of disuse, its actions limited to beating ineffectively against the bars of its cage. The very freedom it craved might prove to be its undoing, rendering it an easy mark for the feral cats that were everywhere to be found in the narrow lanes and courtyards of London. There was a great deal of risk in leaving behind the familiar, even in a good cause—as he and Kit, in their very different ways, were beginning to discover. Kit certainly seemed to be thriving in his new surroundings: he already had the cook wrapped firmly around his little finger, and spent as much time in the kitchen (where he could always count on being allowed to stir the pudding, or given a bit of bread and jam to eat) as he did in the upper part of the house.

For his own part, the transition was not so smooth. The advertisement which appeared daily in the *Times* and the *Morning Post* had failed to yield any results but, as Julia frequently pointed out, it was too soon to find the lack of response worrisome.

He glanced down at Kit and found the boy looking up at him in expectation, clearly awaiting an answer.

"Yes," he told his young brother with a great more conviction than he felt, "he should be allowed to try his wings."

* * *

And so, on a bright but breezy autumn day, Mr. and Mrs. John Pickett and Kit, with birdcage in hand, set out for St. James's Park, it being determined that, although Green Park was closer, St. James's offered a greater abundance of trees from which King George might choose a suitable candidate in which to establish his royal residence. Upon reaching their destination, Pickett turned to his brother.

"All right, then," he said. "Open the cage door."

A moment of awkward silence followed.

"Shouldn't you, I don't know, say something?" Julia suggested. "To make it official, I suppose?"

Privately, Pickett thought it would be "official" as soon as George discovered the cage door was open. However, upon seeing two faces looking expectantly up at him, he said, "Very well, then. Er, um, King George was a—a good bird, and, um—"

"He's not dead!" Kit protested indignantly.

"Do you want me to make a speech, or not?" retorted Pickett. "As I was saying, King George was a good bird, and a friend to Kit when he was very much alone, and for that we shall always be grateful to him. But Kit isn't alone anymore; he has a family now. And so we release King George to live in the open air, as a bird should. Farewell, your majesty. Fly high."

He nodded at Kit, who fumbled with the catch of the

birdcage door until it gave, and the little door swung open with a squeak of rusty hinges.

The goldfinch had been beating his wings frantically the entire time, and once escape was within view, it did not take him long to avail himself of it. Sadly, his bid for freedom was hardly a sight to inspire the heart. After darting through the open door, he lurched drunkenly through the air, to one side and then the other, then plunging precipitately toward the ground before recovering himself and soaring upward once more. Soon, however, half-forgotten habits reasserted themselves, and his efforts became more graceful as he glided away to the west, a small dark spot that grew smaller and smaller until at last it disappeared altogether.

"Well, I suppose that's that," Pickett said, observing the boy closely for any signs of his changing his mind, now that it was too late. Fortunately, there appeared to be none. "Are you ready to go home?"

In answer, Kit turned to his sister-in-law. "Will you read me another chapter of Gulliver?"

"If you like. Or you could read one to me. Or"—Julia darted a glance at Pickett as she slipped her hand through the curve of his arm—"John might read to both of us."

This suggestion found no favor with Kit. "I like it when you read better. You give the people different voices."

"There's gratitude for you," said Pickett, feigning indignation.

"There is one thing that puzzles me," Julia confessed as they set out for Curzon Street with Kit some two or three steps ahead, examining the ground for any interesting leaves, pebbles, or insects and consequently allowing them to converse in relative privacy.

"What's that?" Pickett asked.

"On the night of the robbery, when you held those gold bars in your hands, were you never tempted, not even for a moment, to pocket one?"

Pickett considered the matter for a moment before answering. "No, not in the slightest," he said at last. "Still, there's nothing especially noble in that. One doesn't handle gold bars in the usual manner of things, so I suppose they never seemed quite real. Besides—" He stopped for a moment and tucked a loose tendril of fair hair behind her ear. "—the only gold that interests me is the stuff growing on your head."

Julia rather doubted this; he had entirely too much time on his hands, now that he no longer went every morning to Bow Street, and she had noticed with what impatience he examined the newspaper every day to make sure the advertisement had been printed. Still, the recollection of that night reminded her again of how very close she had come to losing him.

"Oh, John," she said in a choked voice, giving his arm a squeeze.

"Oh, brother," Kit groaned, and skipped ahead with the air of one quite satisfied with the world and his place in it.

About the Author

At the age of sixteen, Sheri Cobb South discovered Georgette Heyer, and came to the startling realization that she had been born into the wrong century. Although she probably would have been a chambermaid had she actually lived in Regency England, that didn't stop her from fantasizing about waltzing the night away in the arms of a handsome, wealthy, and titled gentleman.

Since Georgette Heyer died in 1974 and could not write any more Regencies, Ms. South came to the conclusion she would have to do it herself. In addition to the bestselling John Pickett mystery series (now an award-winning audiobook series!), she has also written several Regency romances, including the critically acclaimed *The Weaver Takes a Wife*.

A native and long-time resident of Alabama, Ms. South now lives in Loveland, Colorado.

She loves to hear from readers, and invites them to visit her website at www.shericobbsouth.com; follow her on social media through Facebook, Goodreads, Pinterest, Instagram, or Twitter; or email her at Cobbsouth@aol.com.

www.ingramcontent.com/pod-product-compliance
Lightning Source LLC
Chambersburg PA
CBHW021308250626
47155CB00002B/432